Rebranding Remy Reilly

Jackie Campbell

Copyright © 2021 Jackie Campbell

Ellendale Road Publishing / Novato, CA
ISBN: 978-0-578-86871-4
Library of Congress Control Number: 2021907936
Title: *Rebranding Remy Reilly*
Author: Jackie Campbell
Digital distribution | 2021
Paperback | 2021

This is a work of fiction. The characters, names, incidents, places, and dialogue are products of the author's imagination, and are not to be construed as real.

Acknowledgement

Thanks to Heidi Shoham at heidishoham.com for all the editing, and Kelly Cozy at booksidemanner@gmail.com for the proofreading. These are the people who take my grammatic mess and make it readable.

A special thanks to Carl Alderete for your patience in helping me understand some winery basics.

Another thanks to Travis Simmons at samsdadgraphics.com for your cover creation.

And again to Erica at newbookauthors.com for putting it all together and getting it print ready and uploaded.

Chapter 1

This was it. This was the day. Six long years of university, combined with six long years of working part time, were finished. And that was after the same heavy load during high school. Long arms extended, ballerina hands perfectly posed, Remy Reilly stood before her audience of three, who waited.

She smiled and twirled her five-foot seven-inch frame for her family's inspection, mimicking the dancer in her prized music box. Her auburn hair was up; not a strand was out of place. A short-sleeved, lime-green blouse topped pleated navy-blue slacks. New black loafers completed the ensemble. She stopped, plucked a lone piece of lint from her leg, and invited approval. "What do you think, Mom?"

"Honey, you look beautiful. The interview will be a snap. All that work and you finally did it—a well-earned bachelor of arts degree in business." Carol Reilly's sharp eyes drifted over her daughter. "Where did you buy the blouse and slacks? I haven't seen them before."

"Target. Seventy dollars for both. Sure, it's a lot, but I want to appear presentable and professional." She stole another glance at herself in the mirror. "Gosh, when was the last time I wasn't wearing jeans and sneakers?"

Remy had an interview with Martha Keating, the owner of Rolling Oaks Winery, one of the highest-rated medium-sized vineyards and wineries in Sonoma County. Remy's advisor at Sonoma State had given her a stellar recommendation, along with a heads-up about the position.

Excited would be an understatement. Remy's final paper had been titled "Marketing for Wineries in a Changing Environment," and she'd focused on promotions on- and off-site and social media presence. The position was only a paid internship to start—another way of saying a probationary tryout—but Remy didn't care. Hope of an actual full-time job, after all those years doing part-time work in burger shops and food markets through high school and college, was reason enough for her current state of elation.

Carol Reilly smiled at her daughter, while Remy's sisters, Roxy and Rita, crammed in against the wall of Remy's bedroom and watched their older sibling prepare for her big day. The family was close, and the excitement and exhilaration infected all of them. The younger girls appreciated all that their older sister had done for them. In the early years, their mom had taken extra shifts at the local hospital where she was a nurse. Roxy and Rita, now teenagers, knew their older sister didn't have to give up her precious Sundays. During their younger years, Remy used to take them to the movies or the beach and watch over them while doing her homework. The joyful air permeating the room even reached Colonel Brandon, their old cat, lounging on the windowsill and no doubt wondering what all the fuss was about.

It had been hard on the family when Remy's dad left and then didn't provide monetary support for the kids. Mrs. Reilly had done her best, had kept their modest house with the hefty mortgage, and she wanted her girls to have all she could afford. Remy, seven years older than the next sibling, was the second breadwinner for the family. Consequently, it had taken her six-plus years to graduate versus the typical four. Remy took her responsibilities seriously. The road to her degree had led through the local community college for three years and then nearby Sonoma State University for an additional three.

Remy watched her image bounce back from the long mirror attached to the back of her bedroom door. She scrutinized the outfit one last time. No price tag scratched at the back of her neck, and no stickers were visible on the bottom of her shoes. A simple pendant, a graduation present from her two sisters, completed her understated appearance. She was ready.

"What time is your appointment?" asked Carol.

"Eleven o'clock."

"It's only ten, honey." Carol pushed loose strands of her graying hair behind her ear. "The place is only twenty minutes away. Why don't you relax with a cup of coffee first?"

"Suppose there's traffic or an accident? No, I can't be late." Remy hoped her anxiety wasn't showing. "I'll stop for some if I get close and I'm too early."

A barrage of good lucks from her mom and sisters pursued Remy out the front door. Even Colonel Brandon stood by the door to wish her well. The cat was named after a character in *Sense and Sensibility*. Remy was the world's biggest fan of the nineteenth-century English romance writers: Jane Austen, the Brontë sisters, and others. The books were her passion, her escape from the daily grind. Remy was the Colonel's favorite human. The cat lifted a paw, mimicking the surrounding humans, and waved goodbye. He seemed to sense that his Remy was happy and excited about something.

Remy waved back at him and said, 'Thank you, Colonel." Then she descended the steps of their modest two-story house on the small tree-lined cul-de-sac.

Skipping along the patterned brick path to her car on the street, she reached out her hand and brushed it along the top of the neatly trimmed hedge next to their small lawn. Many of the neighbors had converted their lawns to drought-tolerant plants, the wave of the future in California, but her mother liked the small island of green in front of the house.

The two parking spots outside the garage door were for her mother's and sisters' cars. Remy preferred her location under the large sycamore tree beside the street. It was a massive umbrella protecting her aging automobile in a pool of shade, blunting the force of the intense summer sun. Even the chirping birds above seemed to be cheering her on. She inserted a worn, scratched key into the ignition of the tired, old Toyota, and whispered, "Please start." It was a mantra that worked most of the time. The car coughed to life to carry her and her hope on their way.

Dreams were there to chase, and Remy Reilly bolted out of the starting gate after hers.

The headquarters of Rolling Oaks Winery would not win any architectural awards. Remy arrived a half hour early and sat in her car across the two-lane road. She scanned the property across from her. The building was a battered, old bungalow house converted to offices long ago. No sign announced the winery, only a street number on a wooden sign below the mailbox next to the road. Probably just as well, considering the condition of the building. Many years ago, it must have been the home of the grandparents or great-grandparents. It was set back about a hundred feet from the busy road. The peeling gray paint and sagging charcoal shingled roof testified how long the company had been around. A new paint job on the sad bungalow would just be lipstick on a pig. Remy knew the building's appearance was misleading. This was a very successful business. To the right of the entry drive stood an imposing barn. Remy could tell it was newer and in better shape than the bungalow. Behind it was the original small family vineyard.

At ten minutes to eleven, she checked her mirrors and drove across the road. Better than a doorbell, her noisy Toyota announced her arrival. It spat her out in the gravel parking lot in front of the offices. Martha Keating herself met Remy at the door.

As she approached, Remy absently brushed down her new slacks, a habit she'd developed whenever she got out of her aging car. "Hi, I'm here to see Mrs. Keating at eleven o'clock. My name is Remy Reilly."

"I am she," said Martha, as she gave both the car and the girl an appraising look. "It's nice to meet you, Remy. Alice Martin says great things about you. Why don't you follow me?"

With long, purposeful strides, Martha led Remy down the narrow hallway to an office. It was one of the old bungalow bedrooms. Remy's mind registered one word as she followed behind Mrs. Keating—fit. The older woman had spent her youth in the fields and processing plant with her now-departed husband. She'd maintained her figure. The short, no-nonsense blond hair was well cut with no gray to be seen. She even had it highlighted. No one would guess she was sixty-five. Taking a seat across from her, Remy saw a lightly lined but firm face with penetrating blue eyes. This woman was still beautiful.

Remy sat nervously on the edge of one of the two chairs in front of the cluttered desk, her back straight, hands folded in her lap, legs crossed at the ankles. This was the proper seating position for a lady, and she wanted to be on her game today.

She had carefully typed out her resume and now handed it across the desk to Mrs. Keating. It was not particularly impressive, but it was who she was, and Remy was comfortable with that—humble, hardworking, and honest.

"Would you like some coffee?" asked Martha.

"No, thank you." Remy thought she might spill it over herself, or worse still, all over Mrs. Keating's desk.

While the older woman examined her resume, Remy scanned the room. Industry awards covered the wall behind the nicked and scratched wooden desk that must have been built sometime in the last century. Clean but worn hardwood floors showed years of wear. Boxes and files were stacked in a bookshelf against one wall and randomly on the floor. Mrs. Keating was clearly in the wine business, not show business. Muted voices, the stutter of a printer, a distant phone ringing, and the hum of a straining air conditioner all registered in the back of Remy's head as she waited, white knuckles betraying the tension in her folded hands.

Martha Keating, matriarch of the respected wine family, studied the resume in front of her, absently tapping her pen on the desk. In truth, she already knew most of it. Martha maintained a severe and stern façade, but anyone who knew her would boast about her knowledge of the wine business and her fairness to her employees.

She reviewed the submission in her hand, along with what she already knew and now observed. The young lady in front of her was almost twenty-six years old, presented herself well, and could sit correctly. She looked to be in good shape, and her jobs in all the burger joints and markets told Martha she was not afraid of physical work. Like Martha in her younger days, this girl was on her feet all day. Everybody in her winery did many tasks. After all of Martha's early years running around the fields, she didn't want to hire any whiney prima donna, someone who would throw a hissy fit and hurl their toys out of the stroller when things weren't going perfectly. Rolling Oaks Winery was not a retreat.

She could tell the young woman across from her was trying to control herself. Nervousness and enthusiasm were dripping off her in equal amounts. Martha's friend at the local university's counseling department had told her all she needed to know about Remy but Martha had to see for herself. Not Harvard or Stanford, but studying six years with part-time jobs and no student loans to earn a degree, backed up by good grades, spoke volumes to Martha over some fancy school. She understood that Remy contributed to the family funds, helping her mother keep their house, and she saw to it that her two younger sisters had some modest luxuries.

Martha knew the time to cut back on her long days was rapidly approaching. Sixty-five years were taking their toll. She needed some competent help to shoulder part of the load. The wine business was changing, and she wanted to usher in some changes of her own before cutting back, giving herself some well-earned free time for herself. Someone experienced with an MBA and preconceived ideas about the company's direction would have nothing in common with Martha and was not on her radar. Their system worked. It merely needed updating. She wanted someone she could mold, someone she could relate to, someone who would be receptive to her method of operation. And, bias be damned, she wanted a young, energetic woman. It was her company, and she'd worked mostly with men her whole life. The company had the products or could create new ones. Marketing and sales were the areas of concern. The wine business was competitive and tough, and the actual wine had less and less to do with it.

The tapping pen took a break. Martha focused on the applicant. "So you're interested in marketing, Remy. Is that correct?"

Remy uncrossed her legs, folded her hands on her knees, and leaned slightly forward. "Yes, ma'am. In school, I did a paper on marketing in the wine industry during these changing times. But I'm really interested in anything in the industry. It doesn't have to be in marketing. I want to get a foot in the door however I can. I've been fascinated by the wine business for years. Any work would be appreciated." She turned the smile up a notch and brushed back a stray strand of hair. "I'll do anything from picking grapes to any office work you have. I know I can do a good job at whatever you may have open, so I can prove myself.”

Picking grapes? Impressed with the simple answer and not having some lofty expectations thrown at her, Martha said, “You’re not afraid of starting with something menial, something below your expectations? This is a physical business. Even if they’re in administration, we expect everyone to spend some time in the fields and in the processing facilities to start with. It’s important to learn what we’re about and earn some respect for what other people in the company do every day.”

“No, ma’am. I want to get a foothold in the business. I’m not afraid of work.”

Martha locked eyes for several seconds with the youngster in front of her—anyone under thirty was a youngster as far as Martha Keating was concerned. She wanted to give this girl a tryout. She didn’t want Remy to take another job before she created the right slot for the girl if she worked out. This was all happening fast. Thoughts about starting a new hire had yet to be sorted. An idea, a test, a project she sorely wanted done crossed her mind. “Did you see that old barn across the way when you drove up? You’re not afraid to start in the wine business by cleaning it out?”

Remy gave a beaming smile. “I’m a cleaning machine, Mrs. Keating!”

Martha almost jumped at the enthusiastic reply.

Not one for dragging things out, she made her decision. Old school, Martha liked being called ma’am, and she liked Remy’s short, direct answers without all the bull. The anticipation gleaming off the “cleaning machine” sold her. She wanted to yank the girl out of her nervousness before she exploded.

“Like I said, around here, everybody does everything. Yes, this is a dirty job to start with, but packed in that firetrap of a barn, along with years’ worth of trash, are a lot of family memories. It’s my latest pet project before it catches fire and burns down half the county. I’ve been putting it off for way too long.” She realized what she was asking the girl to do and softened her delivery. “I’ll need a woman’s eye out there. After that, I can move you up to the tasting room to learn some of the basics about the business. As we discussed on the phone, this is an intern position, a three-month test to see if we're a good fit for each other. Are you good with all that?"

"Yes, ma'am!"

"Can you start Monday?"

"Yes, ma'am!"

Martha almost jumped again.

Remy had told her she made sixteen dollars an hour at the part-time market job. Hell, Martha thought, she'd round it up nine dollars so the girl could eat. "Is twenty-five dollars an hour to start okay?"

"Thank you, Mrs. Keating!"

Martha took a sip of her coffee to hide a smile. She'd been told the girl was energetic, but she hadn't seen this level of enthusiasm since her son got his first pickup truck. Maybe picking grapes wasn't a bad idea. The girl would probably strip the vineyard in a day.

"I won't be here until later on Monday. Drive up to the barn at eight o'clock, and you'll find Juan. He and you can try to straighten that mess out. If it works out, there are plenty of opportunities around here."

"Thank you, ma'am. I won't let you down!"

Straightening out the barn would be a tough task, but Martha liked to see what people were made of early on.

Taken aback by the interview's speed and excited by its outcome, a barely containable Remy bounced up and down in her seat as she drove away from the offices. Even the old Toyota seemed rejuvenated as it purred down the road.

I did it. A mega chance at a good full-time job.

Still doing somersaults in the clouds, she parked the car in front of her house and texted her best friend, Lynn, at her hair salon a few blocks from the center of Santa Rosa.

REMY: What time are u home? I have fantastic news!

LYNN: Six o'clock. Bring some takeout.

Remy scored an empty guest-parking spot in Lynn's condo complex. It was one of the newer complexes in town, two stories high, shaped in a rectangle, with a large swimming pool in the middle. Summers were hot in Sonoma, and pools were a good draw.

She walked along the patterned concrete walkway beside the pool to her friend's ground-floor unit, looking longingly at the water. Over the past two years, since Lynn had purchased the unit, the two busy women rarely enjoyed a day by the pool. Lots of small trees and plants made the space inviting. Six or eight people were relaxing in the late afternoon shade or in the pool after their day's labors.

Remy had her own key. She entered the condo, plopped down the Thai takeout food on the granite kitchen counter, and moved immediately to the fridge, where she knew there was always cold white wine. A glass had been earned.

Lynn watched as Remy walked over to the long leather sofa, kicked off her shoes, and curled up at her usual end, puffing up the throw pillows to her satisfaction.

"Nice outfit," said Lynn. "No jeans and no sneakers. Why are you dressed up? I can't believe you pried open your wallet for some decent clothes. You're almost presentable enough to go barhopping with me."

Their bond, formed in grade school, had never been broken. They shared the same work ethic and dreams. They diverged when it came to fashion and men. Lynn was far more social and continuously frustrated that Remy rarely went out. Her flimsy excuses about working so much were dismissed by Lynn, who worked long days but found time to get out and about. Lynn had decided in high school that she wanted to have her own hair salon, and she'd pursued that goal relentlessly. She now had it.

Lynn was all about chic. The theme of her condo was modern. Contemporary prints adorned the walls, lit by directional recessed lights in the ceiling. A light-gray carpet supported the metal-and-glass coffee and end tables with trendy lamps. No knickknacks, no clutter.

Lynn looked Remy up and down. "Are those shoes Dansko or Merrells? Admit it, they're comfortable."

Both Lynn and Remy's mother, also on her feet all day, had tried for years to get Remy out of her sneakers and failed.

"You win," said Remy, glancing down at her new shoes. "I can't believe how good they feel on my feet. I bought them because I wanted to look professional today. But that's not the good news. I've got a new job! Well, a chance at one, anyhow."

Remy spoke nonstop for fifteen minutes, sharing her good fortune with her friend. She explained she'd been hired on a trial basis, had a chance at a full-time job in the field she'd dreamed about. She told Lynn how fantastic Mrs. Keating was and the things she could learn. On and on she went.

After a while, the ever-practical Lynn said, "Will you be getting a discount on the wine?" She then leaned forward and gave Remy a big hug. "You've just made my day. I'm so happy for you. You've worked hard for years to get that degree. Good for you." Releasing Remy, she gave her an appraising look. "If you're heading out to the business world, it's time for us to do a makeover. I need to get you into the salon for more than a trim. Now that you may have some free time, you can try to socialize more." Lynn's face softened, and she patted Remy's arm. "Leaving the convent won't be hard. I'll be your guide."

Remy balked. "Let's not get ahead of ourselves. I'm cleaning out a barn next week, and I'm not letting go of the part-time job at the food market until I'm sure I have the new job. Things are looking up, but nothing is secure yet. A social life can wait a little longer."

Lynn folded her arms and frowned. "You're cleaning out a barn? Six years of college, and you're cleaning out a barn?"

Remy defended herself. "It's a foot in the door, and I'm thrilled to have the chance. I think it's a test of some kind. Mrs. Keating is very old school."

"Fine, let's get back to dating." Exasperated with her friend, Lynn sang her now-repetitive song. "Remy, there's a life out there aside from work. School is over. You need to relax a little. You can't keep burying yourself in your old romance novels and movies for fun and entertainment."

Lynn didn't read as many of the classic and historical romance novels as Remy, but they shared a passion for TV shows and movies. Remy could probably repeat all the Jane Austen and Brontë sisters' novels by heart. Lynn knew her friend liked tucking herself in bed with one of her books and whisking herself off to a dream place where she could share the trials and tribulations, the sadness and joys of times long past. She thought her friend a little excessive about it, but the diversion kept Remy happy. Lynn's own preferred escape route was to pore over *Vogue* and *Cosmopolitan* during breaks at the salon and fantasize about whisking away on a private jet to a yacht in the south of France. To each her own.

"You need to get out more, Remy. Meet some men. Interact more and expose yourself to the *real* world of romance. Old Darcy from *Pride and Prejudice* and Colonel Brandon from *Sense and Sensibility* won't be coming to Sonoma County anytime soon."

"They *are* here," said Remy. She was still high from her big day. "Put in one of the DVDs. Let's watch *Emma* tonight."

"No! None of that historical crap tonight."

"Okay, you win. It's your house. How about a Hallmark movie?"

Defeated, Lynn shook her head and reached for the remote. "You need to flip that switch, girl. Get that pathetic life of yours out of airplane mode."

Chapter 2

Big Monday. Up with the summer light, showered and teeth brushed, Remy looked out the bathroom window at another calm, sunny day. She had hoped that some seasonal fog would force its way over the hills from the Pacific Ocean to the west. No such luck. Everyone wanted this week-long heat wave to break, and the Pacific fog was usually the tool that did it. Turning back to the sink, she shrugged. *Well, you can't have it all.*

She bundled into the ragged old Toyota and set off to the company offices. Her dark-blue, battered backpack, a part of her since she had bought it when she started college, rested on the passenger seat beside her. Though it was patched in places with silver duct tape, she refused to replace it. It held all she ever needed: her lunch, several pens, a notebook, her wallet, maybe some treats, and a large bottle of water. Dressed for sloppy work, she would meet Juan and dive into the mysterious labyrinth called the barn. Mrs. Keating had said there were no prima donnas and no elitists at this company. Remy was on board with that.

The Toyota muscled its way into the smaller winery property fifteen minutes outside of Santa Rosa. Remy knew that the main vineyards were farther west in the hills. The winemaking facilities and tasting rooms were also at the larger location. Her destination today, the old-styled barn, was near the road on the right side, about thirty yards from the offices. A rutted, gravel driveway and parking area separated the two structures. Beyond the two buildings, toward the rear of the property, lay an ample flat space of approximately eight acres of the original vines, the family's original vineyard. A lush, flat field of big, green leaves danced slowly in the light morning breeze. At the back, the land butted up to the distant golden hills of a typical, hot California summer landscape.

Remy got out of her car and walked toward the barn. She pulled her ponytail through the back of her Sonoma State University baseball cap in anticipation of a grimy cleaning day. Younger than the old bungalow house, the barn was easily over a half a century old, still proudly boasting stability after all those years. It was huge. She approached the weather-worn and time-battered gray sliding doors that had been pushed to the sides. Remy paused and surveyed the interior. It was packed with crates, boxes, and junk almost to the doors. Two narrow walking paths wove their way through the mess. As her eyes adjusted to the dark space, Remy looked up. It was easily two stories high, and massive wooden beams loomed overhead in the undivided space. Very impressive. Grander and bigger by far than the humble old house next door. Remy thought about generations past, when running and growing a business superseded domestic comfort. Everything went back into the business, and families continued to live modestly, building for future generations. The money that went into this barn could have built two or three houses. Several tractors and big trucks could easily fit in the space.

Against the left sidewall, over the mass of trash, she thought she could see old metal racks going almost to the ceiling, probably for the oak wine barrels. She recalled some of the smaller wineries she'd visited while doing her paper in school. Remy surmised this must have been the processing building for the original vineyard. Cobwebs and dust, trash and debris greeted her eyes. Her nose took in ancient smells of mold, mildew, and years of locked-in odors from the vineyard. Barely audible scurrying sounds alerted her ears to what could only be a utopia for all forms of rodents. Her shoulders almost slumped as she took in the years of dense, randomly stacked piles of who knew what from God knows when. This would be no quick cleanup.

Bill Keating, son of the matron, was on his way to the main winery in the rolling Sonoma hills toward the coast. He and Juan handled all the field and processing operations, while his mother took care of administration here at the offices. Making a quick stop at the small shop beside the barn to pick up a few things, he immediately noticed the big dumpster just off to the side. Suspicious eyes then registered a faded old Toyota he didn't recognize parked nearby. His six-foot two-inch frame got out of the truck. He stood and scratched his head through the short sandy-blond hair. *What is going on?*

Curious, he stepped just inside the large barn doors, which were open only rarely in recent years. As he paused and surveyed the dark space in front of him, looking for clues about what his mother was up to, a voice from the shadows made him jump.

Damn!

"Hi, Juan. Sorry to startle you. I'm Remy Reilly, the new girl. Mrs. K told me to meet you here."

A very professional young woman thrust her hand toward him in greeting. She had a firm grip and a friendly smile. "I guess you and I have to clean this mess up. Where do you want to get started?" Remy looked around, raised her hands, and shook her head. "God, this firetrap is a disaster waiting to happen. I hope you don't smoke. Have you got any gloves?"

A bewildered Bill managed, "Well, um, I'm—"

"Wow, one dumpster won't make a dent in this place," said Remy.

"Who exactly sent—"

"Mrs. K, you know, the boss."

"Mrs. K?"

They both looked up as they heard a back door open, screeching on unoiled hinges. Someone moved stuff around, trying to wade through the maze of stacked boxes and equipment. A moment later, from one of the narrow paths, a distinguished-looking Hispanic man with gray hair, in his early sixties, approached. When he saw Bill, he said, "Hey, Chico. What are you doing here?" He then noticed the young lady off to the side. Juan always did the formal act when the owners were with people he didn't recognize. "Oh, sorry, I didn't know you had company, Mr.—"

Bill spoke over him. "Juan, this is Remy. She's here to help you clean this mess up."

Remy, dismissing her mistake, confidently walked over to Juan, once again extending her hand. "Sorry, Juan. I thought

Chico here was you. Mrs. K sent me over to help. I'm the new intern."

Juan's instructions had been that someone would meet him this morning to start the cleanup job. He'd assumed it would be one of the field workers or someone from the production facilities. Confused, he glanced at Bill with raised eyebrows. "Chico? Mrs. K? Intern?"

Bill was standing to the side and a little behind Remy. He gave a slight shake of his head over the girl's shoulder—a don't-say-anything shake of the head. Bill wanted to take a minute to see how this charade would play out, to get an idea of what his mother was up to. This was another secret directive from Mrs. Mussolini, something he, her loving son, wasn't supposed to know about.

Clearly undeterred and dripping with enthusiasm on her cheery first day on the job, Remy turned back to Bill. "Did you get stuck on cleanup too, Chico?" She'd picked up the name when the older man had said it. "You look a little old to be an intern. What did you do to get stuck out here?"

Rapidly trying to sort this out, wondering who in God's name this woman was, Bill thought of his mother. With hidden sarcasm only he and Juan would understand, he mumbled, "Countless things, I'm sure. Let's call it another punishment in my life at Rolling Oaks Winery."

"In the doghouse, huh? Well, let's find those gloves and get started."

Bill glanced over to the nearby workbench, spotted a pair of old gloves, and handed them to Remy. Stalling for some time, he asked, "Can you do us a big favor, Remy? Walk around to the back of the barn. You'll see a wheelbarrow. Could you get that, please? It would be a great help."

"Sure." All smiles, Remy bounded out the door on her quest.

Bill shook his head at all the perkiness and enthusiasm.

Juan started in. "Did she just call you Chico?" It was Juan's term of endearment for Bill since he was a baby waddling between the vines, looking up and reaching for the tempting, round grapes, unsteady baby feet losing their balance in the soft dirt. "There's only about three of us left who call you that, and we're all over sixty. Who the hell is Mrs. K? And what the hell is an intern? Oh, and why are *you* here? You're supposed to be out at the winery today. Your mom didn't want you to know about this cleanup thing. If she finds out you're here, I'm not taking the fall."

"Christ, lighten up, Juan. She can't blame you. Just say I showed up. The girl must be lost. She'll be going back to the mother ship soon. And Mrs. K must be the hip version of my mother. This girl is on a mission. Did you see how cheery and excited she is about going to work? And it looks like she just spits out whatever is on her mind."

Confused, Juan asked, "Why would your mother hire a girl to clean out a barn?"

"I have no idea. Let's let this go for a bit and see where it leads. My mother is up to something." Bill's only thought was, *This can't be good.* "And, yes, I was on my way out to the winery. I stopped by the shop to pick up some things that Skip needed and saw that big dumpster outside. I'm not going anywhere now. What did Mom tell you to do in here?"

"She thinks it's a big firetrap. After the recent fires, she's afraid we'll burn down the county. It all goes. Everything. That's why she didn't want you around. She says you're a pack rat and would just move stuff around."

"*Me*, a pack rat? I didn't put all this stuff in here. I'm the one who told her to throw three-quarters of it out. There's a lot of family stuff in here, which should be sorted out. She probably has my baby teeth in here somewhere."

"Not my problem, Chico," said Juan.

"She can't just throw it *all* out."

"*You* tell her that. Me, I'm doing what I was told. Me and the—what's she called—intern girl."

"Okay, okay. We'll start by sorting through it, see what I can salvage of my existence here on this earth."

Thirty-two years of being on the planet flashed through Bill's head. Thirty-two years of his possessions condemned to the trash heap by his mother, along with all of hers and his deceased father's. Even some of his thirteen-year-old daughter's stuff was in here. No wonder his mother didn't want him around today.

"Fine," said Juan. "You sort. I'm filling the dumpster, and the kid's right, it'll take a few dumpsters."

When Remy returned, Bill turned to her. "Remy, why don't you take all the smaller boxes scattered around and put them outside to the door's right? We can sort through them later. Juan and I will carry the bigger stuff and put it on the left. After we get it separated, we can see what goes to the dumps and what we can donate or recycle." Bill gave the barn an appraising look. "You're right. This might take a while."

"Yeah, right," said Remy. "How many *weeks* do you have? Are there any dust masks? There's probably the Black Death and Ebola hiding in here somewhere."

Remy laughed and started doing her thing as Bill went to his truck for some masks. The three of them were in close quarters, so conversation was easy. The girl seemed to like to talk.

Walking back inside after carrying boxes out together, Remy asked, "So, Chico. What do you normally do around here?"

"Um, odd jobs. I do a lot of odd jobs, running around, things like that. What does an intern do?" Bill probed to find out what his mom was up to. "Who hired you?"

"Mrs. K hired me. Today's my first day. I graduated only two weeks ago, and out of the blue, she called me to come in for an interview. Isn't she wonderful? She hired me on the spot—on a trial basis, but still. My degree is in marketing. She wants to make some changes for the future, but she explained she wants me to do all the things around the winery first, so I understand the business. I think that's great." Remy wistfully looked up to the roof. "She's such a big name in the wine business, one of the industry's top female figures. She might mentor me. How great is that? If this is where she wants me to start, this is where I start. What an opportunity she's giving me."

Yeah, great, thought Bill. He pressed on in his investigation. "Do you know why she's cleaning this barn out?"

"Not a clue. But I want to look good, and you need to get out of the doghouse. So let's do a good job. Wow!" She pointed at an old bicycle exposed behind the boxes she'd moved. "That's an old Schwinn girl's bike from the fifties."

Bill knew it was his grandmother's bike, handed down to his mother years ago. His mom had ridden it everywhere—to school and around the orchards out west before they were converted to vineyards. It must have been in the barn, discarded and abandoned, for half a century. "It must be Mrs. Keating's. How do you know what it is and when they made it?"

Remy looked at him and frowned. "Well, duh, it has Schwinn written on it, Chico." She pointed to the old bike. "It's a Springer model. You can tell by the two suspension springs in the front fork. The Springer girl's bike was made between about '39 to '54. The clue to the year is the inch-and-three-quarter-wide tires and the narrower fenders. They were used after about '54."

A bemused Bill asked, "How do you even know something like that?"

"My neighbor, Teddy, restores old bikes. I've been hanging in his garage for years. You and some other employees should chip in and have him restore this for Mrs. K's birthday or Christmas. I guarantee you she'll cry. You know, there's nothing but memories wrapped inside all that metal."

"But it's a wreck. It's rusted, and the tires have disintegrated, parts are missing."

"No problem for Teddy. He does it all. Sews new seats, re-chromes, fixes all the spokes, paints, and even pinstripes, all in the original colors." Remy paused to think. "Why don't you hide it somewhere while you think about it?"

Somewhat intrigued by the idea, Bill picked it up and carried it behind the garage before the Mad Duchess showed up, saw it, and threw it in the dumpster herself. He took his handkerchief from his back pocket and wiped his brow as he contemplated the rusted metal in front of him. Remy was considerate. In her focused fight to get her job, she still had time to think about making someone else happy. Interesting.

Remy, Juan, and Bill continued to wade through the stacks and piles all morning. At lunchtime, it looked as if they hadn't made a dent. They'd laid out a fair amount in neat rows outside the barn. Ancient vineyard tools and implements, old barrels and wooden boxes, appliances and furniture, pieces of vehicles and heavy, disintegrating cardboard boxes waited for sorting. Everyone had brought their lunch, and they dragged some old chairs to the shady side of the barn for a well-deserved break. Juan found an old card table and brought it out to complete the makeshift dining area. Eating inside would have been like eating in a desert sandstorm after all the dust they'd stirred up. Bill made a mental note to pick up some extra dust masks for the next day.

As they sat and quietly ate, Bill glanced at Remy. She damn sure wasn't afraid of work. He almost felt embarrassed at how he'd had to try to keep up with her pace all morning. Nervous energy alone probably kept her that slim. She was quiet and a little tired now, not the smiley, bubbly, animated energy ball of the morning. Bill noticed her face as she looked absently toward the distant hills. She was attractive. He noticed the long fingers wrapped around her sandwich. She'd taken off the baseball cap to cool her head, and he could see the lovely reddish-brown hair pulled back in a ponytail. He wasn't around attractive women much. His thirteen-year-old daughter and his job limited his private life. He tried to peg her age but couldn't. Thoughts about what job she must've had before to be in that shape bounced around in his head. Her ideas about the bicycle suggestion lingered. He wondered if she had a boyfriend.

Remy watched as Martha Keating drove up to the office and parked her car in the shady spot reserved for her at the side of the offices. She marched directly to the group seated at the side of the barn, surveying the work done as she approached like a sergeant major inspecting work completed by her troops. They had already filled one dumpster.

Ignoring everyone else for the moment, a tall, fit, and imposing Martha towered in front of her seated son. "Why are *you* here?" she asked.

It was said in a tone that Remy had no problem interpreting as a reprimand.

Was Chico in more trouble?

Chico gave Mrs. K a caustic glance before returning his attention to his sandwich. "It looked like they needed some help, and I was *somehow* left out of the loop."

The sarcasm was not lost on Remy. *No wonder the idiot was in the doghouse. That was the boss he was talking to! A serpent of subtlety, he was not. Did they have a vaccine for stupidity?*

Remy had to help. Her mind scrambled for some way to defend her fellow worker. She bolted from her chair. "It's my fault, Mrs. Keating. I asked Chico if he could lend a hand for a bit. Some of this stuff is really heavy, and I'm not strong enough to move it with Juan."

"*Chico?*" said Martha as she glanced between him and Remy.

Remy, seeing the expression on Mrs. K's face, sensed the boss was confused about something. She also wondered what smiling Juan thought was so funny.

Martha directed her attention to Remy. "Are you okay, dear?" She glanced back at all the stuff that had already been placed outside. "Some of this stuff *is* heavy. I'd forgotten what was in this old barn. I can find something else that's easier for you."

"No way!" Remy caught herself. "Oh, sorry, Mrs. Keating, but I've started this, and I want to finish it. Juan and I can sort it if Chico has to do something else."

"Okay," said Martha to the enthusiastic "cleaning machine." She redirected her attention. "Yes...*Chico.*" She pointed a finger at Chico. "Why don't you come into the office for a minute, young man." Juan's smirk disappeared when Martha pointed at him. "You, too."

She looked back at Remy. "Why don't you rest here for a bit longer, dear. They'll be back in a minute. It looks like you're doing a superb job. I hope these two are keeping up." Martha scowled at the two men. "They tend to relax if you don't keep an eye on them."

As she walked to the office, Mrs. K said over her shoulder, "You two men move that old stove to the side. That was my mother's first stove. I can't believe you were going to throw that out. Remy, I'm counting on you to keep an eye on these two. Don't let them throw out anything good. We need a woman's eye out here."

Remy beamed at the new responsibility—on her first day on the job!

Juan and Chico moved the stove two feet before following the boss. In a quiet voice, Chico said to Remy, "Thanks for trying to cover for me. She can be tough sometimes. Last week, I watched while she beat a mother raccoon to death with a metal stake for grabbing a few grapes to feed her children."

Remy flinched before the grin on his face telegraphed that he was winding her up. She gave him a light punch on the arm. "It'll be all right, Chico." During the morning, she had noticed him walking around a lot, talking on his phone. Not good during work hours. She smiled at him. "When you get back, if you learn to keep that phone in your pocket, your production rate will go right through the roof."

Chapter 3

Martha sat behind her desk with the two delinquents standing cowed in front of her. Bill absently slapped his pants and shirt, trying to shed some of the dust and dirt. Martha watched in dismay and shook her head. "Did I raise you like that? Why didn't you beat that dust all over the place *before* you came in?" She rubbed her forehead in despair and turned back to matters at hand. "Explanations, please, and they better be good." She pointed a finger at Juan. "You're supposed to know better. Did I miss something at Comedy Central out there? What's so funny? What the hell is going on?"

Her son spoke first. "Well, *Mrs. K*, I'm a little old to be an intern, and I've just been told that when I get back, if I keep my phone in my pocket, my production rate will go right through the roof."

Both men giggled like school kids in front of the principal.

"What? Enough with you two." Martha's frustration was mounting. "What's with her calling you *Chico*, and who is *Mrs. K*?"

An impish grin covered Bill's face. "You, Mom. You're Mrs. K. Evidently, you're hip now: The modern, progressive female icon of the wine business. A stellar role model for young working women everywhere." He raised his hands, mimicking a camera taking pictures. "I can't wait to see your new publicity shots in all the trade journals. *Mrs. K* did this, *Mrs. K* did that. Remy is going to *rebrand* you for the twenty-first century, Mom. You should buy some of those tight, Spandex gym outfits and get more up-to-date for the photo shoots. Maybe get some trendy glasses." Bill placed a finger on his lip, pensive for a moment. "Maybe a tasteful nose earring. A gold one to go with your lovely skin."

"Spandex, for Christ's sake." Martha shook her head and snorted. "Rebranding? I'll be the one doing any rebranding around here—with a hot iron." Her finger shot out at Juan. "Why is my son still a buffoon? You were supposed to drag him into adulthood when he came back from university. That was eight or nine years ago." She brushed her fingers through her hair as if despair was something that could be knocked to the floor like dandruff.

Bill took up his case again. "That girl reveres you, Mom. I'm surprised she's not out there building a shrine to you." More male chuckling. "When she arrived this morning, she thought I was Juan. Then Juan came in the back door, and she heard him call me Chico. She told me I look old to be an intern. I told her I did odd jobs around here. She thinks I'm in the doghouse because I'm stuck on barn duty."

Juan, a master at covering himself, piped in, "I tried to send him on his way, Martha. Your son is still just a bad penny."

Bill turned to his teacher, mentor, workmate, and friend since he was born. *"Bad penny?* Thanks for throwing me under the bus, Juan. Why don't I get you a blanket so you can cover your ass some more?"

Juan ignored him. "It's just some fun, Martha." Juan had been with her so long, he was one of the few who dared call her Martha. More family than employee, he was essential to the operation and was compensated accordingly.

Bill interrupted. "Tinker Bell out there is a ball of fire. She's so eager. Instead of eating her lunch, she's probably out there painting the side of the barn. And she spits out everything that goes through her mind. You've given her, and I quote, 'a big break, a chance at a full-time job,' and she's not going to let the two of us screw it up for her."

As things sorted themselves out, Martha scowled at her boy. "And you just sat there and let Remy stand up and take the blame for you being here and not where you said you'd be? That young lady out there spent six years getting her degree. She paid for it by herself, not like you and that gravy train ride you had through UC Davis. She's not here for your amusement."

"Mom, we're having a little fun. Don't say anything. Play along with us, just for a bit. She's throwing out ideas about everything, and some of them are good. She won't do it if she knows who I am. And she's funny as hell and doesn't even realize it."

"This will come back to bite both of you." Martha mused on it for a bit, absently tapping her pen on the desk. "Okay, only for a while. Now get out of here."

Her son couldn't leave it alone. "She'll probably want to plaster you all over Twitter, Instagram, and YouTube, Mom. You should get ready. She's determined to make you a major *influencer* in the wine business."

Social media was foreign territory to Martha, and she was happy to leave it there. Barely suppressing a snarl, she looked up and waved her pen at her son. "Is Instagram the same as a telegram? Then I have an *Insta*gram for you two—get out!"

Martha wanted to make sure they got the message. She barked at the two men as they turned to leave: "Remy comes highly recommended, and I'm giving her a chance. She lives with her mother and two sisters. They've fought hard to keep their house and get by over the years. She's the oldest, and a lot of the burden has fallen on her. The degree is a bonus. I'm impressed that this girl worked part time after school throughout high school and college." The pen once again rose to her son. "That young lady has earned a break. You two better not do anything to hurt her feelings." Martha glared at Bill. "It might be good to have some *competent* youth around here with some fresh ideas. Am I clear?"

Respect for the new girl crossed both men's faces.

"Yes, ma'am," they both said.

Bill hesitated. Cautiously he asked, "Mom, why is she here?"

Martha leaned back and relaxed a little in her worn leather chair. "Skip has been here several years working under you and Juan, learning your side of the business. Juan and I will be stepping back soon." The ever-present pen shot out at Juan. "I'm not having him running around in those hot fields eight or ten hours a day at his age. He's done his time. He'll be cutting back, spending more time inside. We hired Skip to fit in easily when that time arrives. I also want to cut back, travel a little, enjoy all the things I've been putting off for years. I want someone young, sharp, and aggressive to carry some of the load. Remy may or may not be that person. We'll find out soon enough."

"Why do you have her cleaning out the barn? That place is a mess. It'll be hard work."

"Everybody's got to start somewhere," was the dismissive reply.

Bill shook his head. "You're a tough old bird, Mom."

Martha lowered her head back to her paperwork. "That's what got me here. And if *you're* lucky, I'll find another tough old bird to replace me."

Duly reprimanded, the two men left. Martha smiled as she heard the familiar banter between the inseparables as they made their way down the hallway. The two of them ran their part of the business tightly and efficiently, but she enjoyed snapping at them once in a while to amuse herself and let them know she was still around. When her husband had died thirteen years ago, the same year that her granddaughter was born, he had insisted near the end that Juan be given three percent of the company. It made a statement about his importance to them, a reward for countless years of dedication. Her husband and Juan had also been inseparable, toiling together for years in the fields and the production facilities as the business expanded. Around the same time, while her son had been away at university, Martha had also made Juan manager of the winemaking facilities.

Juan owning his three percent and being the *manager* of winemaking facilities was the worst thing that had happened to her son. Juan jokingly lorded it over Bill whenever he could. Martha continued smiling and listening to Juan's receding voice echoing off the hallway wall as he started in on her son.

"You hear that, Chico? You've got to step up, carry your share. Listen to old Juan. As a shareholder and *manager* of the production facilities, I think I'm technically your boss. I'm keeping an eye on you for your mom."

Bill shot back, "God, between my mom and you, half the time I think I'm in a daycare center. You two belong in an old folks' home. Leave me alone."

He was ignored. "On top of everything else, now I have to *de-buffoon* you, whatever that is. And the kid's right, keep that phone in your pocket. We need to see your production rate jump up." On and on he droned. Bill had listened to the same broken record since he'd learned to pick his first grapes when he was in grade school.

He shook his head, walked faster, and hummed loudly, trying to drown Juan out, as had been his tactic since he was twelve.

Remy noticed a smiling Juan blabbing away at a sullen Chico as they approached the barn. She wondered if she'd made the situation worse. "Are you in trouble?" she asked.

"Not any more than usual," said Chico. He looked back over his shoulder and lowered his voice. "I don't want to say that the Mad Duchess back there can be mean and evil, but when she goes up into the mountains, the wolves build bonfires to keep *her* away."

Remy scrunched up her face in a dismissive frown. "You're a sick man, Chico. Did you tell Mrs. K to order more dumpsters?"

"Yeah, yeah."

Sweat and brute labor yielded more space in the front of the barn. The battle line moved forward. Piles to the left outside the building awaited more dumpsters. Those to the right needed boxes for sorting. A third row blossomed for recycling. When they sat for their short afternoon break, Remy removed her hat, shook out her hair, and gulped down half a bottle of water. She then announced her opinion. "This barn should be the tasting room."

"What?" asked Chico.

"I drove up to the tasting room at the big vineyard on Saturday to learn a little more about the company before I started. It's a long way out and hard to find up that long single-lane drive. When I got there, they turned me away and said I needed an appointment. I mean, come on, it's not some swanky restaurant in Santa Rosa on Friday night." Remy raised both arms and rolled her eyes to emphasize her point. "This company needs marketing, branding, promotion. This property here is great and is close to town. It's easy to get to." She swept her arm toward the barn. "Look at this place. It's one enormous opportunity waiting to happen. It's a shame Mrs. K has to work out of that old house. They should tear it down and build new offices with a private event center. Rent it out for meetings and special events." Remy was on a roll now. "This barn could be a tasting room closer to civilization. The tasting room is one of the top—if not *the* top—marketing and promotional tools for a winery. It offers an intimate opportunity to impress and hold repeat customers. Why do you think there are so many of them around, littering downtown Healdsburg and Santa Rosa and Napa? Some towns are even passing laws to limit them." She swept her hand around at the sad collection of old wine equipment off to the side. "Look at all that old stuff. It can be used in a small, interesting wine-history exhibit, a mini-museum to set the theme. Incorporate it into the tasting rooms. The wine tourists would love it."

"Customers can't take any of the wine-tour buses up to the tasting room now because, as you say, it's a tough location to get to," Chico explained. "They sell high-end wine and want a selective group coming in. That's why the reservations."

"I'd like to put some ideas together for Mrs. K. If I have any questions, can I ask you or Juan?"

"Ask away," said Chico as they got back to it.

Remy sensed he was a little tense from his meeting in the office. She felt sorry for him. He wasn't afraid of work, seemed bright enough, but he appeared to have some kind of combative thing with the boss. Glancing at him across the barn where he and Juan were muscling some big pieces of equipment, she thought he was fit and attractive. He had no wedding ring on. Her focus returned to work. Romance was definitely not on her radar now. Every one of her thoughts, every aching muscle was dedicated to one goal—to get the job.

Just what I need, thought Bill, a third person telling me what to do on top of Juan and my mother. He could start a new religion around the holy trinity of critics. Remy, this new apostle, was easy. She just wanted to tear everything down around here and rebuild. God knows what she'd say if she ever saw the production facilities. Burn that, too? Build Rome on top of the ruins? Why couldn't people leave him alone?

Bill was happy now. He had his daughter, his job, and a peaceful life. The physical work in the barn settled him. After thinking about it for a few minutes, he had to admit he was impressed by Remy's idea. A tasting room in the barn was an excellent idea for the future. Why hadn't his mom or he thought of it? How did this woman come up with all that after being here for a few hours? Coppola, Mondavi, and many other wineries had created unique spaces, and they were valuable avenues to reaching new customers since the wine tourism craze had boomed. The tasting room being here in the barn, closer to town, would make it more accessible and more public. The barn, larger than the current location out on the hill, could handle more customers. He made a mental note to call Harry Graves, his high school mate who worked in the local planning department. It wouldn't hurt to check out zoning and other possibilities.

He was right about one thing, at least. Remy wouldn't have been so free and easy with her ideas had she known who he was. The young lady was trying to land a full-time job. She'd be much more formal and cautious about speaking her mind if she knew he was one of the owners. A new, accessible, up-to-date tasting room combined with a wine-history museum? He realized Remy's happy, free-and-easy manner disguised a sharp, perceptive brain. The new girl was attractive in more ways than one. And the protective way she'd jumped to his defense with his mother earlier was not lost on him.

Remy had made it through an exhausting first day on the job. In the shower, she used a brush. She would *not* wear a short-sleeved shirt or ankle socks tomorrow. Dust, mixed with grease from old equipment and grime liquefied by sweat, coated her skin. The heat had baked it on like a glaze. She'd been scratching her ankles, arms, and neck all the way home. It felt like all the bugs in the building had a reunion on her body and left their marks. Extra shampoo soaked longer in her hair while the warm water worked on her tired muscles. Finally refreshed, she changed to a T-shirt, shorts, and sandals and drifted downstairs to the kitchen sink to clean her once-blue sneakers that were now a deep, earthy brown.

Exhausted, Remy had a quick dinner of leftovers. Dishes cleaned, she made a glass of iced tea, walked out the patio sliding door, and plopped down on a chaise lounge in the shade of their modest rear yard. Her mother spent her free time on gardening, and the yard, enclosed by a high fence, was peaceful. A small brick path meandered through flowerbeds, shrubs, and two shade trees. Birds chirped above, and bees buzzed among the flowers. The sound of trickling water from the small fountain by the patio's edge poured relaxation into her mind and filtered into her aching muscles and joints.

Old habits die hard. Remy's years-long routine of sitting and studying at the day's end had now changed slightly. She sat with her winery paper from school and penciled changes and additions on the margins. New ideas were added as she revamped and refined the work specifically for Rolling Oaks Winery. Sometimes one of her romance novels would relax her, but today, she wanted her ideas down before she forgot them. Revelations from her first day picked her spirits up until she was tired and put the paper down to reflect on the people she'd met and the work she'd done.

She thought she'd done okay and had held her own. Juan and Chico were nice, fun to banter with. Juan had tons of stories about the old, rusted winery equipment they'd unearthed. He'd explained what he could—some of the stuff was so old even he didn't recognize it. He also promised to show her how things were done nowadays when and if she ever made it up to the production facilities. She had discovered that Juan was an old-school gentleman with two daughters around her age. He proudly boasted about the two of them finishing university.

Chico was strong and helped her whenever he saw her struggling with something. He had a good sense of humor—

almost got her with that horrible raccoon story. He probably wasn't as old as she'd first thought. Lines on his tanned, somewhat-handsome face, earned from years of working outside, gave him loads of character. The tan also made those blue eyes pop. His hair would appall Lynn. She would say the way he'd had it cut made it a wasted asset.

She must have fallen asleep, because the next thing she knew, she felt her mother shaking her shoulder, telling her to go to bed. The sun was setting. The heat of the day had taken a heavier toll than she'd thought. She emptied the untouched ice tea in the sink before climbing the stairs, gripping the handrail for extra support.

Curled up in bed, she made a vain attempt to read a little and find some comfort in *Sense and Sensibility*. After a few minutes, her eyes tired, and she gave up. She placed a marker on the page and closed the cover, thinking more about how nice the two men had been today. Remy reflected on how her old novels highlighted the manners and civility of the times past—manners that were sorely lacking in present day. She'd lived with this contrast daily working in the burger joints and markets, where the use of a simple "please" or "thank you" bounced along the edge of extinction. The two men at the barn were nice and mannerly. Lots of pleases and thank-yous mixed with helping hands whenever she needed it—a welcome change.

The satisfaction of a job well done eased the end of her day. She didn't have to wait long for the sleeper train to pull into the station.

Chapter 4

Wednesday morning, the heat toyed with their endurance. In the afternoon, it punished them. The temperature shot well past one hundred degrees Fahrenheit. Outside in the sun, plant leaves sagged from the strain, birds lost the energy to sing, field mice stayed in their burrows. Even passing cars seemed to move slower. The barn, with no insulation and only one open door, transformed itself into a furnace. There wasn't a hint of a breeze.

Early afternoon, the two men were muscling an old tractor rim onto a cart to move it outside. Juan caught Bill's eye and nodded his head toward Remy across the room. Her shirt was soaked through. She looked pale and was quiet now, not her usual cheery, inquisitive, humorous self. She was fading.

Juan whispered to Bill, "Get her out of here, Chico. She's going to hurt herself or fall down. Chica's not used to this heat, and like your stubborn mother, she has no quit in her."

Bill, upset that he hadn't noticed himself, walked over to Remy. She looked like she was swaying. He wanted to reach out and steady her but decided against it. Instead, he smiled and spoke casually. "Time to wrap it up, Remy. It's too hot. Juan and I can't keep up with you. You're starting to make us look bad. Go home and cool off. We'll pick it up in the morning." When she didn't accuse him of being a wimp, Bill knew she was exhausted. His heart went out to her as she looked at him with poorly disguised relief.

"Thanks, Chico. I don't mind tough days, but this heat is new to me. At least the burger joints and the food stores are air-conditioned."

Bill wiped his handkerchief across his forehead. "Well, Juan and I are giving up. You've outlasted us, and we're used to the heat."

"What about Mrs. K?" Remy asked. "What will she say if she comes by?"

He could see the worried look on her face, the will not to quit, not to look bad in her quest for the job. He raised a finger. "I'll handle Countess Dracula. If she doesn't like it, she can haul her ass out here and do it herself."

"Chico! You can't talk like that about the boss!" She shook her head but maintained her smile. "God, I've got a lot of work to do with you."

He turned to walk away. "Why change now? She won't do anything. Do you know how many times I've testified in court to keep her out of jail? I got that ankle bracelet off more than once so she could go drinking and salsa dancing in San Francisco."

He could see Remy perk up at the thought of his mom half in the bag, salsa dancing. A twinge of guilt flickered through him as Remy once again defended his mother, and he realized some serious explaining would have to be done when his ruse unraveled. He wanted to keep it up a little longer, liking the way she treated him as a fellow worker, feeling amused and comforted by her comment about having a lot of work to do with him. Thank goodness, his mother hadn't heard that one. She'd probably kiss Remy and give her the job on the spot, happy to have another ally in straightening his life out, someone else to badger him into dating and finding a woman to give her more grandchildren.

The few women he had dated either pandered to his ego or salivated over his wallet. Remy only wanted to take his phone away and send him to detention.

Salvation slipped in surreptitiously shortly after sunset. It stirred awake miles away as warm air pulled moisture from the cool Pacific waters. Transformed into fog, it inched eastward on a soft breeze and slipped slowly in the night through the valleys and low hills of southern Sonoma County. Enough, it seemed to say. They deserved a break.

Remy sighed with relief as she looked out her bathroom window. Loaded with mercy, every outdoor worker's friend in Sonoma County was back—fog. If it held true, it would burn off around late morning, defeated by the summer sun. At least the morning would be bearable.

Three relieved workers sat for their morning break as the sun started breaking through. They listened as rafters and beams high above groaned and creaked, surrendering the cool of the night. Soon, sweat would give handkerchiefs their purpose. Energy drinks in plastic bottles would be greedily consumed and refilled with water. Don't touch any hot metal in the sun.

Break over, the three bodies waded back into the mess, combat-ready in masks and gloves. Remy now knew to always wear a long-sleeved shirt and tall socks, preferably not white. Grime etched into her skin, bug bites, and scratches were factors to consider. More dumpsters were lined up along the property and beckoned for their fair share of the load. Bill and Juan started muscling tractor parts, old tires, and heavy metal pieces while Remy moved small stuff and directed them in the sorting process.

Observing all this sporadically from her office window, Martha finally wandered over late in the morning, carrying two cups of coffee. The activity was a magnet to her. It exhausted Martha watching the energetic young lady go nonstop. As she approached, she wondered how her son could have let all this stuff accumulate over the years.

"Don't throw that chair away," she said to Juan as he reached one of the dumpsters. "It belonged to my father." She gestured to Remy. "Come outside and sit with me for a bit, dear. We'll both take a break."

The two women sat in the shade beside the barn, and Martha handed Remy a cup of coffee. "How are things going, dear? Are Juan and, um, *Chico* carrying their share?"

"Chico spends time on the phone, but all the calls are coming in. He's not shirking. I hope he doesn't have problems at home. Juan and I wouldn't make a dent without his muscle. And Juan, wow! That guy never stops. He has this smooth, even flow when he works. He never wavers. How long has he been with you?"

Martha suppressed a laugh. Half her son's job was on the phone, people calling him from the main winery, the vineyards, and suppliers. "Juan has been here for over forty years. He was the first man my husband hired. He and my son, Bill, handle the operations in the fields and production facilities, while I handle most of the administration."

"Oh, so if I have any questions about wine, Juan can teach me?"

"Absolutely."

"Your son, Bill, is he around much?"

"Well, most of the time, yes. But he does spend a lot of time running around." Wanting to change the subject, Martha said, "I know that your mom's a nurse. What about your younger sisters? What do they do? How old are they?"

"Well, we're the three Rs—not reading, 'riting and 'rithmetic—but Remy, Roxy, and Rita. I'm about to be twenty-six, Rita is eighteen and starts junior college this August, and Roxy is thirteen." Remy lowered her head and looked down. "Our dad left when Roxy was one. We don't hear from him." She gathered herself quickly and smiled. "Our family is really close. My mom works hard, and we all look out for each other. We're one of the happiest families I know."

Martha remembered when her son's wife left, years ago when her granddaughter was young. A high school pregnancy every family hopes never happens to them. She smiled back. "I have a granddaughter that's thirteen."

"Whoa, Chico was talking about his daughter yesterday. She's thirteen, too."

"Yes, dear. I know her." Martha knew it was time to move on. "Well, I have to get going. I have to run around a lot this afternoon. You keep an eye on those two."

Remy went back to the barn. Bill came up to her, casting his eye over her shoulder as his mother went into the office. "What did she want? You're not in trouble now, are you?"

"Not a chance, Chico. I don't walk around with a bull's-eye on my back like somebody around here." The comment was accompanied by a soft punch on the arm. "You should follow my example. You might last until Labor Day." She smiled up at him. "I'll make it one of my projects—help Chico last until Labor Day."

Bill leaned over, whispering a confidence in her ear. "Be careful around her. I hear Mrs. K has a secret room in her house where she does blood transfusions during the full moon. They say she was born in the Carpathian Mountains somewhere in Transylvania."

He was rewarded with Remy's back as she walked away, her ponytail waving side to side from the rear of her baseball cap as she shook her head.

Chico, Juan, and Remy bent to their task until lunch. As they sat around in their chairs in the shade, munching on their food, Remy thought it time to enlighten the two men. They had been talking, laughing, making fun of her for three days, speaking Spanish between themselves. She was secretly thrilled that most of what they said was complimentary, but, nonetheless, it was time for a tune-up.

"*Atención, pendejos!*"

Both men's heads shot up—*pendejo* was *asshole* in Spanish.

"Well, *hombres,* I'm glad that Chico thinks I have a *fit figure*, my bubbly manner is *funny*, and that I talk a *lot. Pero esta juera habla español muy bien.*"

Chico and Juan heard it loud and clear—*this white girl speaks Spanish very well*. She even had the accent right.

The two men stopped eating and looked at her with eyes the size of dinner plates, mouths open, like they were trying to remember everything they'd said. They offered mumbled apologies.

"Why didn't you tell us you speak Spanish?" Chico said, sounding rather defensive.

"Don't even try to turn this around, Chico. You two are busted." She pointed her thumb over her shoulder. "Maybe I should go over to the office and ask Mrs. K where the human resources department is and find out how to file a sexual harassment complaint." Remy paused so the full effect would register. "You're lucky I'm too tired to move. I took Spanish in high school and college, but I learned all the questionable words working in burger shops and food markets for the last ten years. You're both lucky my degree isn't in political correctness."

Using Mrs. K, human resources, and sexual harassment in the same sentence had Juan and Chico close to trembling. Guillotines, whipping posts, and shotguns slowly descended from the ceiling, encircling the two terrified men. Little Remy Reilly had the full attention of the adult males in front of her.

She played it out.

"I'm thinking of going out to the Russian River this afternoon and lying on the beach. You guys wouldn't mind covering for me, would you?"

Some form of relief surfaced on Chico's face. "Sure. Sure. Whatever you want, Remy."

"You can count on us, Chica," said Juan.

Remy tapped her long fingers on her lips, and she gave Juan a pensive look. "Mrs. K says you know a lot about wine. If you promise to teach me, I'll let you off the hook. Do we have a deal?"

Juan jumped at the chance to sidestep the boss's wrath and possibly shift part of the blame. "Of course, Chica. You probably didn't hear the countless times I tried to tell Chico it was rude to speak Spanish in front of you. He's still a bad penny."

Jeez, he's called me Chica twice. Maybe he's starting to accept me.

Her focus shifted to Chico. "And you owe me, Chico." Remy rocked her head from side to side.

Chico, the idiot, didn't seem to want to let it go. "How were *we* to know you speak Spanish? How could *we* be guilty? You've deceived us, your fellow workers."

"Yeah, right, Chico. What a pathetic attempt to deflect *your* big problem. I want a ringside seat when you try to sell *that* one to the judge."

Remy leaned forward, close to him, and slowly started swirling both hands around hypnotically in front of Chico's face, freezing him with her blue eyes. This was where her passion for historical romance novels would pay off. He'd learn how his crime would have been handled in years past.

She crafted the scene for him.

"Let me tell you how they would have handled men like *you* in years past. Before your trial, Chico, you'll have already spent weeks in the local dungeon, waiting for the magistrate to arrive for the assizes. He'll arrive in front of the assembly rooms in his shiny, black barouche carriage pulled by two white horses. He'll flick his finger at the jailers as he enters the building, and they'll drag you out of the stocks in the market square where the villagers have been throwing rotten garbage at you for days. His Honor, high up on his perch, will be fixing a white wig on his head when he calls me, the poor, abused country girl to the stand."

Remy stopped hypnotizing and demurely placed both hands on her chest, tilting her head back. "I'll be nervous with all my fancy-dressed betters in the room, but he'll calm me as he asks me to explain my horrible ordeal." She theatrically lowered her head and folded her hypnotizing hands in front of her, now a meek peasant girl. "I know I'm poor, Your Honor, but I'm a good girl." Remy placed one hand back over her breast. Her voice changed to be high, scared, shrill. "*These two—*"

The two men jumped in their seats at the change in volume and passion. They glanced toward the office, clearly praying that Mrs. K couldn't hear the tortured lament.

Remy paused to correct the scene before continuing. "Sorry, I forgot that Juan is off the hook." An accusatory finger shot out like a spear toward Chico. "*This hooligan*, this evil man set upon me in the barn, Your Honor. He was Beelzebub himself. And the language he used. Lordy, Your Honor, it was the likes of which proper people should never hear. He was touching me—please don't make me say where—when this fine person"—Remy scowled at Chico and swept her arm toward Juan—"rushed in and rescued me." Remy paused for dramatic effect, squinted, and reached out her long finger toward Chico. "The judge will ask me if I want to put the rope around your neck myself." Satisfied with her performance, Remy sat back and took a well-deserved sip from her bottle of water.

A smiling Juan seemed happy to be the hero. It clearly amused him, the whole time Remy did that swirling-hand thing in front of Chico's face, a voodoo high priestess. "And that's just the way I'll have to explain it to Mrs. K. Sorry, Chico."

Chico shook his head. "How do you even dream this stuff up?" he asked Remy. "Assizes, wigs, stocks, Beelzebub?"

"Well, I can see you're not a romantic."

"Romantic? Christ, Remy, you just had me hung."

"I read historical romance classics. I love all the old shows and movies, you know, *Downton Abbey*, all the Jane Austen books and movies. *Pride and Prejudice, Emma, Sense and Sensibility*. Also George Eliot's *Mansfield Park* and the Brontë sisters, among others. Back then, that's how they would have handled *you*, Chico." Remy rose from her chair. "Now, it's time for we peasants to get back to work. The manor house needs our production."

Daydreaming while moving between tasks, Remy had a good idea how, years ago, all the scullery maids, charwomen, chambermaids, and others at the bottom of the service chain felt. Years of working in small burger kitchens with inadequate ventilation and an excess of grease in the air wiggled her memory pole. On her feet all day catering to demanding customers at the food market, running back and forth to keep her cheese section pristine, was only a small step up from those burger joints. She knew she had all the opportunities, drive, and skills to "better herself," as they would have said back in the old days. Soon, if things went right, she may have the chance to see how they lived upstairs. Decent hours and a better salary would bless her with time and money to have her hair done, buy some nice clothes, have a fancy dinner once in a while. A vacation wasn't unthinkable. Up until now, she'd only ever been to San Francisco twice and Lake Tahoe once, and she'd never been on a plane.

Her mind jumped back to the present when she saw Chico lifting a heavy wheel rim onto his shoulder across the room. Sun, sneaking through the open doors, bounced off his short sandy-blond hair. His short-sleeved T-shirt clung to his sweaty frame. This boy didn't need a gym. As he straightened under the load, her eyes slipped down, and she noticed he had a nice butt. Thoughts were entertained—immodest thoughts that

Remy immediately dismissed as unseemly and inappropriate. The Bennet girls in *Pride and Prejudice*, the Dashwood sisters in *Sense and Sensibility*, and Fanny Price in *Mansfield Park* would never succumb to such thoughts. Would they? Even with all those tight pants back then? Come on. Would they?

Around two o'clock, Bill heard Remy cry out from across the room. His head shot up. "Are you okay?"

"It's nothing. Keep going." A sharp piece of metal had cut through her jeans and nicked her leg. Blood was running down the inside of her pants and staining the area around the tear. She swore to herself and limped out to her car.

Ten minutes later, her mid-thigh was wrapped with a ripped yellow T-shirt on top of her jeans. She worked her way back to the barn, eager to keep going, finish the day's quota.

"Whoa, whoa," said Bill as he rushed over to her, taking in the blood staining the yellow wrapping. "What the hell happened?"

She dismissed his concern. "A minor cut from a piece of metal. Nothing to worry about."

"Remy, the blood is seeping through that makeshift bandage. It's not a minor scratch. All this metal is rusted. You need to get it fixed properly and get a tetanus shot. Come on, get in my truck. I'm taking you to the doctor." He placed a hand on her shoulder, directing her outside.

"You promise you won't say anything to Mrs. K?" Tears—from frustration or pain—formed in the corners of her eyes. "I can't screw this up. I want this job. I need this job. A girl like me doesn't get breaks like this. I don't want people thinking I'm a screw-up"

Bill could tell Remy was upset—not about the leg, but about the job. It was only her fourth day. He lowered his voice and spoke slowly in an effort to relax her. "This is a winery and a vineyard, Remy. Cuts like this happen all the time. It's not a big deal. It won't faze Mrs. K a bit. Trying to *hide* it will get you into trouble. Now, please, get in the truck."

Remy relented. "Okay, but we have to go to the local hospital where my mother works. We have insurance for that. I can't afford to pay some neighborhood doctor."

"Okay. The hospital it is." Anything to get her into the damned truck. As they limped together to his vehicle, Bill said, "You know, this is a worksite accident. You don't have to pay for it. The company pays for it. They have insurance just for this."

Remy stalled him in the parking area again. A finger shot up beside her frustrated, pained face. "No! I'm not making the rates go up for Mrs. K's insurance. I'll say I did it at home."

Bill gave up. "However you want to do it, but please, get in the truck."

Driving out, Bill didn't know whether to laugh or cry at this girl's fierce independence and sense of personal responsibility. He wanted to put her at ease, make her think about something else. The leg had to hurt. He smiled at her. "You know that you can get workers' compensation for this, spend a few days on that beach at Russian River you talked about. I sure would."

Remy scowled at him. "What kind of wimp are you, Chico? It's a scratch. Do you run off to the palace doctor every time you sneeze or get a scratch?"

Palace doctor? Does this girl live in those old English movies?

A fresh approach was in order—distraction.

"Like I said, this isn't a problem. I'll tell Mrs. K. It'll be fine. You don't want to know what she did to me once when I needed stitches and didn't tell her. It was horrible. I had nightmares for a week. I think she was a matron in a prison camp in a past life."

Visibly alarmed, Remy put her hand on his forearm. "What? What did she do to you?"

Bill pretended distress. "No. I still can't talk about it. It makes the raccoon story look like a child's fairy tale."

His acting must have been appalling. Remy snorted. She smiled and punched his arm. "You can be a real ass, you know that, Chico?"

She was calming down. Bill distracted her more. "Have you come up with any more thoughts about updating the business? Your ideas yesterday were interesting. Seriously, they impressed me."

The tension drained out of her. "I did my final paper at school on marketing options for the modern winery. Yeah, things were spinning around in my head all night. I'm rewriting my paper for this place, to be more specific."

"Can I read it?"

Remy winced and shifted uncomfortably in her seat. "Maybe when I'm done."

Chapter 5

Both Remy's pain and her frustration were building when they arrived at the covered portico on the circular drive in front of the emergency room entrance. Chico eased her out of the truck. It was a high four-wheel-drive vehicle, and the first step down was a stretch. He helped her inside. "I'll park the truck and be right back."

A nurse, a friend of Remy's mother, spotted her as she limped into the lobby and made her way to the check-in counter. "Nicked yourself, Remy?" Clare Hill smiled and put a hand on Remy's shoulder. "That yellow band with the blood on it tied around your leg looks great with those jeans. You can start a new fashion trend. Come with me. The doctor will fix you up, and I'll go find your mother. We're not busy right now."

"Thanks, Mrs. Hill." Remy never wanted to be the center of attention and didn't like people making a fuss. It was nice that Mrs. Hill made light of her plight. A few stitches were water off a duck's back for these emergency room nurses.

Embarrassed, Remy fumed and reprimanded herself. Thank God, there was only one other person in the waiting area. If she was going to keep screwing up like this, maybe she should learn to do some simple stitches herself. Another thing to add to her screw-up skill set. She pictured going back in time one hour. First the cut on the metal, and then a smiling, well-delivered, "Oh, excuse me for a moment, gentlemen. Be right back." A sophisticated walk out to her car to pull out the sewing kit and get on with it. How hard could it be?

Carol Reilly was busy with two patients requiring care. When she pushed the curtain aside, the doctor had finished his work on her daughter. "How many stitches, Doctor?"

"Four, and a tetanus shot, Carol. She's ready to roll. I gave her a prescription for some pain pills. It might act up later tonight."

Remy thanked the doctor as he left. She replaced her ragged, bloody jeans with a pair of light-blue hospital pants, retrieved by her mother from her locker. Remy rolled up her deceased jeans and limped out to the waiting area, mortified by her appearance and predicament. Chico waited anxiously and smiled as she approached. Rising from her funk, Remy smiled weakly back and introduced him to her mother.

"A pleasure, Mrs. Reilly. Why don't you stay here and finish your shift? I'll take Remy home, and we'll bring her car by later on. Would that be okay?" Chico seemed happy to have a new target for his warped sense of humor. His face took on a mock-defeated look. "I tried to tell her about doing recreational drugs at lunchtime, but you know how kids are these days."

Carol Reilly laughed. "I understand, Chico. At least she's off the crystal meth. Life is full of small blessings."

Remy shifted around on the small wooden bench in the stark-white hospital hallway, searching for a comfortable position while being subjected to her mother and Chico talking about her a few feet away. The harsh lighting above made her feel like she was the village idiot on a stage with everyone staring at her.

Carol proceeded to tell Chico stories about all the burns and cuts Remy had gotten over the years working in the fast-food places and playing in the neighborhood when she was a child. "I swear, if she gets any more battle scars, they'll give her veteran's benefits."

Remy swore that half the stories were made up. She sat to the side, bathing in embarrassment. Both of them laughed away, having a good old time at her expense. It was like she wasn't even there. Chico was just busting at the seams at the amusing tales. Maybe they should go out for a cocktail together and drag it out a little longer. She thought about changing her name and moving to Alabama.

Bill organized her in the pickup truck. As he closed his own door, he heard Remy curse as she held her tattered jeans.

"These pants cost twenty dollars at Target, almost an hour's pay. I just got them."

An hour's pay was an interesting way to look at it. His curiosity about Remy resurfaced. "Where was your last job, if you don't mind me asking?"

"I just graduated, so everything was part time. I worked in burger joints for years. Now, I work at the Alderetti market two evenings a week and Saturdays, sometimes Sundays."

That surprised Bill. "You still work there?"

"Yes."

"So all this week, after working in that heat, you left the barn and worked at the market two nights?"

"Sure. I can stash some bucks now. I look after the cheese and pâté section. It's one of those small high-end markets. I've been there for years. The owner loves it because he can trust me to run it, especially on Saturdays when it's busy. If I survive this internship and get a permanent job, I might make around thirty dollars an hour. That's mega bucks for me. And it'll be full time with a real future." Remy paused as if something had just popped into her mind. "Don't you have to pick up your daughter from school, or does your wife do it? I don't want to hold you up."

How would she even think of that, with that leg killing her?

"Relax, it's taken care of. And it's just me and Lizzie, my daughter. The wife is long gone."

Remy said, "Gone?"

Bill laughed. "She left when Lizzie was one and a half years old. It was one of those unfortunate high school pregnancy things to start with. Senior year. We were both so young. Before she left, she announced she couldn't live around here anymore, hated the lifestyle, hated being tied down. She didn't want the same life as I. A fuller social life on a grander scale in the big city called out to her. She always enjoyed being the center of attention."

A sad look flitted across Bill's face as he drifted back in time. They'd rented a house in the beginning, when Bill starting university at UC Davis the following September. UC Davis was *the* school for the wine-growing industry. It was over a two-hour drive to the campus, so he worked his schedule to be home three nights a week. After his wife left, his daughter had stayed with Martha and a nanny when he was at school, the same nanny-housekeeper who looked after his mother's house, his house, and his daughter to this day.

Remy changed the subject. "Your daughter's name is Lizzie, as in Elizabeth Bennet from *Pride and Prejudice*? That's so cool."

"My mother watches Lizzie a lot. She's the one who shortened Elizabeth to Lizzie. And it stuck. My mom watches the same old movies you do. I'm sure that's where she got it from."

"Chico, when does Mrs. K's son show up? I still haven't seen him. How come she does all the work? How old is he?"

Bill went on alert. "Well, he's my age, thirty-two. I, um, went to school with him. This month, he's either playing polo in the south of France, or racing yachts off of Mexico. I forget which. You know how these spoiled rich kids are."

"Huh, Lord Bill the Absent," said Remy with a hint of venom in her voice. "How could he do that to his mother?"

It was time to change the subject. "I'm sure he'll get it out of his system soon and come back to the roost."

They drove up to her house in the old, clean subdivision in the southern end of Santa Rosa. The homes in the area were well maintained. The lawn and shrubs in front of Remy's boasted the care and attention paid to them. Bill walked around and helped Remy out of the truck. He didn't want her stretching the bad leg too far and falling down or pulling a stitch. "Nice place, Remy. You go ahead and open the door, and I'll carry your backpack and jeans."

Walking up to the house, Bill discreetly glanced at the brown-leather tag on the back of the rolled, wrecked Levi's, taking note of the waist size and length. He knew they fit perfectly. He'd been distracted by them for several days. "Give me your car keys. Juan and I will bring it by later."

Remy gave him a shy punch on the arm. "Thank you, Chico. You've been very nice to me today."

"I assume men are nice to you all the time." He ran his eyes down to the baggy blue hospital pants. "Besides, I'm a sucker for a woman in light blue. It goes great with your hair."

Remy blushed.

Bill knew he was on tenuous ground when he blurted out the compliment and she blushed. His mother had made everyone, including him, take a political correctness course. He knew he shouldn't flirt with an employee, but he couldn't help himself. This driven woman was making an impression on him, an impression he hadn't felt in years.

The air conditioner kicked on as Remy sat in her mother's recliner, elevating her leg and finding a comfortable position. The leg felt much better after she wrapped some plastic wrap around it and took a long, hot shower, casting off the day's dust and dirt.

An hour later, Carol Reilly came in carrying some groceries. "Stay there, honey. Keep your leg up. How does it feel?"

"I'm good to go, Mom. Not much pain, a minor setback. I'll be back at it tomorrow."

Remy knew her mother wouldn't try to talk her into taking it easy. She knew how important the job was to her.

"That Chico sure is good looking," Carol said. "And pleasant, too. He has a great sense of humor. What does he do at the winery?"

"Gets into trouble, mostly." Remy turned down the volume on the TV and squirmed around in the chair. She'd been watching Emily Brontë's *Wuthering Heights*. It was dark and wasn't one of her favorites, but it fit her mood nicely after making a fool of herself today. "He says he does odd jobs around the place, but I think he's sharper than he lets on. I think he does something out at the actual winery facility. Juan, the other man I told you about last night, and Chico are both good to work with. They're fun, and they're nice. They try to hide it, but they look out for me and make sure I don't overdo it."

"We're doing a lot better with the money in the last few years, honey," Carol said. "You can slow down a bit, start to enjoy life, maybe start socializing more now that university is finished. That Chico wouldn't be a bad place to start. How old is he?"

"Jeez, Mom, he's thirty-two. He has a kid and is six years older than I am." Her frustration from the day brought out some sarcasm. "Why don't you go over to the retirement home and pick me out a few more geriatric candidates? Besides, we work together."

Carol smiled. "Just a thought, honey." She marched off to prepare dinner.

Remy settled back into the recliner and turned the volume back up. Her focus, however, was drifting.

Oh my God, she thought, *me with a divorced older man? My mother is losing it*. Visions from old gothic romance movies popped up. Remy closed her eyes, drifted off to her long-ago world. She pictured herself being dragged out of her tiny, humble, childhood home with a thatched roof in a small village and sold off to the lecherous eighty-year-old lord of the manor so that her family wouldn't be evicted from their meager tenant plot. It was winter, and the snow swirled around her as she pulled her tattered wool shawl tighter, trudging up the frozen path to the dark manor house. Life in an antique bed with an antique man awaited her. Sacrifices had to be made for the family.

She snapped out of it. *Jesus, I've got to cut back on that dark Gothic stuff*.

After dinner, Remy hobbled up the stairs to her small bedroom, careful not to spill her tea. The beige wall-to-wall carpet was old but spotless. Even as a teenager, she'd kept her room neat and tidy. Her prize possessions—an old, dark four-poster double bed with matching old-world dresser—had been found in a used furniture shop years before. Against one wall was a bookcase that matched close enough. She hobbled over to it. Enough of Brontë. She needed something happier—*Emma*. She'd find comfort tonight in Emma's mischievous matchmaking.

Colonel Brandon, the cat, was very proprietorial about his Remy. He meandered into the room, leaped up on the bed, and settled into his usual spot against one of her legs. He liked it when Remy would sometimes whisper the words aloud and lull him to sleep. The covers were pulled up. She could make believe that the sound of the air conditioner was wind and rain. Book in hand, she—and the Colonel—drifted happily into the story.

The catastrophe of the day, however, refused to vacate her mind. Remy closed the book and put her head back on her pillow. She reprimanded herself again. Remy had a forgiving nature toward others but was her own worst critic.

I like these people. I like this company. I want this job, but they'll think I screwed up, wasn't careful enough. Even Mrs. K, when she finds out, will feel the same. I lost focus for a second and ended up in the hospital getting stitches.

Remy Reilly did not identify herself as a victim. She was from the personal responsibility crowd. Things in life were earned. In high school, her grades would have earned her a place in most prestigious universities. Unfortunately, life's obstacles, notably a lack of money, prevented her from going down that road. Sonoma State University was close by and affordable. So be it. Get on with it. Now she had ninety days to earn the job she really wanted.

Way above average at reading people from an early age, Remy would find out tomorrow what they thought, especially Mrs. Keating. Body language, voice inflections, and tone of the conversations would all be deciphered and evaluated. She reflected back on the game she'd played evaluating people in the burger joints. People would stand in line at lunchtime with a massive menu staring them in the face up on the wall behind her, while she would stand in front of the cash register. She'd divided people into two groups—sharp and dull. The sharp ones knew what they wanted and had their money or credit cards ready. They knew there were people behind them in the same rush they were and were fully aware they were in a fast-food location. They were sharp, quick, and ready. The dull ones, preoccupied with cell phones, chatting with each other, or off in dreamland somewhere, would act surprised when they arrived in front of her and were asked what they wanted to order. They would then ask questions about different burgers when the answers were prominently displayed on the board behind her. Remy would patiently answer their questions and give them the price. The dullards would then start fumbling in their pockets or with their purses to find their money, like it was an afterthought, like they'd forgotten why they were there. The rule of retail demanded that both groups received the same smile and were treated with the same courtesy. She was usually ninety percent right when evaluating them in line before they reached the register.

Tomorrow, she would be able to evaluate Mrs. K's opinion, despite what she said to her.

A positive and deceptively disciplined young woman, Remy knew it was time to relegate these unhelpful thoughts to the side. Random reflections like these were the enemy, clogging the brain and remaining unresolved. *Don't waste the mental energy. Stay positive. Fight for this job.*

Tiredness was creeping up. Shifting around in bed in a futile effort to get comfortable, Remy drifted to more pleasant thoughts—Chico. He was always kind to her, always patient with her. Today had exposed how kind and considerate he was. Him being unattached cast him in a new light. Raising a daughter by himself must be hard. She allowed herself time to reevaluate him. Originally, she'd thought him to be much older. Thirty-two wasn't *that* old. He had a good sense of humor: an unbendable requirement for Remy. He had about four or five inches on her, not bad for her five-foot seven-inch frame. If she ever had a pair of high heels, she'd be right up there with him, almost eye to eye. Well, until she fell over. *High heels?* Remy caught herself before she dared to do the eye-to-eye thing. Picturing herself that close, waltzing inches away from those blue eyes in a country house's grand ballroom was a bit much for tonight. She rolled on her side and tried to conjure up sleep.

Bill stopped by his mother's house to pick up Lizzie. There was always someone around at his mom's, either his mother or the nanny-housekeeper, Gloria. Years before, when Bill had been away at university, Martha had gotten into the habit of bringing work home in the afternoon and working from there in order to watch her granddaughter. The routine had continued until today. Lizzie would go there after school and do her homework or play, rather than sit alone at their own home a short distance away. It was a comfortable, safe bike distance for his daughter.

Martha was preparing dinner for them when Bill plopped down on one of the island stools.

"It's only me, Lord Bill the Absent, your ne'er-do-well son."

"Excuse me?" She noticed her son seemed happier than usual.

"That's my new name according to Remy. I'm never around to help my poor mother. I'm off playing polo in the south of France, or God knows where else. She thinks it's appalling. She does not understand how you can run the empire all by yourself." Bill laughed. "You should hear some of little Miss Perky's ideas. Some of them surprised me. They're good. Evidently, she did her final paper in school on marketing options for the modern winery. She's revising it now specifically for us. See, Mom, I'm glad she doesn't know who I am yet. She's not inhibited when she talks to Juan and me. We're only fellow workers."

Martha studied her son. "You can't keep it up for much longer. If you do, I'll tell her." Martha didn't want to be in town when that shoe dropped.

"Only a little longer, Mom. I want to hear more of her unedited ideas for the place. She's a nice, bright person, an open book with no hidden agenda."

As she watched her son's face, one of Martha's bulbs went on. *Hidden agenda*? His face was as easy to read as when he was five. "You like her." She almost smiled as her boy squirmed.

"Come on, Mom. Let's not get ahead of ourselves."

She pushed. "You like her, and you don't want her to know you're one of the owners. You don't want her judgment of you swayed because you have money."

"Mom!"

Martha allowed herself a small smile as she recognized the lowered head and the embarrassed shuffling from his youth. She turned back to the stove. "Well, you better sort it out."

As Bill continued, Martha detected the hesitancy in his voice. "Um, there was a minor problem in the barn this afternoon." Bill recounted the accident for his mother. He told her how Remy had been forced to go to the hospital and get four stitches, how she was upset about letting the team down and wouldn't allow it on the company insurance.

Martha was wondering which solar system this girl came from. Who had that kind of personal responsibility these days? Most young people would be calling lawyers or booking a week's holiday in Costa Rica. "Did you tell her to take time off?"

"Mom, she's just like you—pigheaded. One, she's not letting a few stitches stop her. Two, she's afraid she'll get in trouble. Remember, I told you she didn't even want to use the company insurance. The poor kid is out twenty dollars—an hour's pay— for her ripped jeans. I already stopped and got her a new pair."

Martha mused on the situation while she laid out some dishes. "Tomorrow, set up a couple of tables and a chair in the shade. Have her sit there and sort through some boxes. Tell her you and Juan will be in big trouble if she runs around. Take her to a long lunch and say it's a company expense. Drag it out so she's not on her feet for the rest of the day. It's Friday, so she'll have the weekend to recover a little more."

A concerned look crossed Martha's face as she stroked her son's face. "I want the three of you to watch out for this heat. That barn is a boiler. Slow down. You've been going at it hard, and I don't want you ending up like your father."

Bill and Lizzie ate dinner at Martha's house at least two nights a week. Their homes were a short distance apart, an easy walk or bike ride. At the table, business talk and cell phones were forbidden. Martha would alternate between doting on her granddaughter's day, or tactfully trying to coax her son into improving his abysmal personal life. She knew the only vacations he took were short ones with Lizzie. She speculated he dated rarely. Even his daughter ganged up on him to "get a life."

Martha Keating had two speeds—work and home. To this day, Bill remained baffled at the difference between work Mom and home Mom. The minute the workday was done, she flipped a switch and was a different person. Today, at work, she'd basically accused him of being lazy, and now, at home, she worried about his health. At work, she was domineering. At home, she sought his counsel on all the business matters, always speaking to him as an equal. She knew she never had to worry about anything in the field. Juan and he were always on top of it. Martha was a poorly disguised control freak, but at least she knew it.

Bill enjoyed sparring with his mom at work. Whenever she got too engrossed in a problem, too worried about sales or the competition, or got tired under the responsibility of it all, he knew he could lighten her mood with some of his comments or antics. He could always make her laugh.

Her comments earlier in the week about wanting to slow down had resonated with him. His mom deserved to have more free time, and he knew she'd spend it with Winston Wright, a family friend she was close with. Proper Martha only referred to him as a *friend*, but everyone who saw them together knew it was more than that. Joking with her about Winston usually got a terse reprimand. Still, Bill knew she enjoyed the teasing, especially since her granddaughter, who adored Winston, would tease her as well. Bill knew his own social life was drab, but he wasn't motivated to do anything about it. He was content with his lot in life.

Chapter 6

Stuck in light traffic on the way to the barn on Friday morning, Remy reviewed her scant love life to date. Chico, so kind to her the day before, had provoked thoughts about having a man in her life—an actual relationship.

A month, maybe six weeks was how long boyfriends usually lasted. Saturdays were what killed them. Saturdays were the problem. The boys wanted to go to the beach and party. It was always work for Remy. Well, time for a change. If this job worked out, she'd no longer let life be a thief, stealing time away from fun and relationships. She'd earned it.

As the traffic moved slowly, Remy daydreamed about the perfect date, sitting in a fancy restaurant with a man she cared for. Not simply a meal, but a romantic night out. Her hair done up in an elegant bun, the fabric of a lovely dress whispering across her chair as he held it out for her. Champagne would be poured, and her hand would be held. Candlelight, glittering off the crystal glasses, would wink at her. The china was so beautiful that food had no place on it. So many silver spoons, knives, and forks on the table would have her delightfully confused. Following a romantic toast, he would kiss her hand and lean over to whisper in her ear. He...

The groan of the old Toyota bumping over the driveway entrance jolted her back to the present, back to real life, where she knew she was still the charwoman, the scullery maid, the chimney sweep. Reality was a bitch.

Her phone rang as she parked. "Why the hell were you in the emergency room?" Lynn was very protective of her friend.

"How did you find out?"

"I have a hair salon, for Christ's sake. I hear everything. Priests in their confessionals might hear juicier stuff, but I doubt it. Are you okay?"

"Yes, stop worrying. I was going to call you later."

"Don't bother. The Wine Bar—five thirty. I'm turning in early tonight. It's been hell week around here." Lynn hung up.

Remy shrugged. "I guess it's the Wine Bar at five thirty."

She noticed Chico smiling at her as she made her way toward the barn, slightly favoring the injured leg. He seemed happy to see her. When she was close, he looked over her shoulder at the fading Japanese jalopy. "I didn't know you collected antique cars, Chica."

She wagged a finger in his face. "Don't get smart, Chico. That Toyota has been my faithful horse and carriage for almost ten years. Don't make fun of it." She pointed over his shoulder at his brown truck, which was probably white underneath all the dust and dirt from driving around the vineyards. "That thing you drive won't win Best in Show anytime soon. When's the last time you cleaned it?"

Chico smiled, conceding a point to her. "You rebound quick. Queen Kong has promoted you. Follow me."

He led her to the shady side of the barn where three large tables were in a row. The two end ones were stacked with cardboard boxes from the barn; the middle one was empty with a chair in front of it. Years of dust had been toweled off the boxes. Remy noted his thoughtfulness in bringing her a cup and thermos of iced tea from the offices. As he tucked the chair in under her, Chico gave her a quick pat on her shoulder.

"Evidently, Juan and I cannot be trusted with important stuff. Mrs. K"—even Juan and Chico were calling her that now—"says you're to sort through the boxes and make a call on what goes and what stays. She'll be back later to go over them with you. If you get out of that chair, Juan and I are in trouble." He gave her a smirk. "I'll have one of the servants bring you a chamber pot if you have to go. You were a trouper yesterday, so I've been instructed to take you to lunch today on the company. Evidently, *you* having an accident is *my* fault for not watching out for you." He pointed toward the offices. "Mrs. Daenerys Targaryen over there threatened to turn one of her dragons loose on me if it happens again. I can't win around here. Any place special you'd like to go for lunch?"

Still worried about how everyone felt about the previous day, Remy was slightly relieved by the way Chico acted. "Thank you. And thanks for the iced tea. Just a burger would be fine. It's very nice of you."

Chico shook his head and ambled back inside the barn.

A few minutes later, Juan came over to Remy. Martha had directed him to put the girl at ease "Fifth day on the job, Chica, and you're already on the gravy train. Mrs. K must be impressed by you." He winked at her and rejoined Chico moving the heavy stuff.

Everyone was getting protective of the new girl. Somewhat relieved that Mrs. K wasn't around, Remy sat and thought about her situation. Half of what Chico had said about Mrs. K's instructions were probably made up, an effort to put her at ease. He could be so nice when he wanted to be, sweet, like a peanut butter and jelly sandwich with the sarcastic crust trimmed off. She sensed he thought she was a good worker and would want her around, but from what she'd seen, that idiot held very little sway over Mrs. K's decisions. Any romantic musings were quickly cast aside. He was attractive, had a good job, and a sense of humor—there must be a girlfriend somewhere in the frame. Her thoughts returned to the job. Getting the job was paramount—the job, the job, just the job.

Noon found Bill holding the door to his truck open for Remy. A lavish burger lunch awaited. They drove to a place where Remy had worked a few years ago. According to her, they were the best burgers in town. It had been years since she'd been there.

It was busy. The line in front of them and the one at the soda machine to the side corralled construction workers in hard hats and orange vests, teenagers on their phones, and neatly dressed office workers. The business looked like it did many to-go orders. Behind the cashier, bodies moved efficiently around the open kitchen area, handling the noon rush hour, dancing around polished chrome tables. Remy and Bill studied the menu hanging over the counter while waiting for their turn.

"Wow, these burgers are ten bucks now!" said Remy. She turned to her benefactor. "Can I get a milkshake? They're not cheap here."

Trying to hide his smile, Bill said, "Hell, get the fries, too."

Bill had been mulling over a few of the ideas that Remy seemed to regurgitate on a daily basis. Change was not one of his strong points, but even he was getting excited about some of them. Seated at the table, waiting for their food, he felt awkward, like a teenager on a date. At least they both weren't both texting. Finally, he said, "Tell me some more of your ideas about the winery. Maybe I can help answer some of your questions about how things work around the place."

No coaxing was needed; Remy lit up and burned ahead. Bill could see this was becoming a passion for her. Thoughts poured out of her head, mixed with questions about many things, all jumbled together, coming in spurts while she consumed her meal. Bill noted that she would not talk with her mouth full of food. Her manners reflected that she read all those old romance novels.

Exhausted just listening to her, Bill finally changed the subject. "I think in the next week or two, Mrs. K wants to put you up at the tasting room to learn how that works and learn what goes into tasting and selling different wines. Then maybe she'll give you a chance at sales. She'll probably want you up there for a few weeks. Do you think you could sell?"

"Did she say that *before* yesterday's disaster?"

"Relax. I told you it wasn't a problem. Now, can you sell?"

"Ha! Me? Sell?" One hand held her burger, so it limited her hypnotizing thing to her other hand. She swirled it around in front of his eyes. "I'm a selling machine, Chico. If I can sell a lump of cheese for ten bucks, wine will be a snap for me."

Well, might as well add confidence to her list of attributes.

"Are you still working at the market tomorrow?"

She looked at him as if he were from Mars. "Absolutely. Need the money. Can't let a scratch stop me. Also, remember, I'm only on trial at the winery. What happens if I flunk out? You always need a backup." He was then ignored while she lost herself in the joy of the pricey milkshake.

Bill wanted to see Remy in her market environment, talking with and smiling at customers, efficiently overseeing her cheese domain. "My daughter and I are going shopping tomorrow, maybe we'll stick our heads in and say hello."

Remy grinned, raised a paper napkin and wiped some of the milkshake off her mouth. It was too thick to sip through a straw. "That would be great. Cheeses are soft, light, and clean with no sharp edges. It's a step up from filling dumpsters."

When they got back from lunch, Remy saw Mrs. K waiting with a look of concern on her face. "Are you okay after yesterday?" Asked Mrs. K. "How's your leg?"

Nervous and worried about the boss's reaction, Remy would now find out. "One hundred percent, thanks, Mrs. Keating."

Martha smiled sympathetically and gave her a pat on the shoulder. "Don't worry about it, dear. When I was young, my father thought he would have to hire a full-time doctor just for me. Stitches, broken bones, I had them all when I was your age. Chico told me you were worried. Don't be. Unfortunately, I doubt this is the last time you'll cut yourself around here."

Remy's fears evaporated. She felt the tension drop from her shoulders. Intuition and observation told her that Mrs. K wasn't lying. She did not see her as a screw-up. A bullet had been dodged.

The two women sat side by side and went through some papers and small objects from forgotten years. Remy could tell it was a daunting task for Martha to see all that history being sorted and saved or dismissed. They laughed over old receipts from a half-century before—a tire for twenty dollars, ridiculously low bottling costs, a gas tag for forty cents a gallon. They shuffled and sorted things for two hours before Martha tired.

"We're both calling it a day," said Martha. She raised her hand to warn against resistance from the young dynamo. "You go now. It's Friday. Rest up on the weekend. I'm putting you up at the tasting room after you sort out this mess. You'll learn a lot there. Don't worry." Martha swept her hand toward the barn. "The two hooligans in there will be around to show you the ropes and get you started wherever you are. They both say great things about you, although I'm not sure if that's a compliment."

"Thanks, Mrs. Keating!"

Martha was up and turning to walk to the office. A soft smile crossed her face as she spoke over her shoulder. "Why don't you just call me Mrs. K, honey. It's easier to say than Keating."

Remy's mouth dropped as the older woman moved away. How did she even know Remy called her that? A look of accusation flew toward the barn.

She grabbed her things and moved to her car. She had been told that the men would move and protect the few remaining items on the table. When she opened her car door, a new pair of jeans covered the rips and tears and duct tape on her front seat. She lifted them and then almost dropped them. She recognized the label of one of the priciest designers around.

These things cost way north of a hundred dollars!

She marched back to the barn and received a blatant denial from Chico. "Haven't got a clue," was his only response. Remy knew he was lying, but she let it go and automatically forgave him. No man had ever bought her a gift before.

Rested and refreshed from a shower and a lazy hour at home, Remy scanned the Wine Bar. Lynn sat alone at the far end. The place wasn't crowded yet. It was too early. Making her way down the long, chrome-and-glass bar, Remy marveled again at her friend's beauty. Lynn always looked like she'd been photographed for a magazine cover. Settling on her stool, Remy smiled as she noticed her friend's outfit. Lynn wore a high-necked pullover from work—no cleavage. She wouldn't be man hunting this evening.

The two ladies' views of romance were polar opposites. Despite her act, Lynn was looking for Mr. Right, and her approach was to get out there and find him. The dating game was a well-managed chessboard to her, and she was approaching grand master status. Remy's attitude was to sit back and wait.

Three years ago, when Lynn had made the move and opened her own salon, Remy had insisted on doing the branding and marketing. She'd created logos, labored over brochures, and launched a website. She'd optimized social media and put a customer rewards program in place. The two of them had labored over the new salon space; it had to be chic. Lynn always chided Remy that for a person so talented at branding and marketing, she flunked it big time in her personal life. Any attempt to get her into the salon for some "rebranding" of her own was rebuffed.

A glass of white wine was waiting for Remy.

"I don't know why I let them talk me into trying all the new stuff they're peddling around here," Lynn said. "Taste this swill. It's fifteen dollars for a shot-sized portion in a glass the size of a fishbowl."

"Jeez, Lynn, my car needs a new battery. Do you know what new batteries cost? Fifteen dollars is pricey."

"God, girl, put your pride in your pocket for a half hour. You did all that work setting up my business and you won't take a dime. I have some pride, too. I figure I owe you about a thousand glasses of wine, so give it a rest and drink up. Oh, and I'm still upset you didn't call me about the emergency room. What the hell happened?"

Lynn milked her for all the details of the ordeal and then said, "Four stitches! A bad day for me is getting some hair dye on my blouse. You need a new job. Maybe needlepoint. No, you wouldn't have any fingers in a week. Professional knitter. That's it. Even you couldn't kill yourself doing that."

Taking the abuse, Remy sipped her fifteen-dollar glass of wine. "Thank you for your wholehearted support and confidence in me."

Sarcastic comment ignored, Lynn moved on. Her eyes moved over Remy's bare arms and up to her neck and face. Concern entered her voice. "Why are you scratching your arms, and what are those marks on your neck and face?"

"Bug bites from that damned barn. The place is infested. They're all over my calves, too."

"Jesus, Remy, you couldn't get that many bites at a vampire convention. How long do you have to do this crap?"

"There's still a lot to do. When I left today, Juan and Chico were setting off a bunch of bug bombs and shutting the barn up for the weekend to try to kill them."

"Six years of college, and you're in a combat zone. They just medevacked you to the hospital. What's the good news? There has to be some good news." Minor stuff clarified, Lynn moved on to more important things. "Tell me more about this Chico guy. From what you've told me, he sounds nice. Is he cute? Nice body?" She lowered her voice, leaned over, and bumped her shoulder into Remy's. "Are you having impure thoughts about him? Sister Angelina would be very disappointed in you, Remy Reilly."

"Lynn!" an exasperated Remy said.

"Hey, just asking. Maybe your problem is psychological. These long, hard, pointy things you keep walking into may be phallic symbols. You're subconsciously attracted to them. It's pent-up carnal energy trying to burst free. Yes, your problem is definitely sexual, Freudian. Get laid more, and you won't have this problem." Lynn tapped her glass against Remy's. "See, aren't you glad you have a friend like me who can help? I should have been a shrink."

"Lynn, I only cut myself *once*, on a rusty tractor fender, *not* some long, hard, pointy thing!"

A patronizing smile accompanied a pat on Remy's shoulder. "Of course, dear. If that's what you think." Apparently she decided it was too soon to let up. "So, back to this Chico guy. Is he good looking?"

"He's a nice man."

Lynn pointed at the fifteen-dollar glass of wine in front of Remy. "Nice man? Fifteen dollars, and all I get is *nice man*? No, no. What's he look like?"

Remy swirled her wine around in the glass, raised her head, and focused off into the distance, collecting her thoughts. "He's attractive, I suppose. In a rugged, manly sort of way."

"Now we're talking! *Rugged, manly sort of way*. You little vixen! How old is he?"

"I think he's around thirty-two."

Lynn was basically a sexual mountain lion, ready to pounce on any tidbit of information about male prey. "Good for you. When it comes to sex, that's when most men get the training wheels off their bikes. Are you going to pursue this?" Time to turn up the teasing. "Tell me, when you're in those close spaces, in that hot, sweaty barn, have you accidentally on purpose brushed that skinny backside of yours up against him? Taunted him? Teased him with those tantalizingly exposed Jane Austen wrists and ankles of yours?"

Remy refused to be provoked. She would not rise to the bait. "Lynn, it's nothing like that," she said in a calm voice. "I work with him."

Lynn shrugged. "Yeah, right, said Monica Lewinsky to Bill Clinton." One last shot for the night. "She was an intern too, you know."

The Alderetti Market, family owned for over half a century, was near downtown Santa Rosa in an affluent neighborhood. In the store, next to the extensive wine section, the cheese corner bustled. Remy had worked there part time for the last three years. The owners had made several tempting offers to bring her on full time—all dismissed by Remy. Her younger sister, Roxy, was occasionally allowed to help Remy on a busy Saturday. She wasn't permitted on the payroll because of her age, but some cash would always materialize at the end of a day and find itself in young Roxy's hand. If Remy left, the owners were happy that a geared-up and ready replacement was being trained. Only thirteen, going on fourteen, Roxy, like her older sister, was a competent and fast learner.

Working his way through the store, Bill stalled his daughter a few aisles away when he saw Remy explaining something to a customer. He took in the friendly smile, the easy manner, the attractive face, and lovely hair. Yes, he would definitely buy some cheese from her.

Remy was about to break for lunch when Bill and Lizzie walked up.

"You made it," she said.

"Hi, Remy. This is my daughter, Lizzie. Lizzie, this is Remy. I told you about her." Bill had cautioned his daughter that he was only an employee if anything came up about the winery. He'd told her it was a game he was playing. "You promised to give me a cheese lesson," Bill said.

"Your timing is perfect. I'm just breaking for lunch. Let's sit for a minute." Remy turned to her sister, made the introductions, and told her to watch things at the counter. "If something comes up, or a customer has questions, I'm right over there. Come and get me."

Lizzie stayed behind with Roxy, letting the old people have some time together.

Bill watched Remy limping slightly as she led him over to the coffee stand and seating area about twenty feet away. He felt sad that she had been standing on that bad leg all morning. Partially trained now, he knew not to say anything. After getting to know Remy over the past week, Bill knew she'd accuse him of being a wimp over a few stitches.

Remy selected a big slice of chocolate cake from the adjoining bakery counter. "What would you like?" she asked.

"Just coffee, thanks."

Remy poured two coffees for them and eased herself into a chair where she could watch her sister over Bill's shoulder. The concerned positioning was not lost on Bill. He trusted she was watching his daughter, too.

"That's it? That's lunch?" asked Bill, looking at the slice of cake. He was wondering how she kept that slim figure. She could burn off anything with all of that energy.

"Don't start, Chico. I watch what I eat all week. On these long Saturdays, I allow myself a treat." She twirled one of her hands around in the air. "Well, perhaps a couple of treats during the day."

They did the small-talk thing. Remy told him funny anecdotes about life in the market, about good customers and bad. They laughed together. Bill once again found it enjoyable talking to her away from work. As he bathed in the animated face while she told one of her stories, Bill wondered about her private life. Was there a boyfriend? With all the work and studying she did, did she have any time for enjoyment, other than those romance novels and movies?

In time, Remy glanced at her watch and declared lunch over. They drifted back to the cheese section, where Lizzie and Roxy were engaged in animated conversation. Lizzie explained to the adults that they had played soccer together on two different local girls teams.

Remy started bombarding Bill with cheese facts. Proud of her work, she rambled on and on about world cheeses. She warned him with a shake of her finger that she was studying which cheeses went best with which wines, especially the varieties at the Rolling Oaks Winery. She informed him he would have to step up his game to keep up with her. She put her coffee down on the counter, raised both her hands in front of his face, and did that swirling, hypnotizing thing she'd done in the barn the day she had him hung. "Hang on to my coattails, Chico. I'll teach you a few things and get you out of the doghouse with Mrs. K. I'll put in a good word for you. Remember, I've vowed to help you make it at least until Labor Day." She followed this with a playful, now-expected, light punch on the arm.

She actually made cheeses sound interesting, thought Bill. He could have sat there all day listening to her, losing himself in the animated energy she radiated from that beautiful face. He knew a formal barricade would rise the minute he told her who he was. Her relaxed, humorous way of communicating would be gone—no more hypnotism. No more punches on the arm. Just a little longer, he lied to himself.

Bill hadn't enjoyed being around a woman in years, especially a woman like Remy. The few times he'd attempted dating, the ladies knew who he was and knew he had money. They'd all reminded him of his wife. From what he'd seen so far, he thought Remy wouldn't even care. He believed she just wanted a good job she'd love. She wasn't the type who wanted a man to support her. He loved being just easygoing Chico around her, always in trouble with the boss. He wondered how she felt about him. He'd watched Remy around his daughter, searching for some subtle reaction, and had only seen how well she handled Lizzie with the same caring attention she gave her sister. He still didn't know if she had a boyfriend, and he didn't know how to ask.

Chapter 7

Early in Remy's second week, the battle of the barn took them deep into the labyrinth. An upholstered sofa and two matching chairs, shredded and nested in by rodents for years, were cleared away to reveal dated wine processing equipment stacked against the back wall. To the side, they uncovered an ancient flatbed truck. Tires flat and looking exhausted, it reminded Remy of an old-time child's wagon with its short oak railings lying broken and rotting on the truck bed. Attached to one rail was a faded old Rolling Oaks Winery sign. Rusted and dented, the vehicle was an immense treasure to Remy, like the Schwinn bicycle she had discovered her first day. She turned to Chico, who had been around sporadically this second week. "Oh, wow, what's that, Chico?"

"It's one of the original vineyard trucks. It's been in here since way before I was born." He scratched his head. "We should call the wreckers and have them haul it away for scrap."

"Are you *crazy*?" Remy grabbed his arm, smiled, and pointed. "This is a big find. You've got to keep your eyes and mind open, mister. The county only allows businesses this far out of town to have small exterior signs to advertise their presence, their businesses." A fountain of ideas surged between Remy's ears before pouring out of her mouth. "From a marketing standpoint, this thing could be a mega *billboard*. How much do you think a *billboard* would cost? Plenty." She squared herself up to face him and raised the twirling, hypnotizing hands. "Imagine this barn as the tasting room with new offices next door. We're on one of the major roads in the area. Right at the beginning of the driveway, next to the street, envision a single parking space with this fully restored truck. Colorful flowers could be planted right in front to call more attention to it. A big company logo painted on the doors.

The oak railing restored with the company sign on it." Swirling her hands, she was quiet for a moment as the fountain recharged. "The bed on the back can be decorated seasonally: Pumpkins and scarecrows for fall, oversized, colorful wrapped gift boxes for Christmas. You can put it in the Fourth of July parade in town for advertising. And those are only a few possibilities. Can you stall Mrs. K until I can put some more ideas in my paper?"

"Leave it with me. I'll take care of it. I'll make something up."

Remy pressed the issue. "And that row of old equipment outside is getting big. Can you stall on that for a bit, also? It will only be for a week or two."

"I know exactly how I'll handle it. I'll tell her we're waiting for the best scrap metal price from several people. She'll wait for that." A mischievous grin bloomed on his face as he leaned over. "I'd be the last person to say Mrs. K is cheap, but I heard she asks the homeless people for change when she's downtown in Santa Rosa. Two weeks ago, I caught her siphoning gas out of my truck. She'll do anything to save a buck."

The twirling hands stopped, replaced by the wagging finger. "Chico! I told you that you can't talk about the boss like that. Mrs. K gave you a job. You should be grateful. No wonder you're in trouble all the time."

The last dumpsters were full by the end of the week. Damp white rags came away covered in dirt and grim. Dust revolted and settled, trying to escape the relentless pursuit of brooms and fans employed for the final cleanup. Breathing eased. Light cleared. Tools rested. Done was another day.

Seven massive dumpsters gone, and the barn almost sparkled in a clean, manageable condition. Remy stood at the large double sliding doors, hands on her hips, and took in the order and neatness in front of her. A handkerchief appeared from her back pocket. Sweat came away from her forehead. She glanced at a wall section near the doors where a group of ancient notices still hung limply from rusted nails on the barn wall. They were illegible now, faded by time and covered with grime. Beside them, a massive hook still held thick, brittle leather harnesses. Were they for horses in years past? She hadn't mustered up the courage to remove them during the cleanup. They reminded her that history wasn't confined to the old English countryside of her novels.

Visions of the new barn space danced through her mind, and her ideas would find their way into her notes at home. Mangled metal, crushed bundles of wire, and scraps of aluminum and iron had all been shipped off for recycling. Outdated paperwork, rotten and moldy fabrics, and old furniture had found a new home at the local landfill. The old winery equipment had a temporary reprieve. For the last two weeks, Remy had hounded Juan to explain what all the old equipment had been used for. He'd fascinated Remy with old stories that went with each piece. Mrs. K had her own pile of memories set aside. Chico had grabbed some treasures and taken them home before Mrs. K could dispatch them. He told Remy they were for Mrs. K's son, who wasn't here to look out for himself.

Bill had popped in and out during the week. His excuse for not being here was that Mrs. K had him back doing odd jobs. In reality, it was a busy time of year with the start of harvest only weeks away. Juan stayed with Remy, while Bill and Skip were at the winemaking facilities. They were installing two new concrete fermentation tanks from Sonoma Cast Stone in Petaluma. Their friend and the owner, Steve Rosenblatt, had finally sold them on the idea. Concrete tanks were becoming a thing in winemaking. Used in ancient times before oak and steel, concrete was now having a renaissance in the industry. They breathed like oak but without adding oak flavor to the wine. Martha, Juan, and Bill wanted to have them along with the stainless-steel tanks already in place to gain more flexibility in creating new wines. Bill and Skip were helping the manufacturer's people install them in time for this year's harvest.

Born and raised in Sonoma, Skip Anderson had graduated college the year before. He was a perfect fit and would be invaluable in the coming years as Martha made Juan slow down. Skip was Remy's age and had started with the company out of high school. His value was clear after his first year. He was quiet, reliable, and a quick learner. Always looking forward, Martha had worked a deal with the young man to go into the same program as her son at UC Davis. Financial support had been worked out with a promise of a substantial wage increase when he was done. It turned out a win-win for everyone.

With the barn now presentable, it was decreed that Remy would start at the tasting room on Monday. Excited, Remy would prepare herself. She had the paycheck from her first two weeks in hand, the biggest paycheck she'd ever earned.

"Wow, Mom, I've never had a check this big. Full time sure beats part time."

Carol Reilly put her foot down. "You're not spending a penny of that around here, Remy. We're doing fine. You spend that on yourself for once. Buy some new clothes for work. Have a spa day."

Spa day? Her mother was definitely losing it. This money was a new battery for the Toyota and then some. She had relented to Lynn's badgering and would meet her at the salon after work, allowing Lynn to do something with her hair. Finished was barn duty. It was the tasting room next week, and Remy wanted to look presentable. After the salon, dinner was Remy's treat. God knows, over the years, Lynn had picked up more than her share of tabs, knowing that Remy was paying for school and helping at home with what money she earned.

Lynn waited for Remy at the salon. She was not going to miss the opportunity to do something with her friend's lovely auburn hair. As far as Lynn was concerned, Remy should have been locked up long ago for not bringing the full force of that beautiful face and hair out for all the world to see. She would also apply some minimal makeup whether Remy liked it or not. The ladies had decided to take advantage of a rare night out together. First would be the hair, then they would catch up over dinner.

Much more direct than reserved Remy, Lynn Klein was not to be trifled with. She was the same height as Remy, but that's where the similarities ended. Long flowing blond hair, always perfectly groomed, framed a strong face. While Remy was sleek and subtle, Lynn's body threw out curves that turned men's heads, and the practiced way she moved across a room encouraged it. Men, easy to attract but deemed unacceptable, were cast off like flies. Lynn had her standards and would filter through them until she selected a compatible mate. She was bright, funny, and generous, but she didn't do nonsense well. These last qualities were shared with Remy, hence their close friendship.

"Finally, I get to do something creative with that worn-out mop on top of your head. I'm taking that dull mess and making you into a magazine cover. Time for you to move out of the slow lane," said Lynn as she settled Remy into her chair.

"Nothing too extreme," directed Remy. She had only ever had it trimmed before and was nervous. "I'm not flashy and naturally beautiful like you."

Lynn had often told Remy she underestimated her own looks. After working on women of all types, week after week and year after year, Lynn found it glaringly obvious that Remy was way near the top in natural assets. Lynn would now show her. The hair first, then some slight makeup. Lynn didn't want to scare her friend with too much or she'd never wear it again. Those wide blue eyes would pop against the new hairdo. It would be cut just below her shoulders so she could wear it down or up comfortably. The ever-present ponytail would be put on temporary leave. Highlights were going into that naturally beautiful auburn hair, along with a light glaze to make it garner more attention.

"Your mother won't recognize you when I'm done." Some logic and rational thinking were called for. "You don't have much of an ass," said Lynn, "so we have to make the guys focus on your head. And don't even think about going to a bar or club without me. The guys will be all over you, and you won't know what to do. I'll be your only defense. All the Mr. Wickhams of the world will be luring you into their carriages, trying to steal your virtue."

"I can take care of myself around men," snapped Remy.

"Yeah, right," Lynn replied as she started snipping away with her scissors. "Being alone in a room with a priest would scare you to death."

"Lynn!"

"Sit still."

The women giggled and gossiped away. What seemed like hours later, Lynn allowed Remy a mirror.

"Oh my God, Lynn! I love it. I never thought I could look like this. It looks...beautiful...elegant...sophisticated. Don't you think it's a bit much for me?"

"You *are* beautiful. Christ, I'm always telling you that, but you never listen." Lynn stepped back and took in her friend. "I think we can save the elegant and sophisticated for later. Maybe when we get you into something besides old jeans and dust-caked shirts on a regular basis. Although what you're wearing does look good on you." Remy was wearing the outfit from her interview. "I have no idea how you picked that out without my help." Lynn stretched out her arms and flexed her tired wrists and fingers. "Okay, we're done. Let's get out of here. I need to get off my feet, have a drink and a decent meal. We'll both be hard at it again tomorrow. God, how we both hate Saturdays."

Lynn had picked one of the hot spots for the young crowd. She was drawn to the bustle and the action much more than Remy. Gliding into the restaurant, head high, Lynn surveyed the crowd. Remy followed, a different Remy in her interview outfit and a blockbuster redo from the neck up. The place was done in a modern style with lots of chrome, glass, and light. A bar at the left wall ran from front to back in the long space. A three-foot-high partition wall separated the bar from the dining area in an open and inviting floor plan.

It was Friday night, and everyone was out. The place was packed, but Lynn had made reservations. Thankfully, their table was ready. Both women wanted to get off their feet and relax. Taking their seats, they were both ogled by the men at the bar just on the other side of the short partition wall. Young businessmen in their suits and ties mixed with casually dressed men with good bodies and tanned faces, a giveaway to

Lynn that the latter worked outdoors and had dressed up for a relaxing night out. As far as Lynn was concerned, they could all wait. One of them *might* be allowed to buy them drinks later.

Remy also noticed the attention being directed to their table from the bar. "You sure know how to attract the guys, don't you?" she said to Lynn.

Setting her wineglass down, Lynn looked across at Remy and smiled. "They're not looking at me, honey."

Remy blushed and redirected her attention to the menu.

Halfway through their meal, Lynn's mood took a serious turn. "I'm starting to feel like I'm living your life. I'm tired, boring, and all I do is work. You couldn't care less, but I'm out there trying to find Mr. Right, expand my personal life, and I'm basically in the same rut as you. What are we going to do? Are my standards too high? I should be able to find a nice guy."

Remy put down her fork. "I'm no expert, but I don't think statistics work when you're talking about romance. You can't push your way through X number of men and assume Mr. Right is in the mix. And I don't think your standards are too high." She took a sip of wine, gathering her next thoughts. "Lynn, I think you need to *reexamine* your standards. I get the idea you want Mr. Right to be rich, gorgeous, funny, and very social. I don't think that's you. You're a worker bee, just like me. You like the success you've created for yourself. Nobody gave it to you. You like quiet nights at home more than bar life, no matter what you say. Sorry, but I'm afraid you're burdened by horrible, boring, traditional values, no matter what you think. You wouldn't be happy sitting around with some rich guy taking care of you. What you really need is a normal, flawed, funny, hard-working guy." Remy speared another piece of chicken with her fork and smiled. "Try not to get sick all over the table, but what you're really looking for is the same kind of guy I'm hoping for."

Lynn paused, allowing the logic to roll around in her head. After a big sip of wine, she said, "You're disgusting. What the hell would I do with a monk in a library? Next, you'll tell me I need to cancel my fashion magazine subscriptions and go work on some organic farm, read about bugs and microscopic slime. You are so screwed up."

Remy flipped her free hand at Lynn while taking a sip of her wine. "Laugh all you want. You know I'm right. Imagine yourself being normal. Now look up and reevaluate all those guys at the bar. Which ones look comfortable and caring, and which ones fit your current pathetic wish list?"

Chapter 8

Early Monday morning, it was peaceful up on the hill around the tasting room. Access to the top of the knoll where the facilities sat was gained by a quarter-mile-long single rutted lane coming off one of Sonoma's winding two-lane back roads. From the knoll's edge, one could see for miles along a serpentine view through the distant hills almost to the ocean. This morning, the hills looked like a quiet, undulating roller coaster of yellow and greens before the amusement park opened. Birds were singing their songs. The resident cat was lounging in a spot of sun before the day's heat set in; soon, she'd have to get back to work mouse hunting in the warehouse. On Mondays, the facilities were closed. Undisturbed, Bill thought it was ideal for getting a jump start on bringing Remy up to speed, and no one would be around to blow his cover.

She was already standing there when he arrived. Little Miss Enthusiasm had probably brought a sleeping bag and arrived last night so she wouldn't be late. Walking toward her from his truck, Bill was surprised again by Remy Reilly. He'd only seen her in work clothes and hadn't seen the outfit she wore the day of her interview. He hadn't seen the new hairdo. The hair framed that face perfectly. This was not Remy from the barn— baseball cap, jeans, and gloves. She wasn't even talking yet. The clothes were crisp, clean, and looked fantastic. Bill didn't have the heart to tell her how long they would stay that way. Tasting-room jobs meant long, hot, hard days in summer.

As he drew near, Remy, a big grin on her face, swept out her arms. "This is right out of a storybook, Chico. All these rolling hills covered with vines and oaks and other trees for miles. Look how far you can see down those valleys. The Pacific fog is even sitting on those hills in the distance."

"I'll admit that I never get tired of the view from up here," said Bill. "On a day like today, when we're closed and it's peaceful, the impact is impressive."

"Where do you live? Is it close to here?" asked Remy.

"Actually, I do live close by, just on the other side of Sebastopol. It's convenient to be between the operation here and the offices at the old vineyard."

Social amenities dispensed with, Remy got down to business. "Where's Juan? Mrs. K says he knows what he's talking about, and I'm ready to go. Over the weekend, I trawled the used bookstores in Santa Rosa for all their wine books. I've been studying."

Bill felt that the Question Machine would chew him up and spit him out before the day was finished. First things first. "Why don't you follow me? I want to make sure nobody stole the coffee machine over the weekend."

Shocked, Remy asked, "People steal things out here?"

Still getting his morning legs under him, Bill just shook his head and marched off toward the building.

Two cups of coffee in his hand from the small employees' kitchen and break room, Bill turned to Remy. "Let's go out to the picnic table by the edge of the hill, and I'll go over the basic layout and what goes on up here," he said, not waiting for her to clean a counter, straighten a trashcan, or do whatever else possessed her. She had no choice but to follow.

Bill didn't want to confuse her with everything that went on, so he explained the layout and the basic duties of the tasting room. She'd learn the rest soon enough. "Any questions before we start on the tasting and selling?"

Remy would not be put off. "Yes. Where's Juan? I want to learn this right. Mrs. K says he's the man. He's the *manager* of the winemaking facilities. He's a pro. I don't want a tractor fixed, Chico." She slowly swirled her hands around in front of his eyes like she was trying to hypnotize him again. "This wine tasting is subtle, sophisticated stuff—clarity, bouquet, hints of exotic tastes, understated high-cuisine stuff, pairing wines with foods, yes, even cheeses. I've spent all weekend reading to get up to speed. When I need a spark plug changed, I'll call *you.*"

Today is going to be punishment for a litany of past sins. I'm looking at a clone of my mother. Both of them were put on this earth to ruin my peaceful life.

Should he try some subtle negotiation? Throw some common sense on the table? "Why don't you let me try to help first, and then when Juan gets here, he'll be impressed by how on top of it you are?"

The logic seemed to appeal to Remy, so she relented. A nod of her head signaled he had permission to proceed.

Once they were settled at the table, the magnificent view was put aside. It was time for work. Bill handed Remy a sheet of wine-tasting terms. "These are some of the qualities that go into the tasting. You don't have to remember them all right now. They'll all come to you over time. The philosophy around here is not to hard sell wine but to approach the task like the marketing courses you took in school. Market the attributes of the wine, and it will sell itself. First, you need to evaluate the visitor—are they novices, enthusiasts, or experienced professionals? If restaurant, hotel, or retail people come in, yield them to one of the more experienced staff. You'll get up to speed quick enough, I'm sure."

Bill shifted around to get comfortable and took in the blue eyes across from him, reservoirs waiting to be filled with additional information. The soft morning sun was on her face and bouncing off her hair. He found it comfortably distracting. Once again, Remy impressed him. She was paying attention, not talking. Her pen was poised over her notebook. The professors at school must have loved her—at least until question time.

"We do whites, sparklings, and red pinot noirs. Each wine has a story. As we go over the wines, I'll tell you the story. We let the client enjoy the wine, tell them the story so they can further identify with it, and explain the different smells and tastes in the glass. We explain how grapes grow differently on flatlands and hillsides and talk about the history of the company. We explain our wine club—don't worry about that yet. It's probably very similar to how you do cheese tastings and sales in the market."

Remy was stoked. "Yeah, it does sound similar. I'm going to enjoy this."

"Okay," said Bill. "Let's go inside and get started."

Remy jumped up, and Bill followed at a leisurely pace. Halfway to the building, Remy looked back. "Let's go, Chico. Time is money."

"Keep your wig on. I'm coming."

They started with the whites. "This one was custom blended for a famous chef who had four restaurants. He went out of business just before the wine came online. We liked it so much we kept in our assortment. What do you smell? What do you taste?"

Remy raised the glass and concentrated on the smells. She took a sip, pondering on the tastes, and swallowed the wine.

"No, don't swallow it. Just taste it and spit it into this bucket. We have a lot to go through, and you'd be drunk by the time we're finished." Not wanting to embarrass her on her first day, Bill volunteered some information. "Did you smell a perfume or floral scent? Did it taste of fruit or herbs? Was the finish soft? Notice it doesn't have a strong acid taste." He suppressed a smile as her pen attacked the notebook.

It was almost one o'clock. "That will be it for tasting today. It's a lot to take in," said Bill. "This afternoon, just roam around and look in the different buildings and go over the paperwork I gave you. I'll be next door in the main warehouse doing some stuff. Write your questions down, find me, and I'll try to help. Now, let's go into the employee lunchroom. I always have some food in there, sandwiches and salads. In winter, the staff takes turns making warm soups."

The summer heat had come up outside, so they parked themselves at one of the lunchroom tables. A soft drink from the fridge and a microwaved dish for him. Remy had water and a premade salad she had brought from home. Exhausted from the morning's interrogation, Bill wanted to change the subject. "So tell me more about your ideas. I may be able to help you fine-tune some of them for Mrs. K. It can't hurt, can it?"

Bang. That was all it took. The starting gate was opened. The dam burst. The tsunami arrived. More ideas poured out of

Remy's head, almost washing poor Bill's lunch off the table. Why Mrs. K deserved better offices—people were stacked on top of each other right now. Why the tasting room would benefit from being at the other location—this place was in the middle of nowhere. How a new building could serve the community and be good for the business. Sure, Coppola, Mondavi, and others had large, swanky facilities, but something smaller and understated would help the company's growth. String quartets or bluegrass on different weekends? Fundraisers for small local charities on-site? Art shows for the local schools? Did they have a newsletter? On and on she went. Bill loved it. He didn't have to talk. Many of the ideas were very interesting, and he loved looking at the animated whirlwind across from him.

Juan arrived around three thirty. He and Chico had to review some options for new equipment, and all the existing equipment had to be checked and rechecked for the upcoming harvest. He walked through the tasting room on his way to the warehouse and spotted Remy busily scribbling away in her notebook. His face lit up when he saw the young dynamo. "Hola, Chica, how's it going?"

Remy barely hid the hurt at being abandoned by Juan in the morning. "I thought you were going to help me with the tasting and sales?"

"Not me, Chica. That's Chico's job. We both have almost the same experience with the different wine qualities, but he explains it better, and as for the sales part, I don't want anything to do with it."

Remy was a little surprised. "He *was* terrific this morning. It shocked me that he knew so much for someone who does odd jobs. How did he learn all that?"

Juan grinned. "Well, Chica, he's studied under me since he was young." Over his shoulder, he added, "And I guess that fancy college degree in viticulture and enology from University of California in Davis didn't hurt."

Remy's mind went into twist mode. *That lying bastard.* Her brain pounded into reverse as she tried to review everything she'd said over the last two weeks. Well, maybe he hadn't *lied*

lied, but there were some serious omissions out there somewhere. Remy Reilly had been raised on accountability. Accountability she would have. *Was everybody just getting a kick out of the new girl?*

She took some time to settle, braced herself, and then went hunting. As she exited the tasting room, she glanced over to the parking lot. She saw the Great Deceiver talking to a woman who had driven up in a very pricey Mercedes sports car. He had greeted her with a big hug. They appeared to be talking intimately with each other. Remy knew he was divorced, so this was probably the girlfriend. From the looks of her, she seemed way out of Chico's league. Or maybe that league was changing? The sports car was worth a major chunk of Remy's mom's house. The shoes cost more than Remy's entire closet. And she was a tall, stunning blonde with an impressive body. The jewelry looked like it belonged in a safe-deposit box. She was dressed in light tan, just like the color of the car. Even the vineyard dust couldn't make her look bad.

A slight twinge of jealousy squirmed through Remy. Watching them, she found her opinion of Chico continued to evolve. In recent days, he had been in her thoughts more and more, being reevaluated, being reconsidered. He appeared to be taken now, and by someone who Remy could never compete with. Another fantasy dashed. Remy would deal with it, just like she always dealt with disappointment.

Bill gave Maggie another hug and kiss on the cheek before she left and then ambled back to the warehouse. He noticed Remy standing in the shade of the tasting room porch and walked over. "Are you okay? You look a little tense."

"I'm fine."

"Okay. Well, what did you think of your first day up here?" asked Bill.

"It was very nice of you to take time from your *odd jobs* to help me today. Were you ever going to mention that you do other things around here, like training? *You*, with your degree in *viticulture* from UC Davis?"

"Well, that's technically not true," fumbled Bill, wondering where she'd come across that tidbit of information. He noticed

Juan over her shoulder waving at him from a safe distance away. "Sarah is the one who runs the tasting operation, and she normally does the training. She'll be the one watching over you from now on. I just thought I'd step in today since we're closed and give you a good head start." He was treading carefully. "We're almost done for the day. Would you like to stop off in Sebastopol and get something to eat on the way back?"

Remy wasn't finished. "You lied to me. And you and Juan made fun of me. You're just like *Mr. Wickham.*"

Bill's finger came up and wagged in her face, accompanied by a firm voice. "I don't know who the hell Wickham is, but, Remy, I've never lied to you. Yes, Juan and I pick on you, but that's because we like you. You're the new guy. We both think you're bright, a great worker, and have a nice personality. If we didn't like you, if we didn't think you were a good worker, if we didn't think you had potential, we would barely talk to you." Bill didn't want to overstep. He was technically her boss, and his attraction for her was growing. He tried to take a mental breath, wanting to be politically correct, but he was getting flustered. "While we're on the subject, I personally like you very much. You have an effect on me. That's why I wanted to take the time to get you started today. And if it's not inappropriate, I have to tell you how great your hair looks."

Bill noticed her slumped shoulders, sensed he might have overloaded her with info today, as she said, "I'm sorry. I overreacted. Thank you for taking the time to help me. I'm nervous about starting in the tasting room. You can see I have no idea what I'm talking about, but I want to learn. I don't want to let Mrs. K down. I want this job, Chico."

"Honestly, don't worry. You're actually catching on faster than most people do. It's a lot to take in." Bill softened his tone. "Now, how about something quick to eat on the way home? We can talk more about your ideas, and I can answer more of your questions about how things work up here."

Bill watched a mix of emotions do a slideshow on Remy's face. "What will your girlfriend think?"

"Girlfriend? Oh, no, no. That was my ex-wife, Maggie. I told you about her before. She lives in San Francisco. As you can see, she remarried well. She's taking Lizzie for the week and wanted to sort some details out with me."

"You seem to get along well with her."

Bill made sure his face had the neutral look of a Las Vegas poker player. "Yes, we get along fine." He noticed that Remy looked both relieved and still a little upset.

Finally, she said, "Okay, then. Yes, I'd like to stop for something to eat. I do have a few questions."

Bill was already picturing "a few." His deception had almost unraveled. Thoughts about coming clean about it were shunted aside, since he reasoned it was not the time, what with her being upset and stressed about her first day in the tasting room. She was so focused on the job, and he still had no idea about her private life. Confused about his feelings, he was glad he'd told her he liked her, but he was somewhat surprised he had.

His big excuse was that he'd take a little more time so that she'd see him as a regular guy, and then he'd tell her.

Chapter 9

They arrived at the restaurant—not a burger joint—in separate cars. Bill knew he had to be at the top of his game if he wanted to rebound from the ex-wife thing and Juan's big mouth. He walked over and opened her car door, offered his hand to help her out. At the entrance, Bill pulled back the restaurant door and ushered her in front of him.

It was an old-world, romantic type of place in Sebastopol with soft lighting, white tablecloths, and candles on the tables. They were early, so it was only half full. It was French; Bill had gambled, thinking she'd like it better than fish and chips, eel, boiled potatoes, or some other god-awful meal from the distant past, where she seemed to enjoy spending her free time. He would show her there were also gentlemen in this day and age.

"Permit me," he said as he held the chair out for her. Mannerly.

A smile and a thank-you told him it was going well. He was working his way out of another doghouse.

"Would you prefer red or white wine?"

"White, please."

"A sauvignon blanc is not too dry for you?"

Her formal guard from their words earlier was still up. "That would be fine. Thank you."

He handed her a menu. "The veal cordon bleu is excellent." Suave, sophisticated.

A perfect setting. He watched her beautiful hair glistening in the candlelight. Enough work talk. He would be sensitive, attentive, and caring.

Remy sipped her wine and looked around as they waited for their food. "My, this place is lovely. It's old-world romantic. I'm impressed."

Bill *was* on his game tonight.

"Do you bring all of your girlfriends here?"

That was an unanticipated curve ball. The truth never hurt. "No, I haven't dated in years. Too busy with work and my daughter."

"Oh."

He could feel the appraising look across the top of her wineglass.

The food arrived. More wine was poured. He gave a toast to her successful first day at the tasting room. Bill Keating wanted to learn more about Remy Reilly, but he knew to be subtle. His focus would be on her. He would relax her. She would loosen up with the excellent wine and fine food, reveal some of her personal thoughts and feelings. He hadn't realized he could be this suave, this smooth. Years out of practice, he thought he was regaining the magic. She was quieter than usual. Less wired. The ambiance was working. "So do you have any more questions, or can we talk about you?" asked Bill.

She slowly lowered her glass to the table. *Here it comes.* Those lovely eyes embraced him. An intimate conversation would soon break over the horizon. Bill sensed romance blooming, intimacy revealing itself, vulnerability on display.

Remy reached down to her side, fumbled around in her backpack on the floor, and withdrew the dreaded pen and notebook. "Yes, Chico. What's the difference between viticulture and enology?"

Oh God. What did it take to turn off the Question Machine? She probably still has notebooks from grade school.

Ever the gentleman, Bill felt a headache coming on as he graciously launched a detailed response to her question. When he finished, having thought the night was lost, he was rewarded.

"That's fantastic. All that work at UC Davis, and you got a job in the field you love. I hope I'm that lucky." Very observant, Remy had piled today's information on top of what she'd seen over the last few weeks, analyzed it, and rendered her opinion. "You know, Mrs. K should just give her son, Bad Lord Billy the Absent, his trust fund and cut him loose. Dump him. You and Juan seem to be able to do everything in the fields and at the winemaking facilities."

What a nice compliment, thought Bill. "Thank you, Remy. That's a nice thing to say." He tried to steer away from all the questions and move the conversation back to her. "How long have you been thinking about your dream?"

She spoke slowly and quietly, pulling up her memories from past years. "I decided when I was a senior in high school that I wanted to work in marketing. After my first year in college, I became fascinated by the booming wine business here in Sonoma. Anything growing that fast needs up-to-date marketing and branding..."

He pulled out family details, surprised at her school and work history. "What kind of grades did you get in school? It had to be tough working so much."

"I never got less than a B." She rested her hands on the table and raised an eyebrow. "What about you at UC Davis?"

"Let's skip that for right now," said Bill.

"Spit it out."

"Okay. If a course was about wine, I got an A. Anything else... Well, let's just say my grades were *flexible*."

Bill hadn't enjoyed himself this much in years. It was a wonderful dinner with a beautiful woman, an almost forgotten pleasure for him. They exchanged stories from their pasts. Laughs were had. After a strenuous day, her bubbly manner had been put on hold. He could tell she was tired from her first day in an unfamiliar environment. When making a point, her hand and arm movements were slower, more sensual, as were her facial expressions. Bill enjoyed this calmer version of Remy Reilly. The wine somehow tasted better as he relaxed and enjoyed himself. He thought about making his confession tonight but decided against it. She'd had a stressful day, the meal had settled her, and there was no need to burden her with his guilt and deception. Soon, very soon, he told himself.

After dinner, Bill watched Remy drive away from the restaurant. He harbored concerns about how her wreck of a car would make it home in the growing dark.

Martha was waiting for an update on the equipment issues Bill and Juan had discussed that afternoon when she looked out her kitchen window and saw her son drive up to pick up Lizzie. They reviewed each other's day while Bill settled at the kitchen island with a cup of coffee.

Supply and equipment reports received and digested, Martha asked, "How was Remy at the tasting room?"

"Voracious. She's a black hole for knowledge. Ideas keep spewing out of her head." He told his mother about the clever, creative truck idea that he'd forgotten to tell her about the week before. Bill looked up and beamed at his mother. "I can't believe what a great idea of mine it was to bring her on board."

Martha lowered her head and gave him *the eye*—the don't-push-it look from his childhood.

Bill ignored it. "Her grasp of my invaluable contributions around here was summed up by another of her brilliant ideas. At dinner, she told me you should give Bad Lord Billy the Absent his trust fund and get rid of him. She decreed that Juan and I know how to run everything around the winery, and you should just dump ungrateful Bill."

Martha saw pride blanket her son's face. She said, "The only one getting a trust fund around here is my granddaughter."

It was always *my* granddaughter. Over the years, it was only *your* daughter if Lizzie brought home a C on her report card or spilled something on a Persian carpet when she was a baby.

Proving she still had a step or two on her son, Martha said, "At dinner with Remy? Let's skip back to the at-dinner part." She enjoyed watching him fumble.

"Well, um, jeez, Mom. We stopped for something quick to eat. That's all. It was a long day."

Martha wanted to warn her son that his deception was going to blow up in his face if he kept at it much longer, but she decided to let him off the hook and returned to the issues at hand. "I can't believe how simple that idea about moving the tasting room is, especially coupled with the new building. A fresh set of eyes, as they say. You know, I've been thinking about renting space for the office. We're on top of each other now. I definitely like the idea of an expanded new building to house us, along with rooms for community functions, things like art exhibits or business functions for other companies. After Remy said it, even I realized that many big vineyards are doing this type of thing to expand their brand and contribute to the area. Has Harry Graves from the county offices gotten back to you about the feasibility?"

Bill poured himself some more coffee. "Harry feels it shouldn't be a big deal. Zoning is perfect for a new building. He thinks the community service angle would help blunt any opposition. He suggests going ahead with some rough plans, and he'll line up people at the city to talk to."

"Well, the directors' dinner is coming up. I'd like to have the ideas better organized so we can give them a picture of our expansion plans. Put it together. We'll go over it, and you can do the presentation."

Bill asked, "Who's Mr. Wickham, Mom?"

"Excuse me?"

"In those old English books you read and movies you watch, who's Wickham? Juan threw me under the bus again today and told Remy that I have a degree from Davis in viticulture. She accused me of lying to her, said I was just like that Wickham guy."

Martha laughed out loud. "Wickham is the bad guy in Jane Austen's *Pride and Prejudice*. He's a lying opportunist, an evil womanizer, a villain." Another laugh. Martha got a kick out of that one. "I'm Wicked Wickham's mom. Ha! The dear girl may have a point."

I have an effect on him? He likes me? I have a lovely personality? Remy Reilly was exhausted from the long day. The old Toyota groaned along home, its various noises and complaints ignored while Remy sifted through the new small treasures in her mind. The restaurant had been wonderful. Most of her dinners had sell-by dates on them. She usually enjoyed them with budget wines from Trader Joe's, accompanied by one of her historical novels or shows.

She realized Chico and Juan hadn't been making *fun* of her, just picking on her because they thought she was a good worker. No problem with that. Chico would just have to learn that she could give as good as she got. He was so nice at dinner. He wouldn't even let her pay half. There were hints of a gentleman there. And he'd taken the time to help her tweak some of her ideas. At dinner, that tan had looked terrific with those blue eyes.

Her mood dropped as she recalled the ex-wife. She'd looked like she had it all—sophistication, beauty, money. If that was the kind of woman that drew his attention, Remy felt destined to be just a good friend and workmate.

Finally, she arrived home. Movement was slow as she made her way into the house and up the stairs to her room. Fatigue weighed down on her. Enough. Time for sleep.

Monday of the following week, a week's worth of tasting-room experience under her belt, Remy reported to the offices for her time with Martha.

"I thought following me around on Mondays when the tasting room is closed would give you a glimpse of how the administration end of the business works," said Martha. She poured two cups of coffee, came back to her desk, and placed one in front of Remy. "Did you have an enjoyable weekend, dear?"

Remy didn't mention she still worked Saturdays at the market. She also didn't bring up the paper that she was still fine-tuning with her winery-expansion ideas. "Well, on Sunday I sinned and spent the entire day watching *Pride and Prejudice*, the Colin Firth version, all six episodes. It's probably the tenth time I've seen it. I think it's better than the book, and that's saying something."

"Oh! My granddaughter and I have watched that several times," said Martha. "Do you read a lot, too?"

"Too much. I love all the classics. Jane Austen, the three Brontë sisters, George Eliot, and others. I like historical romances, all the books, all the videos." She sighed. "I guess I'm just a romantic at heart."

They rattled on about their shared interest a bit before Martha got back to business. "Let's walk around, introduce you to the people here."

Martha's office was the old master bedroom. It maintained a sense of space by having only her desk with two chairs in front of it, and a small table off to the side with four chairs. Cluttered bookcases and boxes were off to the opposite side of the room. The second bedroom, brimming with file cabinets and shelves, served as storage. Sue Weaver, the bookkeeper, occupied the third bedroom. Finance needed its privacy. The clean, dated kitchen still functioned well for the staff. A large table and chairs filled the dining room; stacked papers covered one end and there was an intimate group of three coffee cups on the other. Reception, a third desk with a few folders on it, and a fourth spare desk crowded the living room. Lack of additional space necessitated that other staff work out of the production facilities.

Noon was on them in no time. "I normally eat at my desk," said Martha, "but let's get out of here today. I can explain things better without interruptions, and I'll be able to answer any of your questions."

An old-time diner was a short distance away on the road to Santa Rosa. Clean and quiet, it served good, reasonably priced food. It was a landmark in the area because of its shiny metal exterior with the enormous, nostalgic neon sign next to the street announcing it was *Angie's Diner*. Sometimes basic communications were best.

The smell of coffee and items on the grill welcomed them as they entered. Beside the cash register was a corkboard with multicolored tacks holding notices about events in the area. On the other side of the entry stood a coatrack, now holding only an old multicolored scarf, probably left last winter. Long counters with fixed stools ran left and right from the entrance. Booths with upholstered bench seats and backs ran in the same directions next to the windows. It was a classic example of diners that had been stamped out up and down the East Coast in the middle of the last century. Men relaxed over coffee, reading newspapers at various spots along the counters. In a few of the booths, families with children entranced by their phones represented the newer generations.

Martha headed to a corner booth overlooking the road and the cars and work trucks parked out front. She stalled several times along the way, saying hello and exchanging banter with other customers and staff. She'd been coming here for years.

Once seated in the booth, Martha could spend some private time with Remy. If she was going to be tied to this young lady, grooming her to take some of the burden, Martha wanted to pry out more about her, bounce ideas off her, and grade her responses, evaluate her input. The hubbub of the office would be a distraction. This was a big step she was taking. She wanted to be confident she could work with and enjoy the company of this candidate. She knew the girl had book smarts and drive. Did she have the common sense to match? Did she have the street smarts to survive? Glowing reports from Bill, Juan, and Sarah at the tasting rooms were undoubtedly in her favor. Still, it was not some clerical job she would be filling.

Martha had worked with men her whole life. If she was to train someone to take over a portion of meaningful items, working in close quarters with them every day, she wanted a young, energetic, positive woman—biased be damned. She wanted someone hardworking and loyal, someone she could enjoy time with, someone who shared her passion for the company and life in general.

Coffee arrived first, and Martha started. "So explain all this branding and rebranding stuff. I'm behind on all the new marketing terms. Content marketing—is that what it's called? The social media approach to moving a business ahead. Customer retention and loyalty, I get, but a lot of the other stuff evades me. Can you break it down into simple English for me?"

Earlier, when Martha was chatting with the waitress, Remy had noticed a blue-and-white PG&E utility truck pull in and take up two parking spaces out front. It was a big one with a battered white lift to move men up to the power lines. Two large spools of cable hung on the back. Four doors opened, four men got out, four yellow hard hats landed back inside, and four men in orange vests made their way to the door. When they entered, the men walked to a booth at the far end of the restaurant. Remy was relieved. She knew they'd be loud and didn't want them close by where they might break her concentration.

Martha could tell Remy was nervous. It was, after all, her first actual business meeting with the boss. She sensed that Remy appreciated being taken out of the office to a more relaxed environment where there wouldn't be interruptions.

"Okay," said Remy. "I'll go over the basics of what's out there and do an example of how it relates to Rolling Oaks Winery specifically. Let's start with social media."

She gave a concise, clear summary of social media outlets. She asked Martha questions about what the winery currently did on social platforms—very little, as it turned out. Her explanations were professional and carefully worded. She explained search engine optimization and other terms obscure to Martha. An hour passed before they knew it.

"I have more ideas about the tasting room. I know how key it is to wine marketing. Can I have another week to organize my suggestions better for you? Some of them may be extreme, but I'd like to have them laid out clearly so you can grasp the whole concept."

The lunch put Martha at ease. She was impressed. Remy didn't know it, but Bill had already told Martha about moving the tasting room. When the logic of it registered with her, Martha thought it a brilliant piece of thinking. She noticed Remy could shunt aside her light manner and sense of humor when the conversation turned serious. Other scenarios presented by Martha were quickly evaluated, and several options or directions were offered in return. Martha thought about the upcoming directors' meeting and dinner in two weeks. She wanted Remy to attend and see how she would fare among the group of investors, finance, and salespeople. She also wanted to encourage Remy more about her tasting room ideas, push her to concentrate on them.

"You're right about how important the tasting rooms are to marketing," she said. "They lock in loyal repeat customers and growing sales. Remember, these direct sales at the tasting rooms and our wine club are a lot more profitable than sales through wine shops or restaurants. With them, we get about half the bottle price, since those other outlets have to have their markup." Martha was pensive for a moment. "I want you to stay up at the tasting room for two more weeks. That following Friday night, we have the directors' meeting and dinner. I want you to attend and meet some of the people who aren't in the office."

"Is it dressy?" asked Remy.

"The men wear jackets, and we wear dresses. Not formal, but an attractive, young woman like you will brighten up a room full of us old people." Martha smiled at her. "The meeting is very informal and short. This isn't General Motors. It's a combination of legal requirements, explaining the company's current state and direction, and rewarding ourselves with a fun night out. There'll be about a dozen of us. The dinner is always fun."

Remy hadn't seen much of Chico since the night of their dinner a week ago. He, Juan, and Skip were busy at the winemaking facilities and in the vineyards now that the barn cleanup was completed. She missed him and wondered if she'd see him again socially, but after seeing his ex, she didn't hold out much hope.

Sarah, the head of the tasting rooms, had been terrific. She'd guided Remy through the subtle ways of helping visiting wine enthusiasts, the finessed way to guide them through the tasting experience.

Instituting the reservation system a few years prior had made life in the tasting room less hectic. An appointment schedule, like a doctor's office, rendered it much more manageable than the previous potluck system where large groups could materialize on top of each other. Today, a group of five were a no-show. Remy and Sarah stole a few minutes, grabbed some coffee, and took a break at one of the small tables outside in the shade. They'd been there about ten minutes when a stretch limo pulled into the parking lot. Four well-dressed people got out. There were two fit men in sports coats and pressed slacks, and two women in pricey dresses carrying Louis Vuitton handbags—not the cheap ones.

Remy started to get up, but Sarah put a hand on her arm. "Stay close by and listen," she said. "These are the types you hand off to Carl or me. I don't recognize them, so someone must have told them to make the effort and come all the way out here. These are people who know about wine." She gave a casual nod in the guests' direction. "Those handbags the women are carrying, what do you think those cost?"

No dummy after leafing through Lynn's fashion magazines for years, Remy glanced over. "I recognize the Vuitton logo and style. They're worth more than my car." She picked an obscene number from the air. She would impress Sarah with her worldliness. "Twelve hundred dollars," she said with authority.

Sarah moved her head slightly so Remy would block the approaching visitors from seeing her face. "Ten thousand dollars—each," she said, her voice low. Her face brightened as she whispered, "Imagine if they own several restaurants back home and decide they like our wine."

Dumbstruck, Remy didn't even notice Sarah rise and greet the group. The two women with bags worth a year's salary at the market Remy worked at walked by. Remy didn't have the courage to look at their shoes. It dawned on her why the bags were so big. They needed room for their heavy platinum or black credit cards.

Bill caught Remy in the parking lot at the end of the day when no one was around to blow his cover. "Sorry I haven't been by. Is Sarah taking care of you?"

Remy beamed as he drew closer. "She's the best. She knows how to teach and make sense of all this stuff. I've seen Juan a few times, and I've met Skip. He seems nice. Everyone around here seems very good at their jobs." She gave him the kidding punch on the arm. "You seem to be the only one who can't stay out of the doghouse. Are you keeping out of Mrs. K's way?"

"As much as possible. I think she's in a good mood today. She shot a family of skunks in her backyard before breakfast."

Bill was nervous. He'd thought about this for a week, and now it was time. Their first meal, aside from the burger lunch, had been spur of the moment, two fellow workers grabbing a bite after work. Now, he would ask her out on a date, foreign territory he hadn't tread on in years. "Listen, Remy. My daughter doesn't get back until Sunday. Would you like to go to dinner with me on Saturday night? I understand if you're busy." There, it was out.

Tension dissipated when he received a bright smile. "Yes!"

Bill said he'd pick her up.

"We can take my car if you'd like," offered Remy.

"Ha! Not on your life. Bring your revised paper. I'll go over it for you."

Chapter 10

On Friday night, Lynn met Remy at the pizza parlor near her salon. Already tired, both women had another busy Saturday looming in front of them and were not up for a night in the bars. It didn't take long for observant Lynn to see Remy was holding on to something. Her friend was still as transparent as a ten-year-old. Time to pry it out. "Let's have it, Remy. I know you too well. You've got something on your mind."

Remy shifted in her seat and folded her hands together. "Chico asked me to dinner tomorrow night, like an actual date. I think I'm starting to like the guy. He's still a bit of a mystery, but he's been extremely helpful and nice to me. He seems to be showing a little interest." She then explained about the ex-wife and all the doubts she was harboring.

"Jesus, girl, you still don't know that you're a real catch. If you'd give any guy a chance, he'd be all over you," Lynn teased her. "Let's face it, reading men hasn't found its way into your skill set yet." She leaned back and folded her arms. "Admit it. This Chico guy must have perked up when he saw the new hairdo, didn't he? Relax and roll with it. Are there any other available men around that place? Pickings are getting thin on the ground around here."

"Funny you should say that," said Remy. "Last week at the tasting room, Juan introduced me to a guy called Skip. He's our age, and I guess he helps Juan and Chico on the production end of the business. He's cute, seems sharp, but he's a little shy." Remy fluffed her hair like she was preening in front of a mirror, mimicking Lynn. "If I decide I don't have any use for him, I may throw him your way. You really must get out more, Lynn. I can't keep finding guys for you."

Lynn let out a snort. "Yeah, in your dreams. The last guy you landed on your own was in eighth grade. You'd be in a convent by now if it weren't for me. Where's this Chico guy taking you for dinner?"

"Sebastopol, one of the chic, new restaurants in that new Barlow complex. What should I wear?"

"No jeans! Please! I think it's time for you to graduate to a low-cut blouse and a short skirt. Hell, make it a miniskirt. Give him lots of cleavage and a mile of leg. You'll need a crowbar to pry him off. Then he won't notice when you order the most expensive thing on the menu."

"Lynn!"

"Just saying. If you want to take this guy on a test-drive, you've got to make him want to get into the car."

"No, thank you. I don't have a parking garage at home like you do."

Exasperated, Lynn rolled her eyes before returning to the menu. "Look presentable and act like yourself. That's all you'll need to do. That's all you've ever needed to do."

Orders were placed. Remy glanced over Lynn's shoulder as a man walked into the restaurant. "Well, speak of the devil." She waved, got his attention, and motioned for him to come over to the table. "How are you, Skip? This is my friend Lynn. We just sat down and ordered. Why don't you join us?"

Lynn focused—quickly. *This guy is cute. And the body. Oh, yes! Eye candy in a pizza parlor—who'd have thought? I wouldn't find many like this on Tinder.*

Stammering slightly, clearly unsettled by one of Lynn's mega smiles, Skip said, "A pleasure to meet you." He dragged his eyes away and addressed Remy. "Well, I was just getting something to go. It was a long, hot day."

Lynn decided this thing wasn't going anywhere. She reached out and put her hand on his arm to make sure he'd stay. "Oh, you poor thing. You look exhausted. No. We can't allow you to drive on an empty stomach." She slid over one chair and patted the vacated seat. "Why don't you sit right here next to me?"

Is there such a thing as a lucky Friday night?

The poor boy looked nervous, and Lynn thought it best to put him at ease. It had been another hot day, and she could see poor Skip was sweating through his tight shirt—his form-fitting shirt. She turned toward him and gave him a better view. Would you want to look at the Mona Lisa sideways? "Skip, why don't you relax and unbutton that shirt?"

"*Lynn,*" Remy reprimanded. Her friend was doing a preliminary assessment of a potential victim: Medusa soothing her snakes while twirling her spear. Pandora toying with the top of her box.

An angelic face turned to Remy. "What? Someone should look after the poor thing. You never told me you worked in a sweatshop. Aren't there laws against abusing hard-working, handsome men like this?" Her attention returned to Skip, sultry now, and she laid a soft touch on his arm. He fidgeted in his chair, and the glow of a blush worked its way through Skip's tanned skin.

Remy tried to distract her friend and change the subject. "Lynn has her own beauty salon just around the corner, Skip. We've been friends since we were kids."

It didn't seem to be working, but Lynn's focus would not be deflected. "Let's get Skip a beer." She gave him big, concerned green eyes—one of the best tactics in her repertoire. "Or are you a wine guy, Skip?" The brushing-nonexistent-dirt-off-his-shoulder trick followed.

"Um, beer. A beer would be good."

Lynn's gaze moved up to the medium-length blond hair. It was lovely but all over the place. Combs or brushes were obviously not in his budget. The slow, seductive voice slinked out of the repertoire. "Oh, Skippy, what I could do with that hair. You're a tanned Greek god waiting to be pulled to the surface."

There was more male squirming. More Remy squirming. Hair was safe. Remy backed off. "You're right. Skip has lovely hair. What would you do with it? I think it looks fine as it is."

Lynn's palms came up to shoulder height, a connoisseur lost in studying a masterpiece. She was going to have a little fun with these two. "Let it grow. Long, *very* long. Then fill it with a cascade of highlights, a flowing golden river cascading down from that handsome head." Lynn knew Remy was nervous since Skip was a coworker, but what the hell—and he *was* cute. She did the slow, weaving-hands thing she'd learned from

Remy. "Picture him on the cover of one of those erotic historical romance novels you read. Imagine him wading out of the raging ocean surf with the wrecked sailing ship behind him. Naked. Those long, wet, flowing locks molded to the curve of his muscular buttocks."

Skip couldn't speak. Remy almost gasped. "*Lynn*, leave him alone!"

Lynn patted Skip's cheek, almost bursting out in laughter at the look on both their faces. "Okay. Okay. Just having a little fun with the both of you. Back to business. So, Skip, tell me about yourself. What do you do at the winery?"

He was so shy Lynn felt like a dentist pulling teeth, trying to wrestle out details about his work.

Eventually, their orders arrived. Lynn could tell she'd wound him up enough. "Could you bring this man another beer, please?"

She decided to take it easy on both of them. Christ, Remy belonged in a convent, and poor Skip belonged in the monastery next door. Lynn found his shy, soft demeanor a refreshing change from the ordinary guys in a bar. There could be some potential here, but she knew there was no way this guy would make a move on her. He needed help. Lynn would help.

Once she got the two of them relaxed, it was a fun meal. As they got up to leave, Lynn turned to Skip. "You're not going to try and hustle me up for my phone number like a guy in a bar, are you?"

"No. No, of course not. I'm not like that," stammered Skip.

Lynn gave him a stern, appraising look. She knew how to drag it out for just the right amount of time. "Good." She handed him a salon card with her cell number written on the back. "If you're interested, call me." She sensed the poor thing might be a little confused. "Not for a haircut. For a date." Lynn almost laughed. Like the old cliché, he was actually looking at the card and scratching his head with a perplexed look on his face.

"Why...why would someone as beautiful as you want to go out with a guy like me?"

Lynn glanced around, looking for a spaceship nearby. Suave, this guy was not. It was a great line, but she sensed the idiot didn't even know it. "Well, dial the number, Skip. Maybe we'll find out."

As she walked to her car and looked back, she giggled at the bewildered look on poor Skip's face.

A concerned Remy called Lynn at the salon the next day. "God, Lynn, Skip works with me. You can't make him another one of your conquests. What are your intentions?"

Oh, she's been reading those books again, thought Lynn. *What are your intentions?* "Well, Remy dear, if he calls, we'll meet for coffee or something. I have it all planned out. I'll tell him I have a grapevine planted in a pot at my condo, and it doesn't seem to be doing well. Could you please come to look at it, Skip? He will—"

Remy interrupted. "Lynn, that's a *palm tree* in that planter!"

"Who cares? By the time he tells me that, I'll have already set the dead bolt on the door."

"Lynn!"

She enjoyed winding her friend up. A few more cranks were in order. "Take it easy. Hell, I thought I was very restrained at the pizza parlor last night. I left out the good bit about him wading out of the surf on that book cover thing."

"And what was that, God forbid?"

"How we would gaze longingly at his... How do they say it in those books you read?" Lynn put on her slow, sultry voice. "We'd gaze at his *swollen member.*"

"I most certainly do not read books about *swollen members!*"

"Huh, you can say that again. I'm sorry. Maybe it was *pulsating loins.* You should read this Sunday's *New York Times* book section. There's a great article about some newly discovered Jane Austen personal letters. She wrote about both of those items, quite vividly, as a matter of fact."

"Jane would *never*..." Remy caught herself. "Stop. I'm not going to let you emotionally abuse me with all that garbage piled up in your sex-obsessed brain." She fired a shot back. "You're going to be reincarnated as an alley cat."

Lynn laughed down the line. "Relax. If Skippy calls, I won't embarrass you. Let me know how your dinner goes with that Chico guy tonight. I have to go. Don't forget the low-cut blouse and miniskirt. See if anything 'pops up.'"

The Barlow complex in Sebastopol screamed trendy with new buildings in a hip warehouse theme with high ceilings, exposed ductwork, and chic lighting. Large glass roll-up doors filled the main wall. They were opened, weather permitting, to bring the outside in or vice versa. Multiple restaurants of every type were peppered between art galleries, clothing boutiques, and craft stores. Narrow streets wove an intimate web throughout the entire area, and strings of large white lights spanned overhead, giving the space a festive feel. The streets teemed with people milling around. Fortunately, Chico had secured a quiet table in the rear of a new California cuisine location.

Remy wore a dress. She had stopped by Target on the way home from the market and found a simple summer dress on sale. It was a patterned light green with short sleeves and a respectable neckline befitting a lady, not some trollop outfit like Lynn had teased her about. Seated at the table, she was still smiling to herself about how Chico had stared openmouthed at her when he'd picked her up. He'd stuttered the nicest "You look beautiful" she had ever heard. Her books were right. Presentable was a good thing.

She reached down to her bag. "Here's my paper. It's finished."

Chico was having none of it. "I'll take it with me and read it later. Let's make a pact not to talk about work tonight. I'm sorry, but you look much too lovely to waste the night and this restaurant on work talk after a long week." He shunted the Question Machine off topic.

Chico seemed to deflate as he read the menu. "Do you know what any of this stuff is? What's a fusion? What's a reduction? What's a medley? Where's the steak or chicken? Are potatoes banned now? What's a cream sauce of organic alpaca milk?"

Remy looked up, sensing he was not much of a foodie. "Stop whining. Look on the bottom right. There're eight words, and 'fillet' is one of them. Tell the waiter to leave off the other seven words and just bring you the steak part. Or take a chance. You can scrape off the rosemary cabernet sauce. And the bed of Egyptian caramelized rice is just rice."

"Why don't they ruin the steak completely and cover it with shredded bat wings in kangaroo snot? Why don't they just serve it with aged grape roots in sterilized organic mulch?"

"Chico, be nice." Men could be such children when it came to food. She heard her phone ding in her bag with a new text. It would wait. "Save your breath to cool your porridge. You can get through this. We'll get you an ice cream cone when we're finished."

Chico wasn't letting up. "And the salads. Look at the salads. Doesn't anyone serve lettuce anymore? Where's the romaine, the iceberg? These are all weeds from someone's backyard."

Well, at least he'd be easy to cook for, thought Remy. A slab of meat in a frying pan and a head of lettuce with some bottled Caesar dressing, and she'd be elevated to queen. He needed some historical perspective. "You don't know how good you've got it, Chico. Centuries ago, you'd be eating jellied eel, mutton as tough as a leather seat cover, sheep's head, or parts of a cow you never heard of."

Drinks arrived, and Chico asked, "So, tell me where have you gone on vacation? What's your favorite place?"

Remy folded her hands around the glass of wine in front of her. "I've been to San Francisco a few times, but I guess that doesn't count. I've been to Lake Tahoe for four days. That's about it. Just haven't got the time or the money. If I get this job and make some money, I'd like to travel more." A glint bounced off Remy's eyes. "Let's see how sharp you are. Now that you know me a little, where do you think I'd like to visit more than anyplace else?"

"Bulgaria," answered Chico with a deadpan face.

Remy raised an eyebrow and deadpanned him back.

Chico smiled. "Okay, okay. England. Not real tough after all those books you read and the TV shows you watch. You want to see the land of Oz, see London, see the history and places those characters come from."

She beamed. "And someday, I'll do it. You just wait and see."

The waiter placed their salads in front of them. Chico poured her more wine. "You'd love London," he said. "Many of the areas are the same as back then. Lots of the stores and buildings date back to the seventeen and eighteen hundreds. It's a wonderful big city."

Remy's mouth opened. Her eyes went wide as she leaned forward. A pot of golden knowledge was sitting at the table across from her. "You've been there? Doghouse Chico has been to London? Did you go there to get away from Mrs. K?"

"In a manner of speaking."

"Oh, please, tell me all about London," begged Remy as she reached down to her purse.

Bill frowned. "You're not going to bring out that dreaded notebook, are you?"

"Relax, it's just my handkerchief."

"Okay, What do you want to know?"

Bill finally had a chance to do his own mesmerizing. He tried to copy Remy's hypnotizing handweaving, but he was so clumsy, she broke out laughing when he started. He held her with every answer, excited her with his descriptions of a city and country far away. He dazzled her with stories of Buckingham Palace and the Queen's Gallery, beautiful shopping streets, Selfridges—she'd seen the TV show—the Assembly Rooms at Bath, the costume section of the Victoria and Albert Museum, on and on. As she was drinking in the images, Bill felt a twinge of sadness. This woman had had but one vacation and was fascinated by his stories. He'd never known anyone so positive and easy to please.

The night flew by. After coffee, she again impressed him. "Can we move to the bar for a glass of wine? They're busy here tonight, and I don't want to tie up one of their tables."

So few people would think of something like that.

He remembered she'd had a long day at the market. It was ten thirty when he dropped her off. On the way home, tension built inside Bill. Any thoughts of telling Remy who he was had, once again, been shunted aside. No way was he going to spoil their night, the happiness, by owning up to it now. Nerves, however, were fraying. As they grew closer on a personal level, the game was shifting. Had he left it too long? Was it getting past laughing it off as a minor deception? He decided to confess in the next day or two. From her accusations the day she'd found out he had a degree in viticulture, he sensed Remy could be a little volatile. Best find a private moment and a private location, not the tasting room. If she momentarily lost it, bottles of pinot noir cost money. He briefly pictured her hurling them at him while customers scattered and the room was transformed into a blood-red Quentin Tarantino movie set. Guilt and tension ramped up a notch. He had to wrap this up soon.

What a dream dinner, and it had been a date! Remy lay in bed staring at the ceiling. He'd been even more handsome tonight. How did a guy get more handsome? Never mind. Unfortunately, with the admission of caring, doubts surfaced. She liked Chico, but feelings often fostered questions. Her mind flashed back to when he had told her about his wife leaving. She'd sensed sadness. Did he still have feelings for her? If that woman hinted she wanted to get back into his life, Remy felt she was way outclassed. Why was he even interested in her after being with a stunner like his ex? Her mind drifted to the hug and kiss she'd witnessed when the woman had talked to him at the winery. Remy Reilly had never been in a situation like this. These were all new feelings, all new sensations. Was she making too much of it? Was there even something happening here? Confused happiness finally saw her off to sleep.

"You'd better read this," said Bill, handing Remy's revised report to his mother. It was the following morning, and he had stopped by on his way to do some errands before picking up Lizzie from his ex. "It's terrific. It's all logical and well organized. I'm running late. I'll swing back later today."

"Make it dinner time. Winston is coming over. We want to hear all about my Lizzie's trip."

Five o'clock found Martha at the stove preparing dinner for the four of them. Her granddaughter was coming back after a week away, and Martha had missed her. Winston Wright, whom Martha still insisted on calling "a friend" to everyone's amusement, sat at the nearby breakfast room table poring over Remy's paper.

He was sixty-eight years young, slim, and fit, and Martha thought him an elegant and mature version of Cary Grant. She loved seeing him at her table concentrating on Remy's paper. She loved seeing him at her table anytime.

Originally from London, Winston had made his money in finance at one of the big Wall Street firms in New York. At fifty-three, he'd abruptly decided to semi-retire and manage his own money in a more relaxed environment. Winston was a wine buff. He'd moved to Sonoma to look for smaller investment opportunities. Fifteen years ago, he had invested heavily in Rolling Oaks Winery's last expansion with the Keatings. They had become friends. Two years later, Martha's husband died, her granddaughter was born, and her son had started at UC Davis. Young Bill was home three nights a week, but a lot of the burden of looking after the child had fallen to Martha. A complete gentleman, Winston had helped Martha through the next four years. He had also lost a spouse years before and knew firsthand the devastation it could bring. When Bill finished with school and Martha had more time of her own, she'd realized she had formed a mutual bond with Winston, and she had no desire to break it.

Lizzie burst into the house ahead of her father, rushed over to Martha, and gave her a big hug. Martha let her get the initial burst of energy out before telling her to let her finish dinner preparations. Lizzie then went over and hugged Winston before sitting in the chair beside him. Winston was the closest thing she had to a grandfather.

Martha occasionally glanced over at Winston as he doted on the girl. She smiled to herself, remembering all the years she had to softly caution him against spoiling the child. Most of the time, Winston ignored her. Never having children of his own, he looked for any excuse to buy Lizzie something. Last November, the girl had complained about her old computer. The next day, Winston gave her an Apple laptop loaded with enough stuff to run a corporation. He couldn't even wait a month until Christmas.

Back from getting a few things from his truck, Bill leaned against the cooking island by his mother while Lizzie harangued Winston.

"I had Winston over early to look at Remy's report," said Martha. "Some of those ideas are so different from what you and I had been thinking that I wanted his opinion. He's extremely complimentary. Says we better not let Remy get away, especially if she could put up with me." Martha smiled. "Winston's still very subtle about pointing out any of my perceived shortcomings."

"Jesus, Mom. When are you two just going to move in together and get it over with?" Bill had been watching with amusement this *friend* act of his mother's for his daughter's entire life—thirteen years. "You and Winston love each other. Lizzie and I think he's the best thing that could happen to you. What's the holdup?"

Martha blushed. "Enough of that talk, young man."

One of Bill's small revenges came in making his mother blush. With a sly smile, he lowered his voice. "Winston didn't come over early to do anything else, did he? I mean, like fix the dishwasher, or something like that?"

Martha gave him a glacial gaze along with a terse, "Be careful, young man."

Bill snorted and moved out of range to the table with Winston and Lizzie.

After the meal was finished, Lizzie went to the TV while the adults had coffee and talked. Martha patted Winston on the arm. "Tell Bill what you think."

"I must say this is wonderfully thought out and precisely presented. From what you've told me about this young lady, she sees a lot more than she lets on. An organized mind did this report. I can't wait to meet her." Always one to throw humor into a conversation, especially after hearing that Remy was fascinated by the English romantics, Winston added, "Naturally, having an appreciation for our classic English literature, I knew straight off the lady was intelligent."

"I agree," said Bill.

"She hit one of my major concerns about prices," said Martha. She roughly summarized one section of Remy's paper.

"The younger generations aren't into expensive bottles of wine. Craft beers and cans of hard liquor mixed with juices are attracting their attention. Additionally, we've been on a great economic recovery. When the next recession hits, everyone will watch their wallets. We're headed for the same affordability problems that the restaurants are now facing with food. Our concentration should be on more affordable varieties."

She looked up at her son. "God, did she nail that on the head," Martha mused. "Look at the details about making the barn into a tasting room closer to town. Incorporate a small wine museum. Have flat-screen TVs showing both old black-and-white and current films showing ways of picking, destemming, and crushing. Why didn't either of us think of this?" She turned from the paper to her son. "I guess we're just a little too close to it all to see a broader picture. We all ignored the potential of that old barn we see every day. A fresh set of eyes and some creativity sure puts a different light on things."

Bill threw in his observations. "The section on content marketing impressed me. We need to build better brand awareness through social media, lead nurturing, customer retention and loyalty, hold more events and promotions during the slower winter months at the tasting rooms. Coppola has a museum of all their movies, Sonoma-Cutrer has worldwide recognition through its croquet tournament. Iron Horse has been very successful with their Oyster Saturdays. Remy's list of ideas to make us stand out more is very creative. She suggests we use the event center for local arts and craft shows, fundraisers, even local book club meetings. We can rent it out for business conferences and seminars, not just weddings and birthday parties." Bill laughed. "She didn't just take marketing in school. It looks like she eats and breathes it when she's not buried in those old romance books and movies."

Focusing on his last comment, Martha looked at her son. "Think it through, Bill. This young woman never had much. She's always put in long, hard days, and she took on the role of partial breadwinner for the family at a young age. Those books and movies are her only escape. They give her happiness and hope that life can be better. She can't just up and fly to Europe or the Caribbean like the three of us. She hasn't the money or time." She reached over and patted her son's hand. "I want to give her the job now—*full time* as she calls it. I like Remy. She's a hard worker. I don't want to take the chance of losing her. Are you good with that?"

"Couldn't agree more, Mom."

Seeking final affirmation, both personally and because Winston was a substantial stockholder and she valued his opinion, Martha turned to him. "Your thoughts?"

"I'm afraid that I'm biased. Hiring anyone to free some time up for you is one of my dreams. This Remy appears to have all the requirements and more. She's a worker. She's bright. She's enthusiastic. Paramount from what else you've both said, she's responsible." Winston held Martha's hand. "If she can put up with you, you've hit the lottery."

"Good," said Martha as she stood to get coffee and kissed both her son and Winston on their heads. "I'll get the architect to draw up some rough ideas. We'll need some graphics for the directors' meeting so everyone gets these ideas better."

Winston was one of the family. He knew about Bill's ongoing subterfuge with Remy. The potential outcome amused Winston, but it worried Martha. Bill felt comfortable talking about it around him. Nervous about reality closing in, Bill said, "Mom, I haven't told her yet about me."

Martha raised her palms, shook her head, and gave her son a mischievous grin. "Not *my* problem. *You've* had plenty of time. Now I guess she'll find out at the meeting. I don't want you upsetting her before then. This will be a big, happy surprise for her. I want to announce her great ideas and her new job in front of everyone. You dug yourself into this hole, now you can figure a way to dig yourself out." Martha grinned at her son and gave him a motherly pat on the cheek as another creative light bulb flashed on. "I know what. *You* can do it. *You* can make the announcement." Martha turned back to the stove, obviously thrilled that she could shove her son

under the shiny new bus coming down the street before Juan
had a chance.

Oh, Christ, thought Bill.

Chapter 11

Monday of her third week on tasting-room duty found Remy with Martha at the offices. The two of them were brainstorming final preparations for the upcoming Friday night directors' meeting. Equipment for the PowerPoint presentation working—check. Reservations for dinner confirmed—check. Topics to cover—check. Everyone attending—check.

Important items resolved, Martha said, "Okay. Let's go have lunch at the hotel. I want to see their menu and decide on the food for Friday night. I'm still up in the air about having limited selections or offering them a full menu."

Settled at their table, they both ordered salads. Remy asked the waitress to please leave the menus. Small talk swallowed the time during the meal. Martha was enjoying Remy's company more and more. Other women to talk with were limited in her world. She found it easy to discuss things with the young lady across from her, and she enjoyed her opinions on how younger women viewed the world.

They studied the menus over coffee. "What do you think, Remy?"

"I'd make limited selections, Mrs. K. Have them choose a salad and choose an entrée from a shortlist. No need to drag it out with people taking forever reading the menu. This menu is big. People would waffle over selections forever." Remy paused for a few seconds. "Some of them might even order appetizers. We should pre-select some appetizers and have them on the table as soon as the dinner orders are in. For the main meal, I'd go for the usual chicken and steak, but throw in a third, maybe a seafood dish or pasta."

"Great," said Martha. They were on the same page. She loved the quick answer and the idea for a third option. She would have stopped at chicken and steak. "Let's make it a seafood pasta dish for the third. If anyone starts with the vegetarian organic thing, I'll tell them to order a head of lettuce or macaroni and cheese. Prepping and doing these meetings strains my patience. You've helped make that part easy. Call them tomorrow and sort it out." This delegating stuff was growing on Martha.

They settled the check, and Martha gathered her things. "Let's go. Time to shop. We ladies should look stunning on Friday night. It's rare for me to go out in a group." Martha gave Remy a winsome smile. "Winston takes me out a lot, but he wants me all to himself."

Winston? Who is Winston? A lover? Chico had told her that Mrs. K slept alone in a coffin in her closet. Remy thought it best to let it go.

They arrived at Martha's favorite boutique dress store close to downtown Santa Rosa. When they entered, Remy noticed it was definitely upscale. It was filled with spaced racks of women's wear and shelves full of high-end designer items. Three other customers prowled the store. None of them looked like they used their hands for anything other than carrying around nail polish on long, manicured fingers.

The owner came up to Martha. Introductions were made. "Two cocktail dresses for a nice dinner out, June. Not fancy, something understated," said Martha to her friend. She turned to Remy. "June is a mind reader. She'll show you two or three dresses, and you'll pick one of them, no problem."

"You, I know," June said to Martha. She shifted her gaze to Remy, took in the tall, slim figure, the lovely auburn hair. "Let me get Remy started, and I'll find you in a bit. Follow me, Remy."

She moved Remy through the store to dresses in her size. "I do the store in sizes to keep it simple. Look through these, pick out a couple, and Martha and I will help you with a decision." June moved on to catch up with her friend and to have a gossip and a cup of coffee.

Oh God, thought Remy. She'd only seen dresses like these in magazines. She promised herself not to tell Lynn about this place. She'd spend her life savings here.

Remy fanned the hangers back and forth. Not a procrastinator, she pulled the first three that appealed to her, laid them over the rack, and critiqued them. Curious, she flipped over the price tags. The rack behind her almost fell over after she jumped back and hit it. *What the fuck!* These dresses were all over six hundred dollars. One of them was close to a thousand! Jeez, they were *dresses*, not used cars. Surely nobody actually wore them? Were they wall hangings? How could she get out of this? No way could she afford this place. Panic was setting in.

Martha noticed Remy's stress as she and June approached. Best put the girl at ease. Men were inept at picking the right woman, even when they were standing right in front of them, and her son topped the list. Martha thought Bill needed an extra push in Remy's direction; she couldn't care less about a new dress, but it always pumped Winston up a notch, and she enjoyed pumping Winston up a notch. This stop was about putting the final varnish on a beautiful painting for her son. Time for him to get a life.

"June, could you please bring over the one I like?" said Martha. "I want to see what Remy thinks about it."

With June out of earshot, Martha's voice was stern as she spoke. "This is my treat, young lady. Call it a bonus for barn duty. I know this isn't in your budget. I was young once, too, you know." Remy started to object, but Martha's finger came up. "Not a word."

When June returned, they all approved Martha's choice. That out of the way, Martha decreed, "I like the green for Remy. It's form-fitting, shows off her figure, and accents those hard-working calves." June agreed. Remy stood there in silence. "Well, go put it on, dear. We'll get it fitted."

Remy returned from the dressing room, careful not to bump into anything and snag the small fortune covering her skin. Both older women were impressed. She had a figure, and this dress was hiding none of it. *Even that idiot son of mine won't be able to ignore this package*, thought Martha.

"Perfect," she said. "Just one or two alterations. The high heels will be up to you, Remy. Thursday okay for pickup, June?"

"Easily, Martha."

In her car on the ride home after work, Remy thought, A *fitting*? Target and Marshalls didn't do *fittings*. The green dress was over six hundred dollars. A new battery, a new muffler, and probably a new paint job for the Toyota. She'd have to get a white sheet for her driver's seat on Friday night. High heels? What was Martha talking about! Remy had never even worn high heels. Would she have to practice? Lynn, she needed Lynn.

"Meet me at five thirty at the salon," said Lynn. "We'll go down the street to the shoe store."

Remy heard Lynn stifling a laugh.

"Let's pick out some heels to go with that green dress." They were in the shoe store. This wouldn't take long. Lynn could navigate a shoe store like a merchant marine behind schedule. "No need to get too fancy. You'll probably break them anyhow. Now stand up." Remy started stumbling around. Lynn shook her head. This was like daycare for an adult. "Wear them at home every night this week. You'll get used to them. You'll be fine. Hell, it's only for a few hours. You're not running a marathon. We'll pick out some of my jewelry later this week." Lynn was getting a kick sorting her friend out. A big grin covered her face. "You're finally going to the prom. It's a shame you missed the one in high school. Don't forget the garter belt and stockings."

"What are you talking about, Lynn? I'm *not* wearing a garter belt and stockings!"

Time for the needle. Lynn said, "Jane Austen confided in her lost letters that she wore them all the time."

"Stop it, Lynn. I'm nervous enough as it is."

"Okay, just pantyhose then. God, you are so boring." Her friend was going to pay for dragging her out to the shoe store. "Can't you picture yourself in a dimly lit bedroom with that Chico guy naked on the bed in front of you, letting the dress slip to the floor and then climbing on top of him wearing a garter belt and stockings?"

"Lynn!"

Remy missed Chico. It was Thursday, and she hadn't heard from him since their dinner the weekend before. She'd sensed he might be interested in her, and she was definitely interested in him. A new side had been revealed that first day in the tasting room when he'd professionally taught her the basics. When she'd asked Sarah about what Chico did, Remy thought she'd been a little vague, but Sarah did say he was good at his various jobs.

Remy was now getting the idea he was not the odd-job guy who was always in trouble with Mrs. K. Had he lost interest? Was she utterly unimpressive at dinner? Did he think he should aim higher? He'd have no problem doing that if he wanted to. She tried to calm herself, knowing there wasn't anything she could do about it. To compound everything, she had no idea what she would be doing next week. Mrs. K wanted her at the meeting, but what did that mean? Nothing had been decided about where Remy would go after the tasting room. It had been well over a month since she'd started working for Martha, and Remy knew she was liked, but what about the full-time job prospects? Would she stay up at the tasting room? Would she be let go? She tried to lose herself in her work, oblivious that Chico hadn't returned her paper.

In the afternoon, Skip stuck his head into the tasting room. Remy could see he was tentative as he approached. He fidgeted a bit in front of her before saying, "Your friend Lynn seems nice."

Remy cut right to it, knowing what the issue was and sensing he might take a while to get it out. "Do you mean she's absolutely beautiful, and you're wondering if you should call her?"

"Well, um, yes. I don't know if she was serious when she gave me her number. Why would she want to go out with a guy like me?"

The poor thing seemed genuinely confused. Remy knew what Skip was going through based on her own jumbled thoughts about Chico. "By 'a guy like me,' do you mean a nice man, attractive, with a good job, and not sporting a massive ego?"

Skip just stood there, so Remy continued, "Dial the number, Skip. Give it a try. Lynn is a great woman, despite that act she puts on at times. She's not seeing anyone. I think she wants you to call. Just be yourself, and you might hit it off. What have you got to lose?"

He shuffled back and forth for a moment. "Thanks, Remy." And then he meandered off.

Well, thought Remy, he won't be a speechwriter anytime soon.

Friday morning, Martha called Remy and told her to work only until noon at the tasting room. The meeting was tonight, and she needed Remy for an hour or two to prepare. The old Toyota belched its way through Sebastopol toward the office. The muffler was failing, and the noise almost drowned out her phone ringing.

"He has such wonderful taste."

It was difficult to hear over the racket. "What? Who is this? Speak up."

"It's Lynn. Skip called. The song of the sirens is luring his ship to the rocks. He wants to take me to dinner tonight. The idiot let me pick the restaurant."

"You be nice to him, Lynn. He came by yesterday and asked about you. I lied and told him you were a good woman. I almost went to the bathroom and threw up."

"Relax, mom. Tonight, I'll give him the clean-clothes, clean-vehicle, and restaurant test. I always like it when they open that little black folder at the end of the meal and that tab jumps up and smacks them in the wallet. If he passes that, I'll decide how nice to be to him."

Remy refused to be dragged into another of Lynn's adventures. They were two adults. "Lynn, I don't have time for you to torment me right now. I have to get ready for tonight's meeting and dinner. I'll see you later."

Chapter 12

Remy's old Toyota grumbled toward the impressive, columned portico protecting the hotel entrance. She forced it to the self-parking area off to the side of the building since she didn't know what to tip the valet parking in front, and it was money she couldn't spare anyhow.

The agenda spun through her head one more time. Eight to attend the meeting; double that for dinner, when spouses and significant others would fill out the table. Martha and Winston, Chico and Juan, and an Uncle Keith, who owned five percent but could care less—he was here to visit the family and enjoy himself. The accountant of twenty-five years, the head of sales, and Remy completed the group.

The meeting part would be held in one of the function rooms with dinner afterward. The meeting would be short—a formality to comply with corporate law. It was a small group who knew each other well. No surprises would rear their ugly heads.

High heels found tentative footing on the asphalt outside the car. The lovely green cocktail dress followed. At home, she'd felt like Cinderella putting it on. Remy held the clean white sheet in place on her car seat so it wouldn't follow her out of the car. Her balance was quite good as she walked in short steps to the hotel entrance. Delicate bracelets, borrowed from Lynn, jangled on her wrist. She'd been told they would call attention to her graceful, long-fingered hands and freshly painted nails, both finally recovered from barn duty. Her hair was down, and she wore a pair of Lynn's tasteful earrings.

She and Martha had been there earlier to check the final arrangements. Remy knew where to go. Yielding to Lynn's badgering, she'd allowed her friend to apply minimal makeup after sorting her hair out before she rushed off for her date with Skip. This was a dress-up fancy dinner, and Remy felt she would fit in, another first in her life.

The usual pre-meeting milling around was under way as people arrived and exchanged greetings. Remy had just walked up to Martha and Chico standing in the front of the room by the PowerPoint screen when Winston entered the far end and stopped to talk with Juan.

Remy, noting Winston's arrival, said, "Wow. Who is that gentleman?" Elderly movie-star handsome in a perfectly tailored suit and tie below an attractive tanned face framed by perfectly combed salt-and-pepper hair, Winston radiated elegance.

Chico leaned over as Martha smiled with pride at Remy's comment. He spoke softly to Remy, but loud enough for his mother to hear. "That's Winston Wright, the company's biggest investor going back many years. He and Mrs. K have a thing going on. Rumor around the company is that she sleeps with him to get lower interest rates."

Completely taken aback, Remy was appalled that Chico would dare say something like that in front of the boss, especially since he already spent most of his time on eternal probation. She didn't understand why he was even at the meeting. He was an employee, just like her. She didn't understand why she was here, either. Still, Mrs. K had insisted on it, something about meeting the people involved with the company.

Remy was about to pull Chico aside when Mrs. K put a hand on her arm, turned to Chico, and gave a reprimanding glare that would melt ice. Martha turned and smiled at Remy. "Winston and I do occasionally go out together. We enjoy each other's company." She gave Chico another reproving glance. "Don't believe any rumors spread by gossipy ne'er-do–wells around here."

"Wow, good for you, Mrs. K, he's gorgeous." She added her own glare toward Chico. "*Some* men should learn lessons from a gentleman like that." Remy pointed across the room. "Look at that posture. Look how dignified and gracious he is talking to those people. I doubt *he* would make tasteless remarks about a woman."

It was time. They took their places. The function room was set up with water, glasses, pens, and paper for all. At one end, a screen would show the PowerPoint presentation so all could see the facts and figures Martha wanted to convey. A long conference table comfortably accommodated four to a side for the eight people. The head of the table had no chair so the screen would be unobstructed. There was one additional chair at the opposite end for Martha when she finished her part. She didn't like craning her neck to see people, so she sat on one of the sides. Remy sat at the far end next to Martha, and opposite her sat Chico.

As Martha was getting ready at the front of the room, Remy leaned across the table. "I have to say, you sure clean up well, Chico. Nice shirt and slacks. That lovely sports coat goes perfectly with them."

Remy wondered why he seemed so nervous when he said, "Thanks, Remy. But tonight, you outshine everyone in the room."

Bill tried to focus on his presentation but was distracted by that stunning dress and who was in it. Remy looked fantastic in that dress. He'd never seen her with her hair down. It looked wonderful. He caught a sparkle flash off an earring. It brought more attention to that beautiful, animated face, which tonight had a slight application of makeup. Bill didn't even think she needed it. The dress, cut just at the knees, showed her lovely calves, firm and well-shaped from years on her feet. The fabric clung to her waist and caressed her hips as it flowed down over her thighs. She didn't get that for twenty bucks at the outlet stores. How could he have missed those graceful hands and long fingers before, especially when she was always doing that hypnotizing thing to him? God, she was lovely.

He'd kept his distance from Remy this last week. Thanks to his mother, fixing his great deception was out of his hands. The Mad Duchess had decreed he not upset her and not tell her about the job. It would all come out in the next few minutes—the information about Remy's new job and Remy's new boss—Big Bad Billy the Absent. How was that going to go down? Memories of everything since he'd met her ran through

Bill's head. Mr. Deception. He would make evil Wickham look like a choirboy. He glanced around the room, wondering if there was any escape. Where could someone pick up a six-pack of Valium? Or some cyanide, for that matter.

He slammed back to the present when Remy asked, "Why are you and Juan here at a directors' meeting?"

Bill, getting more nervous by the minute, said, "Juan actually owns three percent of the company. He's a shareholder. It goes back to all the years he worked with my...with Mr. Keating when he was alive." He then stammered, "Me? I just do what I'm told."

Martha started as soon as everyone settled. Remy was excited. This was a real business meeting, not a pep talk in the stockroom of a market or burger joint. She noted Juan sat beside Chico. The two of them always seemed to be joined at the hip. As Martha spoke, Remy enjoyed herself, fascinated by all the financial mumbo jumbo, projections, crop yields, new varietals, the usual stuff of these meetings. She watched the people taking notes, drinking water, making facial expressions as each agenda item got its due and faded.

"Now to our expansion plans," announced Martha. "We've gotten down to the broad strokes, but there's still a lot to do. To get you up to speed, my son, Bill, will lay it out for you."

Surprised, Remy leaned over the table to Chico. "Big Bad Billy is back?"

Bill, starting to rise, mumbled, "In a manner of speaking, yes." And then he made his way to the front.

The light bulb went on—hell, let's not understate it, the whole damned chandelier exploded in poor Remy's head. Her database was shredded as subtle hints blossomed into hard facts—Mrs. K's tolerance of all of his smart-aleck comments, the degree from UC Davis, how he seemed to go wherever he pleased, whenever he pleased, everything he knew about the business... Reality was a pinball machine between her ears. Horrified at the sudden revelation, Remy shrank inside herself at the mind-numbing ramifications of what was going on. She was mortified.

Martha tactfully hastened around the table and sat down beside her. She leaned close to the young woman, put a reassuring hand on her knee, and whispered. "Relax, dear, all will be clear in five minutes. It's all going to turn out great. I'm shocked that my son and Juan kept up their subterfuge for so long. Naturally, I was against it from the start."

Remy half listened, head down, not wanting to look up as Bill started with some new equipment expenditures and something about a reorganization at the production facilities. He spoke well, was clear and precise. Snippets of past comments fast-tracked through her mind, adding to her humiliation and isolation.

No wonder everyone was laughing at the new girl. How could he? How could he? I thought we were friends. I thought we could be more.

At the small podium, Bill started outlining plans for the new offices, a function center, and the tasting room. He held them in his grasp. Nods and murmurs of approval were heard and seen around the table. Details were offered—all Remy's ideas. Marketing ideas were gone over next. Social media presence, new branding, community involvement—again, all Remy's.

Abject Anger was rounding the far end of the track, catching up with Mounting Mortification.

That horrible, deceitful creature was getting ready to wrap up his victory speech with a beaming smile on his face. Mr. McPerfect would probably take credit for the sunset if he could get away with it. That day at the market with his daughter, Lizzie—he must have rented that girl for the day. No way could this vile man have a daughter that nice. He looked like a politician vacuuming up adulation for someone else's work. All this time, he'd just been using her for her ideas. He'd been milking, coaxing, twisting them out of her for weeks. He should bite his wicked tongue off.

Martha felt Remy's trembling and gripped her leg again to settle her. "Easy now. We're almost there."

Almost there? Christ, almost where? What the hell was she talking about? What else could they do to her? Burn her at the stake? They'd probably fan the flames by pouring their pricey eighty-dollar pinot noir all over her. No. Not for insignificant

Remy Reilly—they'd use a cheap white. And sow salt over her ashes to appease the gods.

Mounting Mortification and Abject Anger were sprinting neck and neck down the stretch. Who would cross the finish line first? Would it be a photo finish? Somewhere behind, Stupefying Sadness was limping into third place.

"My mother and I have wanted to embark on this new expansion for quite a while, but we could never come up with a comprehensive, coherent plan. We wanted to embrace the changes in the industry and give something back to the community, but we were at a loss about the right direction, the right changes, the right timing. Our knowledge and education in many of these areas are limited, our eyes clouded by our usual, comfortable routine. Fresh eyes and creative outside help were needed." Bill paused for effect and glanced around the room, everywhere but at Remy. "All of these brilliant ideas that you've just heard from me, and some of the ones my mother spoke of earlier, came from one person who created them with logic and order and presented them to us clearly and succinctly in an all-encompassing report. I'm sure you'll agree this is a wonderful and profitable avenue she'll be leading us down. She will be working hand in hand with Martha to launch and implement this, quite frankly, ambitious project. I would like you to recognize our newest full-time employee, now executive assistant to Martha Keating, and hopefully our future head of marketing once she learns the ropes and this expansion is up and running." Bill smiled and pointed. "Miss Remy Reilly."

Thoughts of payback had distracted her. Thoughts of how when she finished with him, he'd think Guantanamo Bay was for preschoolers. She was dreaming up answers for when the prison psychiatrist asked her about the murder. "And how did that make you feel?"

Something made her snap back. Why was everyone looking at her? Why were they clapping? People cried, "Hear, hear!" and, "Well done!" She was drowned in a cascade of praise. Sweating, she hoped they couldn't see her shaking.

Did he just say "full time"? Did he just say "executive assistant"?

Remy's world exploded around her. She pulled herself up from the depressing black hole she had lowered herself into only minutes before. A smile was mustered. She blushed. Nobody had ever recognized her for anything before.

Martha leaned into her and gave her a hug. "I hope you still want to be around us. I'll need a lot of help with all this, and I want no one but you by my side. We'll talk details later."

With that, Martha rose. "Let's all move to the bar before dinner and have a drink." She looked down at Remy. "And it doesn't have to be just wine for anyone who needs something stronger."

In a light fog, Remy got up and followed Martha. Elation started filling her bones. She'd wait until later to decide about *him*. As of right now, if that user, that manipulator, ever considered assisted suicide, she would happily volunteer.

Martha hit the door first. Over her shoulder, she said to Remy, "I like to be first at the bar." Shepherding the bundle of nerves to the waiting barman, she said, "A Maker's Mark over for me and a shot of Maker's for her."

Christ, thought Remy, she owns a winery. Why was she drinking bourbon? Wasn't that sacrilege or something?

A protective arm went around her shoulder. "Drink it down, dear. It will help settle you."

Right out of a movie scene, the shot disappeared, and Remy scrunched up her face and shook her head. "Damn!" The last time she'd had bourbon was ten years ago behind the stands on the high school football field on a rare Saturday off. She vaguely remembered making all kinds of promises to the Blessed Virgin the next morning, if she would only remove the anvil from her head.

Bill knew to give her some space. The next punch from her might not target his arm. Should he at least offer a hand in congratulations? Bad idea. He might not get it back. The last fifteen minutes had to have been a lot to take in and digest. He didn't know how far her forgiving nature went and, right now, he wasn't in any hurry to find out. Everyone stopped at the bar before sitting down to dinner. All the wives and significant others had arrived. Bill left Martha to make the introductions.

From the back of the room, he watched as everyone lauded Remy for her brilliant ideas and the new job.

It was assigned seating at the dinner table. Martha and Bill would split up. It was a business dinner, after all. Bill stood behind his chair, waiting for the women to be seated. Remy eased by to her place at the opposite end of the table.

He gave a cautious nod of his head. "Remy."

"*Mr.* Keating." Prime and proper and dismissive, she continued past him.

The look he got reminded him of how someone would look at a target through a sniper scope. *Oh Christ.*

Martha sat at the head of the table, flanked by Remy and Winston. Bill oversaw the opposite end with Uncle Keith and the accountant. The others filled the middle.

Bill watched Juan lean over and offer congratulations as he passed by Remy. He noticed Juan point in Bill's direction. He knew that Juan was giving her the bad-penny thing, dumping all the deception on him. Great. His own mother and best friend had abandoned him. All of a sudden, they were shocked and appalled that he could deceive this lovely girl. He was now Trash Can Keating—out in the cold by himself. His life was falling apart faster than the chest of drawers he'd bought from Ikea.

The shot of bourbon—well, two shots, Martha had made her take another—seemed to be working. Her wits were returning. Remy took a moment to survey the table while Martha and Winston exchanged a few quiet words. She made an effort to rechannel her thoughts. She'd never been at a fancy dinner with this many people. Two low, lovely flower arrangements set off the center of the table. White and red wineglasses glittered in the light from the large chandelier in the private dining room. Smiling people were starting small talk with their neighbors. Waiters moved efficiently around the guests, offering wine, water, or mixed drinks. She brushed her hand along her thigh, feeling the fabric of her new dress, still not sure she was worthy enough to wear it, absently wondering when she'd be able to wear it again.

Sitting across from Winston Wright was like sitting with royalty to Remy Reilly. For a few moments, she was upstairs, not belowstairs with the servants. Winston's elegant, relaxed manner and his lovely, upper-crust English accent fascinated her. "Mr. Wright, Martha tells me you're from England. Did you live in London?"

"Please, Remy, it's Winston. After reading your wonderful paper, I couldn't wait to meet you. It's an honor to be seated near you at dinner. Yes, after Oxford, I lived for years in London before arriving here via New York. London is still my favorite major city in the world. Martha has been there several times, as has Bill." Winston couldn't resist a friendly jab. "Or, should I say, Chico, as you so affectionately call him."

"Affectionately? When I'm through—" Remy remembered where she was. She was sitting beside his mother. "Yes, *Chico*. What a *charming* young man he is."

Martha and Winston exchanged a humorous glance. No need to call up any more buses for her son. It looked like an entire freight train was headed his way.

They added more detail to the picture of the great city that Chico—Bill—had painted for Remy at their previous dinner. "When you go," Winston said, "definitely travel around on the subway. We call it the Tube or the Underground. It's perfect for people watching, permeated by young and old from every country in the world. And it's actually the fastest and cheapest way to move about the city. Cabs are expensive." Winston reached across the table and refilled Remy's wine. "Don't even think about planning your first trip without speaking to Martha or myself. You'll stay in my flat, of course."

OMG! London. A lifelong dream suddenly appeared on the horizon. *Not anytime soon, but now more than a fantasy. I'll be able to save money. Maybe in a year or two. Lynn will go with me. I'll make Lynn go with me.*

Sense was slowly being made of all that had transpired. Boundless Joy snuck into the lead. Abject Anger, Mounting Mortification, and Stupefying Sadness were temporarily falling back in the field. They'd probably catch up later. She gave smiles to Martha and Winston and scowls to the opposite end of the table. Every time she cut her chicken, Remy tested the weight of the knife and calculated the distance. Options about where to put Bill's dismembered remains bounced back and forth between her ears. Temptation was a bitch. She remembered a TV mystery show where the murder victim was found at a vineyard floating in a vat of wine. Options were a good thing.

The dinner was a huge success. Everyone embraced the new ideas. As people started leaving, Martha turned to Remy. "Walk me out to my car, dear."

Martha had asked Winston to give her five or ten minutes before following. She had something for Remy, and she wanted to make sure she was okay after all that had transpired in the last few hours.

As they neared Martha's Range Rover, the older woman fumbled in her purse, found the keys, and handed them to Remy. "It's important to me that you stay with us, dear. I'll let you two young people sort the situation out between yourselves." She made a modest attempt to save her son, Wickham. "It was an innocent deception, dear. I hope you have it in your heart to forgive him."

Remy walked up to the Range Rover door and was about to insert the key. "No, dear," said Martha. "The keys are for *that* car." She pointed to a small Honda SUV parked beside her own. Winston had driven it over behind Martha earlier. "It's your new company car. You can come back tomorrow with someone and pick up your old one. We'll be doing a lot of driving around, scoping out and evaluating the competition. *You'll* be driving. I don't think I could get in and out of your old car too easily. At my age, I'm used to certain comforts."

Remy looked dumbstruck. This was an added shock on top of everything else. "A company car for me?"

Martha wanted to give her son some kind of help in the coming conflict. "It was actually *Chico's* idea. Don't be too hard on him. I think he's quite taken with you. The insurance is taken care of. We had all the information we needed on your employment application. We'll be getting you a credit card for gas. Obviously, it's for your personal use also. It's an SUV type with better storage in the back. Over time, you'll be hauling a lot of stuff around. It's the nature of this business."

Remy's eyes teared up. She grabbed Martha and gave her a massive hug. "I'm so sorry, Mrs. K, all I can think of is thank you. This is all way too much."

As Winston approached, Martha said, "Go ahead now, dear. Get some rest. You've had a big day. We'll talk Monday."

Seated in the passenger seat of the Rover, Martha rolled down her window and watched Remy try to get into her new car. "No, dear, you don't have to put the key in the door. Just push the unlock button on the key fob." It was all said with a loving smile. Always three steps ahead on the chessboard, Martha lowered the window again when it was halfway up. "And when you're inside, you don't need the key for the ignition. Just press the start button."

As they drove away, Remy tried to figure out the key fob. Her Toyota was so old that the key did everything. What were all these other buttons? Why would you *push* on a key? It was a *key*. It was supposed to go *into* something.

Finally, after figuring enough out so she could leave, Remy reveled in her new wealth. Company car *and* gas *and* insurance? She allowed herself to feel the weight of her purse getting soaking wet from all the extra bucks pouring into it.

Chapter 13

Remy's gleaming new carriage delivered her safely home. She parked under her sycamore tree and searched for the interior light switch. Giving up, she opened her door to bathe the inside in light so she could take in how everything looked. Still not believing her good fortune, she locked it up and headed into the house.

Everyone was asleep when she entered. The good news would wait until morning. Tucked in bed, covers drawn up to her neck, she knew there would be no time for reading tonight. She was coming down from the elation that had been coursing through her veins, her bones, and her mind. All that hard work, all those years in school had paid off way beyond her expectations. In the basement of the manor house, the scullery maid was peeking up those stairs, up to a fuller life above. To get up there, Remy mentally reviewed the upcoming work required to achieve her goal. It was daunting, but she was up for the challenge.

Finally, casting aside the thoughts of all her good fortune, she decided it was time to focus on *him*. Evil Willoughby in *Sense and Sensibility*, Evil Wickham in *Pride and Prejudice*, Evil Crawford in *Mansfield Park*, all of them amateurs compared to Mr. Keating of Sonoma County.

"Quite taken by me? No harm meant? Just an innocent deception?" Did he really see it that way? *"I made a fool out of you, but no harm meant."* No, no. That's not going to fly. Like every villain in her books, there were hints of a dubious character that needed addressing. Deceit and treachery, she would not abide.

As she lay with her arms folded behind her head on the pillow, delicious revenge options intertwined together, a ballet dance in her mind. She pictured him in the stocks at the center of the old market square, or in a dank, dark dungeon cell with rats laughing at him, dampness sweating off the walls. He'd be fed scraps of gristle and rotting mutton washed down with putrid water from a rusty, dented metal cup. Or he was on a chain gang of prisoners swinging pickaxes and shovels, repairing dirt roads, choking on dust rising from the passing carriages of his betters. Or at the end of his grueling day, ankles bleeding from the manacles and chains, exhausted, crawling back to his cell with cuts and blisters on his bare feet, bruises on his knees from collapsing on the cobblestone square from the heat and thirst.

A smile grew on Remy's face. This was definitely going somewhere. Her revenge blossomed into a movie scene.

She'd tap the ceiling of the carriage with her parasol, signaling the driver to pull up the horses and stop. The window lowered, she would toss the odious creature a box of bandages for his bleeding, shredded knees. A thimble of water would follow, but, as planned, it would spill it all over the ground in front of him. Despair would drip off his parched, swollen lips. She would tap the roof of the carriage again and be off, laughing loudly, on her way to visit with other ladies of her elevated station.

Remy's head shifted around on the pillow. Be fair, she thought. Both sides should be considered. After all, the car was his idea. He had helped her a lot since her first day at the barn. He'd taken the time to jump-start her education at the tasting room. He was probably the one who'd bought her the new, expensive jeans when she'd cut her leg. Suddenly, Remy caught herself. Magistrates had to be fair, *not* sentimental. No. No. None of this could possibly balance the ledger for his gross deception, his disregard for her feelings, his shaming of her—a copper penny on one side of the scale, a block of iron on the other. No. Go back to thinking about the rats in the dungeon. The rats in the dungeon were creeping into first place on her revenge list. She liked the option with the rats in the dungeon.

Abject Anger was definitely leading the pack tonight.

How about more modern alternatives? Waterboarding seemed an attractive option. How about...

Colonel Brandon, the cat, probably feeling the tension permeating the air, pushed himself slightly away from Remy's thigh.

On Saturday morning, Remy dispensed a hurried version of her news to the family over a cup of coffee. She was running late for work at the market. They showered applause on her as she drove away in her new car.

Tucked way in the back of the market parking lot, her car out of danger of being scratched or nicked by carelessly opened car doors, she texted Lynn and arranged for an emergency dinner later—she had a mix of terrific and bad news. Meanwhile, she'd do the right thing today and give the appropriate two weeks notice.

The pizza parlor was the right choice. Remy wasn't that hungry, and her stomach hadn't fully settled from the tension of the night before. She was in her familiar uniform of jeans and sneakers. Cinderella's dress was carefully boxed up and tucked away. She sat in the booth across from Lynn and poured out her good news about the job, followed by another bucketful about the new car.

Lynn said, "Wow, how could you have any bad news after that? You even got a new car. Can we have a party and burn that old Toyota?"

Remy deflated, a tire going flat. She sank down in her seat. "It's him. It's Chico—or should I say Bill—I never even thought to ask him his real name. I was really starting to like him, and now I find out he was deceiving me the whole time. He's actually Mrs. Keating's son. He's one of the owners."

Lynn looked down and rechecked the menu. It said nothing about bombs like this at the dinner table. "Well, that means he had a say in getting you the job, doesn't it?"

"Well, yes, but that's not what this is about. He's just another Mr. Wickham thrown into my life. I can't believe the way he manipulated and used me."

Lynn looked confused. "Why don't you go back and explain everything that he said at this meeting. Everything."

Remy gave a detailed summary of Bill's presentation—how she found out who he really was when he popped up out of his chair and proceeded to outline all of her ideas, how he'd praised her work, how he'd given her credit, and then announced her new position.

Lynn still missed the logic in all this. "Both he and his mother loved all of your ideas so much they're going ahead with most of them?"

"Yes."

"And he praised you and gave you complete credit for everything, and he obviously had to be part of the decision regarding the job?"

"Well, yes."

"And it was his idea about the new car?"

"Perhaps...well, yes."

"Help me out here," Lynn said. "What's the problem?"

The real problem finally nosed itself into position. Mounting Mortification, Abject Anger, and Boundless Joy were falling back in the field. Stupefying Sadness, the fourth horse in the race, was pulling ahead.

"It's all clear to me now. He's the boss. He's way up there. Why would he be interested in me? No. He was just using me for my ideas." A feeble hand was raised. "I'm not saying it didn't work out great for me. I just thought he liked me, not just my ideas. I sure liked him. I thought there might be a future there." Remy cast a sad eye down to her wineglass and lifted it for a sip while pondering how she felt. "I'm not an idiot. He deceived me into thinking he was just a regular guy so I wouldn't be intimidated by him being the owner while I just kept babbling on about my ideas for the winery. I'm mortified about the way I spoke and acted around him. God, the first day I told him if he stayed off his cell phone, I could help get him out of the doghouse with his mother." Other humiliating conversations poured out. "At the tasting room, I told him I only wanted Juan to teach me because he was only good for fixing tractors. I basically insulted both him and his mother by ranting on about what a dump the offices and barn were."

Lynn stepped back in. "Okay, let's focus on just him. Remember those first days, when they were speaking Spanish and didn't know you understood, did he say anything bad about you?"

"He said I was funny, worked hard, talked a lot, and had a nice ass."

"That sounds far from bad to me. At least he noticed that scrawny thing you call an ass." Lynn laughed at her own wit. "When you cut your leg, who calmed you down, took you to the hospital, waited for you, and saw you safely home?"

"Well, yes. That was nice."

"And the designer jeans?"

Remy didn't like this logic. A more robust response was called for. "That was probably guilt."

"Was that Costco twenty-dollar guilt or designer-jeans big-bucks guilt?"

Remy sniffled, shook her head, and looked up at the ceiling. She felt fully entitled to push aside logic and common sense if she wanted to.

"No," Lynn said sternly. "We're not done. Who took a day to help you at the tasting room when he didn't have to? Who took you out to a few lovely dinners when he didn't have to? Who took all your ideas to Mrs. Keating, thought they were great, lauded you with credit, and was instrumental in your good fortune when he didn't have to?" Lynn reached for her own glass and summarized. "It sure sounds to me like he cares for you."

Remy allowed it to come to the surface. "It was probably all just guilt. Don't hurt the new girl's feelings." She flipped her hand up to the side. "Buy the poor thing a few dinners. Size her up for the new job. Sort out some more of her ideas. It's my fault. I read too much into it. He was just being nice to the new girl. I'm sure he likes me as a person the same as he likes the receptionist or the bookkeeper. I thought he liked me *romantically*." Her shoulders slumped, and her face saddened. "I saw his ex once. She's stunning, sophisticated, worldly. She could be on the cover of *Vogue*. He probably has lots of women like that. How could Remy Reilly compete with women in that stratosphere?"

Lynn reached across and covered Remy's hand with hers. "You still don't get it, honey. You're better than any of them." Time to lighten the mood and get her friend back. Lynn grinned at Remy. "What are you going to call him now? Chico, Bill, Mr. Keating, or asshole?"

"The hell with him! He was Chico to start with, and he'll be Chico still. I refuse to lose *all* of my dignity!" Remy caught herself. Enough about her problems. She'd vented enough and wanted to put the brakes on the personal abyss she was falling into. She needed to change the subject. "How was your date with Skip last night?"

"He wears jockey shorts. There are so hard to get off, don't you think?"

"Lynn. Not tonight, please."

"Okay, okay. Jeez, lighten up, Mother Teresa. It's called humor. Remember when you had it?"

Remy shoulders sank as she sighed. "I'm sorry, you're right. I could use a laugh. I'm just a little disappointed with the whole Chico thing. Tell me about your date."

"We tried that new Italian place up the street. I made Skip pick me up at the salon so I could see what kind of car he drove, even though it's only two blocks away. You can tell a lot about a man by his vehicle. He drives an old pickup truck. It's cute, reminded me of high school. It was clean, and he cleaned up well too, didn't have that dust-storm look he had when we first met him after work. Can't you people put carpets in between the grapevines or something?"

Remy sighed. "Now that you've got all the *material* things out of the way, what did you think of him as a person? I assume he generated some feelings in you."

Lynn's hand moved to her breast. "Aren't we Miss Sensitive today. Anyway, I could see he was embarrassed to tell me he still lived at home with his parents, but he's saving up to buy a condo or small house. I like that he's responsible, focused, and he could have lied about living at home. His clothes were Target or Costco but neat. We had a good time. He opened the truck door for me. How nice is that these days?" Lynn sipped her wine while gathering her thoughts. "I did the fake-stumble thing so I could reach out and grab his biceps. Tactfully invading a man's personal space is one of my strong points. He's fit. Maybe if he passes his first test-drive, I'll buy him a fancy shirt."

Remy finally laughed. "God, Lynn. Saying your mind is in the gutter is an insult to the gutter."

Lynn clinked her glass on Remy's. "Jesus, girl. You are so old-fashioned. Your dildo probably doesn't even have batteries."

Chapter 14

Remy's new car cruised silently into the parking area, a ninja with tires. Remy could tell it was in stealth mode since Mrs. K didn't look out her window at the approaching noise normally delivered by her old Toyota.

On Sunday, job secure, Remy had shopped for some appropriate work outfits.

There were two different-colored pairs of slacks and four shirts on her bed Monday morning as she'd opted to wear the pricey jeans Chico had surprised her with when she'd cut her leg.

Remy stood in the office doorway waiting for Mrs. K to get off the phone so they could leave. They were supposed to go somewhere, but she forgot where. Thankfully, Chico, or Bill, or whatever the hell his name was, was nowhere to be seen. The wound was still fresh, and Remy, while thrilled with the business part, was still chewing over his personal deception. She would have to corral her feelings as things moved forward. She had no idea what turmoil would surface when she next saw him.

Martha said she wanted her at the tasting rooms for one more week to get a good understanding of how things functioned. She would get to know the people better, how hard they worked, how important they were to the company. She'd be working closely with Sarah during the coming changes. Sarah's input regarding the new tasting room would be invaluable, and Remy wanted to develop a good bond with her.

Today, they would drive up and check out the Coppola Winery in Geyserville, just north of Healdsburg. They would check out the facilities, see how it varied from Rolling Oaks Winery, and have a lovely lunch, and Martha would go over her plans for Remy.

"Let's see how this new car does," said Martha as she headed for the passenger door. "I'm killing two birds with one stone today. We're having lunch with my best friend in the business, Helene Schneider. She's also one of the best growers around, and the most important one for us. She never had any desire to start a winery of her own. We buy almost all she grows. Her vineyards are just over the hill from Coppola in the Dry Creek area. Over the years, we've served together on more committees in the wine association than I care to remember."

Small talk got them onto the freeway and heading north. "I'm curious," said Martha. "I've heard you have a passion for the old English romance novels and movies. Why do you like them so much?"

That son of hers and Juan must have been blabbing, thought Remy. "I'm probably too taken by them," she said. "But it's my form of escape. I really get lost in the manners, the costumes, and the lovely country houses. I'm fascinated by the different lives upstairs and downstairs."

"Well, I enjoy them, too. My granddaughter and I let them swallow us up on our nights together. When she was young, I would read her a book and then make her wait a week before watching the movie or the miniseries. Now, they're safe books for her to read at her age."

They rattled on about their shared interest all the way to Geyserville. They picked out characters in the various books and discussed how the actors portrayed them in the movies and miniseries versions.

A turn off Highway 101 took them right to the entrance of the Coppola Winery. Martha gave Remy a heads-up about her friend. "Helene is my age, and no one ever has a problem figuring out what's on her mind. She's extremely direct, but she has a terrific sense of humor and a caring heart, although one may not always be able to see that. Be on guard."

They parked the car. Remy looked up at the imposing structure in front of her—Coppola Winery. Big and proud, standing in the middle of the vineyards, it was a lovely, two-story, modern interpretation of a classic mansard-roofed French chateau. The roof, a mix of slate and metal, was punctuated by a tasteful balcony and window openings. The walls below were a deep, earth-toned stucco. Corners of steep, four- or five-story pitched spire roofs locked the building into the landscape.

They mounted the sweeping curved stone staircase leading up to the entrance. An array of small outdoor seating areas surrounded the building, all tied together with an assortment of olive trees and trimmed hedges. A massive pool was available for guests. Small, cream-colored changing rooms with brown doors flanked the pool. They looked like someone had snatched them from an Italian beach.

"Jeez, no budget problems around here, huh?" said Remy.

Martha just laughed. "Wait 'til you see the inside. We're early, so we'll do the tour on the inside first."

They entered the gift shop. The famous Tucker automobile from the movie by the same name captured Remy's attention. It rotated slowly around on its own platform. As they moved through a few of the rooms in the large building, Remy's head cataloged all the stuff for sale—books and DVDs, wineglasses and coffee mugs, corkscrews and cuff links, cookbooks and cheese boards, marmalades, and brandy sauce.

Is this a winery or a mall?

The two women moved on to the two tasting areas. Martha watched Remy as she took it all in. There were around eighty different wines on the sales list, maybe half from other growers. There was a thirty percent discount for guests, and forty percent off for wine club members.

Damn, these people know how to market. Remy grabbed any brochure she could find.

They entered the restaurant right on time. The hostess directed them to a table where Helene was already seated. The wine people looked after each other, even someone as big as Coppola. These two ladies were known. Their table, tucked in a corner, offered some privacy for their conversation.

"About time," said Helene as she paused writing some list and looked up.

"I want you on good behavior today, Helene," cautioned Martha as she and Remy settled into the chair opposite. "This is Remy, the young lady I told you about. I'm trying to impress her, so don't scare her."

Remy beamed. Another female icon of the wine business. "A pleasure to meet you, Mrs. Schneider."

Helene eyed Remy up and down while talking to Martha. "Where the hell did you find her?" She turned her attention to Remy. "The only one who calls me Mrs. Schneider is my banker, and that's because he's afraid I'll move my accounts. You can call my Helene, or 'hey, you,' or anything but Mrs. Schneider."

"Helene, go easy on her," said Martha.

Helene looked at Remy with mock surprise while pointing a finger at Martha. "Wait. Is she still doing the prim and proper winery boss act with her new star employee? Don't fall for it, dear. Her sense of humor is a lot sicker than mine. She just does a better job of disguising it when she wants." She reached across the table and patted Martha's hand. "We older women in the business have survived because of our twisted senses of humor. We're not really up to date on all that PC stuff. We were always capable of looking out for ourselves in the workplace, as they call it nowadays. If we thought men were being sexist, we'd just run them over with a tractor."

Martha changed the subject. "You're always writing those damned lists. What is it this time?"

Helene scowled and glanced down at her list. "I'm making a list of people I want to fire the week before Christmas, right after I shoot the Little Drummer Boy and feed the Nutcracker termites." Seeing the look on Remy's face, Helene patted her hand. "Just kidding, dear." She leaned back in her chair, pounded down the rest of her martini, and said, "Let's order. I'm starving."

Small talk between the two older ladies filled the time waiting for the food. Helene seemed to think Remy was being left out of the conversation. She turned to her after she finished with her salad. "You hit the lottery, young lady. You couldn't find a better or more knowledgeable mentor than Martha. She knows how to run a vineyard and a winery. She's been successful at it for years."

Martha said, "Cut the crap, Helene. I'm not paying you more per ton for your grapes."

The two older women had a laugh before Helene asked Martha, "Will she be active in the association? We need some young blood. You and I are running out of energy, and it's time we both started enjoying the fruits of our labor."

"One thing at a time," Martha said. "We want to get Remy up to speed on the business. For the immediate future, she'll spend all her time on the expansion. Hopefully, she'll want to take part in the association. When the time comes, you and I will have to school her on how to deal with certain male members."

Remy felt like she was on the auction block as Helene gave her a slow, appraising look. "She's a good-looking girl, Martha. Be perfect for your Bill." She turned to Remy. "Have you met him? He's a hottie, isn't he? And a gentleman, too. Start wearing shorter skirts, dear. Get his attention." Helene looked at Martha. "They'd have some great-looking kids, wouldn't they?"

The two older women giggled to themselves while Remy turned red. *This Helene talks like Lynn. She wants to make a broodmare out of me.*

Martha stepped in. She was, after all, Remy's boss. "Christ, Helene, you can't talk to people like that these days. Apologize to the young lady."

"Yeah, yeah, sorry, Remy. I know humor is dead." She turned to Martha. "Jesus, Martha, I'm afraid to say good morning half the time at my own office. Forget 'nice shirt, Joe', or 'beautiful nail polish, Francine.' I'm thinking of building a safe room for myself."

"You don't have to walk on eggshells around me, Helene," said Remy. "I've spent years working in burger joints and markets. Humor helps gets us through the day. I can give as good as I get."

Helene snorted. "Is Healdsburg too far to drive, Remy? I have a job offer for you."

The lunch lasted longer than any of them had expected. Remy was in heaven listening to the banter, the reminiscing, and the serious business talk between the two veterans. It was like sitting with a couple of stars in Hollywood. The food, the service, the room's ambiance, all made for a perfect afternoon.

When it was time to leave, Helene held Remy's hand. "Martha says you're sharp and creative. I want to figure out a way to give Santa's sleigh a flat. Let me know if you come up with anything."

They descended the large, curved staircase and arrived back at the car. It was midsummer and the parking lot was full. It amazed Remy how this place drew potential customers. A lot of these people wouldn't be buying just today. Remy guessed they'd be back in the future as well.

In the car, Remy turned to Martha. "Thanks so much for lunch, Mrs. K. It was an experience listening to you and Helene. She's a character, isn't she?"

"Don't be fooled. If you go to her house at Christmas time, you have to wear sunglasses. The entire house is done up with lights. Inside, outside, on the roof, they're all over the damned place. Last year, I think she even put lights around her toilet. She has a fake reindeer head with massive horns for her Mercedes grille. Everyone in Healdsburg scatters when she drives down the street. I'm surprised she hasn't impaled someone by now." As they drove out of the parking lot, Martha said, "One more stop in Healdsburg. I'll tell you where to go."

The short ride to Healdsburg was quiet. As she cruised down the highway, nature took its course with Remy. Happy thoughts about the lunch, Helene's take on Christmas, and the stories that were exchanged eventually dropped away as other memories intruded unannounced. The Great Deceiver still weighed heavily on her mind. Maybe she should start her own Christmas list. Something for her other boss. Perhaps a cute new backpack filled with Semtex? A shiny new timer tucked in the side pocket? Maybe a razor-wire hammock to catch a nap in?

They arrived at Holdredge Wines. Tastings were by appointment only during the week. Martha found the front door locked and marched Remy around to the back to a big open warehouse door. She'd called ahead and said she'd be stopping by.

They entered through the large open warehouse door. Casual as could be, Martha called out to John, who was up on one of the wine vats. "I'm going to show someone around, John. Is Carri here?"

"She's gone today. She runs around like you. You know how it is. She said to say hi. I've got coffee on, Martha. Don't even try to sneak out without sitting down with me."

Inside the modest-sized warehouse, Martha swept out her hand. "I wanted you to see this place so you could appreciate another approach to the wine business. John and Carri used to have a small vineyard years ago, growing some other types of grapes, but then they fell in love with pinot noir. Now they don't grow. They buy first-class grapes from select growers like Helene and make award-winning pinots. It's great wine, top of the line every year. And they're both active in the industry associations." Martha pointed out all the state-of-the-art equipment. "They process everything in this space. Look how clean and efficient it is. When it comes time for bottling, the equipment is set up in a truck by the back door. I wanted you to see the stark difference between a big operation like Coppola and a smaller, quality producer like Holdredge. We're in the middle range. John and Carri Holdredge have a following most winemakers only dream of. They're old school like Helene and us. Most of their business is done on a handshake. There are lessons to be learned from inside this space."

Happy to take a break, John came over, wiped the sweat from his brow, and poured coffee by the staff kitchen area. He graciously gave Remy a quick tour of the place before sitting on stools around one of the tables off to the side. More banter, gossip, and updates were shared by old friends before the two women were on their way.

They arrived back at the office around four. Martha beckoned Remy inside. "Come into the office. We'll go over a few things."

Martha took her messages from the receptionist, and the women went back to her office. She reached into her desk drawer and took out some notes. "We're at the end of July now. The harvest picking might start around the last week of August. That's only about four weeks away. This is your last week on the hill. After this week, I want your focus on the details of the new tasting room. I want to keep the integrity of the barn structure, but if you think any small additions are needed, think about them. There's a desk out there that Juan and Bill rarely use. Set yourself up there, or if the weather is nice and you need more space, use some of the tables out in the barn. At least it will be quiet out there, and you'll be able to concentrate. We'll sort something more permanent out later."

Fully focused on the boss's instructions, Remy said, "Don't worry, Mrs. K. I'll find a nook somewhere. I know space is tight around here."

"When the harvest starts next month, you'll spend a morning picking grapes. It's not for your production value, but for experience and knowledge. Like your time in the tasting room, you'll get an appreciation for the work that happens during a harvest. You'll be seeing all the processes at the production facilities up close. When things settle down a little around October, you and I will also have to be done with the guest list, invitations, and details for the employee's harvest dinner and dance. It's for the employees, their families, some friends, and key customers." Martha looked up from her notes. "Your plate will be full. Are you up for this?"

"I already have some ideas sketched out. You're right. Sarah's input will be invaluable. I'm on it, Mrs. K. There's a lot I don't know. I'll have a lot of questions. I hope that's okay?"

"My door is always open. My cell is always on. I'd worry if you didn't have a lot of questions. And, Remy, at this point, why don't you call me Martha? Now, let's go over your pay."

On the drive home, Remy Reilly was the only one smiling in the bumper-to-bumper traffic; there'd been an accident up ahead. Life was good. She'd figured out how to turn on the Honda's air conditioning. Already up to around thirty dollars an hour—she always thought in terms of per hour from years of part-time jobs—up from the twenty-five she'd been making last week. It was almost double what she'd made at the market. Working at the winery was providing a cornucopia of cash, a bucketful of bucks, a deluge of dollars. All that from doing something she loved! She imagined the size of the piggy bank she'd have to get for her dresser. Jeez, maybe a floor safe.

Chapter 15

The joy of the new job settled in over the weekend, bolstered by her lunch with Martha and Helene. Lying in bed Monday night, Remy had time to reflect further on her disappointing excursion into romance. Lynn's talk at dinner Saturday night had added some confusion, but Remy now decided that her relationship with Bill had been, unfortunately, misinterpreted on her part. They hadn't been on the same track personally. She was convinced that his interest in her was strictly friendly and business oriented. No denying he'd been kind to her, but she had distorted the reasons behind it. The problem was hers. She would now be pleasant and formal with Mr. Keating. Boundaries would be observed. Both could move on with their lives. After all, they did have to work together. Abject Anger and Mounting Mortification were safely back in their stable stalls. Stupefying Sadness was still being walked off in the pasture. Disappointment would diminish with time.

Tuesday morning of her last week in the tasting room, she shifted boxes in the back when young Lizzie popped her head in the door.

"Oh, hi, Remy. How are you? Are you working up here now?" said Lizzie as she crossed the room.

"Yes, Lizzie, for the rest of the week, and then I'll be with your grandmother at the offices and the barn. What are you doing here today?"

The girl looked bored. "All my summer activities are over. Now, Grandma and Dad take turns watching me until I start school in two weeks. This week it's Dad's turn, and he has me up here so I don't get into any trouble." The frustration of youth showed. "They both think I can't take care of myself."

Remy smiled at the youngster. "Well, young lady, you can spend your time throwing rocks at squirrels, or you can help us out, if you want."

Lizzie's face brightened a little. "What can I do?"

"This morning, I'm sorting out the stock for the tasting room, checking inventory, and then cleaning up the employee kitchen and break room." Remy had volunteered. The rest of the crew were happy to let her do it. "You can help me if you want."

"Sure! I'm sick of walking around looking at barrels and bottles."

Remy had an idea. "It's ten o'clock now. We'll write your hours down when we finish, and you can give them to your father. You do the work, so you should get paid for it."

"Wow. I've never had a job before. I can earn some extra spending money?"

This was not a spoiled child. Father and Grandmother had instilled values and the concept of personal responsibility in young Lizzie. Every new gadget was not purchased, every whim was not indulged, her allowance was modest.

"You can, and you've got a job for the day if you want it. Longer if you get your father's okay." Remy handed her a pad and pen. "I'll sort the stock. You write down what I tell you. Then take the list next door and tell Mark what we need for restocking."

They labored together all morning, had a fun lunch outside, and continued into the afternoon until three. Lizzie told Remy that her dad would meet her in the parking lot to take her to her grandma's, where Gloria, the housekeeper, would watch her until Bill or Martha finished their day.

Tired but smiling, Lizzie climbed into her dad's truck outside the warehouse. "You look happy," said a suspicious Bill. "What did you do today?"

Little Lizzie fastened her seat belt. "My job, just like you." An animated Lizzie then told her dad about her exciting first day on the job. "I have my hours written down. I'll give them to you when I'm finished."

"Your hours?"

"Yes, Remy said, if I do the job, I should get paid for it. Minimum wage will be okay. Remy said that's a fair place to start since I don't have any experience. Remy said that, if that's a problem, she can refer me to a child labor law attorney. Remy said I can come back tomorrow, and she'll find me something else to do if I get the okay from you." Lizzie turned to her father. "What's an attorney?"

"An attorney is a lawyer," said Bill. "A job, is it? Well, good for you."

Oh God, thought Bill, *Monster Number Two is creating Monster Number Three, and Monster Number One, the Mad Duchess, will think it's terrific.*

Bill briefly wondered if he should look for a job at another winery. Still unsure about what awaited him, he had stayed away from the tasting room and Remy. It had only been four days since his unmasking at the directors' meeting. Some might refer to his conduct as cowardice, but at least he was still alive.

He gave Lizzie permission to keep working. If he casually stuck his head into the tasting room to check on her, surely Remy wouldn't clobber him in front of his own daughter.

Bill vowed to take a chance the next day and test the waters. Around eleven, he worked up the courage to go into the employees' kitchen adjoining the tasting room. It was also the location of the washing station for all the glasses used for the tasting room. Lizzie was there. It was late summer, and business was brisk. His daughter, apron on, was taking racks of glasses out of the washer, giving them the once-over, and readying them for a return journey. As he drew close, before Bill could say anything, Lizzie instructed him, "Remy says I should check them close, make sure there isn't any lipstick, grease, or dirt still on them. Careful where you put your hands, Dad. You're not tracking dirt in here, are you?"

Careful where I put my hands? Tracking dirt? From my thirteen-year-old?

As he snorted at his daughter, Remy came in with a tray of glasses, a big smile on her face. "Good morning, Mr. Keating.

Are you here to see our new employee?" A shop owner reeking with politeness, greeting a customer.

Okay, good, thought Bill. It was a nice Mr., not the accusative, admonishing Mr. from Friday night, the Mr. that heralded all kinds of possible terror. And a smile, too. Okay, okay.

"Hi, Remy. Yes, I wanted to see how she's doing in her first job." He glanced at Lizzie. "Congratulations to both of you on your new positions." Nervous, he looked back at Remy, groping for some way to start a conversation. "How were Holdredge and Coppola?"

"Very informative. We had lunch with Helene Schneider. It made me realize how much there is to learn about what goes into producing and making wine." She put the tray down, primly folded her hands in front of her, and turned to face him.

Were those fists? She never talks without moving her hands.

Bill unconsciously took a half step behind his daughter as Remy continued.

"The experience up here has been great. I've learned a lot. Thank you for all your help, Mr. Keating." Very prim, proper, and professional.

"I always liked Helene," said Bill. "Her sense of humor can't be matched." He tried to cut into Remy's formality. "You know that you don't have to call me Mr. Keating, Remy. I'm still Chico or Bill." An attempt at humor. A big smile of his own. "Heck, even Mr. K is better than Mr. Keating."

Remy beamed back at him, standing straight, hands still folded in front of her. "Mr. K? Well, a lofty appellation like that should be earned, don't you think, Mr. Keating?" Still with the big smile.

Bill missed her weird mannerisms—a light punch on the arm to make a fun point, a pointed finger to make a strong one, the voodoo hand-waving thing when she wanted to mesmerize him, the old-world references from her books. Bill wanted her to understand. He started to sweat. "Remy, I'm sorry about the deception." It came out like a plea. "It got out of control. I wanted to tell you, but—"

She cut him off, raised one hand, palm out—a benediction from the archbishop. "No need to apologize. I completely understand," she said with her smile still in place. "Well, it was lovely chatting with you, Mr. Keating. We must do it again sometime. If you'll excuse me, please." Remy turned and disappeared into the tasting room.

Cold, proper formality—an iron ball in poor Bill's heart.

Remy and Lynn celebrated Remy's last week at the tasting room Saturday night at the pizza parlor. Lynn asked Skip to bring a friend. She wanted to expose Remy to some male company and take her mind off the disappointment with that Chico guy. Frank, Skip's friend, worked for the company that serviced the equipment at the production facilities. Decent looking, he had a pleasant sense of humor. No harm would come from a simple dinner and drinks.

Entering the restaurant to meet the guys, Remy asked Lynn, "Why did you have Skip bring his friend?"

"You know what they say the best cure for getting over a guy is," said Lynn.

"I can't wait for this bit of philosophy," said an exasperated Remy.

"To get over an old one, get under a new one."

Remy ignored her.

It was about seven as they sat at the long table for eight in the center of the room; all the smaller tables were full. Remy smiled as she greeted Skip, happy that he was still around for his third date with Lynn. She fumbled over introductions with Frank. Remy had him explain what he did with the wine equipment. He did sales and service. The busy time of the year was upon them, and he was on call seven days a week. For the next couple of months, he would be available to several wineries.

Orders were placed. Drinks arrived. Relaxation was setting in after everyone's long week. Suddenly, Remy tensed when Skip, sitting across from her and facing the door, raised his hand and said, "Hey, boss. Over here."

Bill walked up to the table with Lizzie. It wasn't until he drew close that he noticed Remy from the back.

Fumbled greetings were exchanged, and Remy introduced Bill and Lizzie to Lynn.

Skip teased Lizzie. They'd known each other for years. "Big night out with the old man, Lizzie? Going nightclubbing?"

Lizzie, by now standing beside Remy's chair, unconsciously put her arm around Remy's shoulder. "Dad just took me to a five o'clock movie. He promised we could come here afterward for pizza."

Lynn jumped right in. She was finally face-to-face with the Chico guy! "You have to sit with us, Bill. We've just ordered. I've been dying to meet you. Remy's said so many good things about you."

Remy flicked stern eyes from Lynn down to the knife she was now holding in her hand, while Skip and Frank cajoled Bill and Lizzie to join them.

Remy, thankfully seated at the opposite end of the table, lowered her hands and started tearing at the paper napkin in her lap, all while maintaining a serene, dignified smile. She couldn't very well get up and leave. She decided to conduct herself in a proper, friendly, and formal manner. She held her head a little higher as she corrected her posture in the chair.

Lizzie pulled a chair around and asked if she could squeeze in beside Lynn next to Remy, leaving her dad at the other end with the men.

They shifted chairs around and things settled. Lynn, always one to liven up a party, beamed at Chico. "Well, Bill, I've heard you've been a naughty little trickster with our Remy the past few weeks, haven't you?"

Bill shifted in his seat, cleared his throat, and mustered a stiff smile. "Yes, I accidentally took it too far, entirely my fault." He glanced quickly at Remy and then back to Lynn. "I hope all is forgiven. As far as my mother is concerned, Remy's the best thing that's happened to the company in years, and I agree. I'm sure if I got hit by a truck, and Remy had a splinter, Mrs. K would worry about Remy first."

Everyone laughed.

As only a child could fan the flames, Lizzie said, "He didn't mean it, but it was the wrong thing to do. My grandma told me." Little Miss Brutus, last in line to say hello to Caesar.

Bill flinched.

Remy smiled. Gracious and dismissive, she said, "Absolutely nothing to forgive. Things have worked out extremely well for me, and I hope I'll be an asset to the company."

The men talked among themselves, while Lynn and Remy fussed over Lizzie and asked her about the movie. Remy made a point to focus on the young girl so her interaction didn't have to extend to the far end of the table.

Lynn kept it light, not wanting to add to her friend's discomfort. She charmed Bill with humorous questions like Remy's discount on wine. She explained how long she and Remy had been friends and how Remy had helped her set up her salon. She confided to him about how grateful Remy was about the job. All the time, Lynn was trying to pry out nuggets about Chico to size him up and see if her interpretation of the Great Deception was on the mark. Was there a hint of feelings there? Gestures, body language, and small comments told her there was.

As the meal progressed, Lynn saw the subtle, strained look on Remy's face. The encounter tonight had her uncomfortable. Lynn decided to wrap it up quickly. After the meal finished, she waited an appropriate amount of time and then said, "Well, this was lovely. Unfortunately, I'm exhausted." The catalyst broke up the gathering.

Disheartened, dejected, despondent, despairing—hell, just wrap them all together and call poor Bill miserable. Throw a capital M on it.

Why was she out with Frank? Were they dating? Bill liked Frank. He was a nice guy. He was closer to Remy's age and single. It made sense. Sinking into his swamp of misery, he groped for justification. Why would she want to saddle herself with an older, divorced man with a teenage daughter? Did he have any chance? Had he ever? He'd thought they were going somewhere before the deception was unveiled. How could he turn this around? Could it be turned around?

Overall, it was not a particularly good night for poor Bill. On the way home, he muttered to himself, "Baby steps, baby steps."

"What did you say, Dad?"

"Nothing, honey."

A new week kicked off, and Remy immersed herself in the first major task of the new job—converting the barn into a tasting room. Over the weekend, she decided not to use the desk in the office. There were too many papers and drawings that needed to be spread out. Inside the barn, off to the side of the massive doors, she set up two long folding tables in an L-shape. The barn was empty now, and she didn't want to waste time running back and forth with a tape measure while she laid out her ideas. Hands on hips, she surveyed the challenge. It was one big open space now. Heavily cracked with chunks missing, the concrete floor was stained with oil, paint, and grease. New plumbing and wiring would have to go below. It would have to be replaced or overlaid with a durable polished concrete to go with the new theme. Old metal racks for wine barrels lined the long wall to the left. Exposed studs, rafters, and beams showed the strong skeleton of the structure. As it creaked and groaned with the rising temperature, Remy felt it was trying to breathe life back into itself, getting ready for its second coming.

She reviewed some of her ideas. Lighting would have to improve. She didn't want the massive beams and exposed rafters overhead lost in shadow. Some form of lighting up there would help expand the space and draw the eye to that unique feature. She had already decided that the massive doors would stay but be fixed open. Her design included a new glass door just inside the wood sliding doors. It would let in much-needed light and provide a small overhang to protect against the summer sun and winter rain. The floor-to-ceiling wine racks going along one wall would be filled with old empty barrels, a backdrop behind the long tasting counter and tables. She had to get the flow of the business right first, then work her museum ideas around that.

Since the tasting rooms were closed on Mondays, Sarah had volunteered to come to the barn and meet with Remy about her plans and give her input. Thirty-five, married with two children, Sarah had been with the company for years and loved her job. Her finely tuned palate put her on the tasting team for new varietal wines with Bill, Juan, and Martha. She and Remy had become close during her three weeks out at the old facility.

Coffee was ready when Sarah drove up. Remy had purchased pastries on the way to work.

"Well, congratulations to you, Remy," said Sarah. "I got a hint from Juan. He and I get on really well, and he told me Martha had plans for you. He said you were a good worker, and that's about as high praise as he can give. Most of the young people are careful around him. He doesn't do lazy very well."

Remy moved two chairs to the opening of the big barn doors so they could have a better view of the space. The large portable lights, set up by Juan and Bill during the cleanup, were still there. The original lighting in the barn was useless at best. Gazing at the pristine space, Sarah said, "I never knew what was in here. The space is fantastic. Oh, Remy, you dream! What a great idea. Working closer to civilization will be wonderful. When we move down here, I can actually go somewhere local at lunchtime, not stay trapped out on that hill all day."

"I hope it gets better," said Remy. "I really need your input. This will be your domain, and I want to make sure it has everything you need. My ideas are to make it attractive and interesting for the customers. After working with you up on the hill, I want to improve the traffic patterns. Hauling those cases of wine and racks full of wineglasses those long distances is just one of the things I want to improve for you and your crew."

Sarah took up her cup of coffee. "Well, fire away. Let's see where you're at now."

"Mrs. K says we can make some extensions on the building, but she wants to maintain the original barn's integrity. I need a list of everything to make things easier for the workers. I need to know about storage space, refrigeration for the whites and sparklings, kitchen and break room requirements, how much office space you'll need, things like that."

The two women spent the morning roaming the space and going over Remy's ideas and Sarah's wish list and input. The old flatbed truck had been moved outside. Martha had told her to talk with Bill and Juan about restoring it and who should do it. "Dump it on Bill," was how the boss had put it. Martha had expressed as much enthusiasm as Remy about the idea. She'd remembered the truck doing its job out in the vineyards in her youth. She'd enjoy helping Remy with her idea of decorating the big truck bed for holidays.

Lunchtime found Remy and Sarah in the old diner down the road. They sat in the corner booth overlooking the street. Remy found the retro, padded, red plastic seats and Formica table fascinating. There was even one of the mini old-fashioned coin jukeboxes with songs from the fifties and sixties next to a table with mustard and ketchup, salt and pepper. Black-and-white checkered linoleum squares covered the floor. The two women reviewed ideas, and Remy wrote comments in her notebook. Over coffee, the women had time for some relaxed talk and gossip.

"I'm sorry about Bill's little subterfuge with you," said Sarah. "Martha told me it came as quite a surprise at the meeting. I hope it's all good now. Bill is a dream. He's one of the nicest people I know. He's always there when you need him, always helpful and kind."

"It'll be fine," said Remy. Not so sure it would be.

Clearly, Sarah's curiosity was piqued. "What other projects will you be working on? Fill me in on the other changes."

Remy told her about the new offices, the event center, and some marketing ideas for later. "I'll be bouncing a lot of stuff off you. I hope you don't mind. My plate is full. Martha's embraced delegating. This week, I also have to search for temporary office space so that when plan approval is received for the new office building, things can move forward quickly. She doesn't drag her feet."

"She's always been like that," Sarah said. "No vacillating. Give her a problem with some options, and she'll make a hundred-thousand-dollar decision in minutes. I've seen her do it up at the production facilities and with field equipment."

The ladies spent time getting to know each other away from work. Sarah mentioned that lunch in a restaurant was a dream for her. It differed from eating something amid constant interruptions up at the employees' lunchroom. "When you need some more meetings with me, schedule them for noon. I can slip away from the hill, and we can meet here. Do you know how long it's been since I've had a decent burger for lunch?"

As Remy lay in bed that night, Sarah's lofty monologue about Bill weaseled its way back into her head. She'd gotten similar speeches from Skip and Juan. Even Lynn said she liked Chico after talking to him at the pizza parlor. She'd lauded his attributes and self-effacing humor. Everybody gushed over him. Were they all in the same cult of Bill Keating worshippers? It was like everyone was collaborating on a book or indoctrination video just for her. Nice guy? Well, even Stalin and Ivan the Terrible and Wile E. Coyote had acolytes. Everyone seemed to want her to jump on the Bill Keating tour bus. Maybe we should bring over some Morris dancers from England, maybe an Oktoberfest beer garden from Munich. How about throwing a big old pep rally for the Great Deceiver, give out those nested Russian dolls with his picture on them? Remy Reilly wasn't buying a ticket.

Keeping her current view of Chico was comfortable. Doubts about how long she could maintain this mind-set were already gnawing at her. Still, it diverted Remy's mind from considering her woeful shortcomings on why she didn't measure up romantically. Flashes of the ex-wife in her Mercedes and clothes, her perfect figure and expensive hair, would occasionally find space in her mind. She wasn't in that league. Minor league ball was her lot in life, and she was comfortable with that. Someday, someone would want her for who she was.

Lynn was right. She'd make the effort to get out more. The romance closet had been thrown open by a few meals with Chico. She had time now. A quiet dinner, pleasant conversation, and a few laughs with a man were enjoyable. Yes, she'd make the effort.

Chapter 16

Two weeks later, August sixteenth, was Martha Keating's sixty-sixth birthday. Remy had promised Lizzie she'd help with decorations, flowers, and food. Bill and Winston had organized a guest list and delegated the rest to the young girl to make her feel included. She'd reached out to Remy in a panic, nervous about the responsibility.

Typical men, thought Remy. Organizing meant coming up with the idea and dumping all the work on the women. If it were up to Chico, the guests would munch on mini hotdogs and chips and dip, and there would be a case of beer on a plywood table.

Remy and Lizzie forced Martha off to a spa day on Saturday so they could decorate and prepare. The spa gift certificate was a birthday present from Lizzie and Remy. Lizzie, barely concealing her pride, made sure her grandma understood that the money had come from her job. Martha begrudgingly complied, mumbling something about unproductive time. Old people were like that. She forced Helene Schneider to go with her. A concerned Helene had called Remy. Spa day? Should Martha be checked for dementia? She'd go along just to keep an eye on her.

The caterer was arranged, decorations organized. A gentleman like Winston Wright would not be eating pigs on a stick. At home, preparing herself for the evening, Remy was tense. She had only seen *him* a few times, always blunting the conversation anytime it drifted into the personal. Knowing that she'd be trapped in the same room with Bill at the party, Remy was happy Skip would bring Lynn as his date. Backup never hurt.

The group of family and friends numbered about twenty. The buffet-style food was artfully laid out on the dining room table. Drinks were on an antique trolley in the adjoining living room. Martha's house was right out of one Remy's dreams.

Everything was done in the traditional English style. Polished mahogany smiled at you in every room. Persian carpets complemented the hardwood floors. It was elegant. Winston's influence had to have helped.

Martha, Lizzie, and Helene were upstairs preparing themselves while Remy, supervising last-minute details, noticed Bill pulling up in his truck through the kitchen window in the rear of the house.

Her attitude toward him had softened in the past few weeks, notably from her friend's constant badgering. Lynn resisted no opportunity to point out what a fool Remy was. Lynn was up to date on all of their interactions, simply because Remy always talked about them. "At least give him an opportunity to explain rather than cutting him off all the time," Lynn had said. "He seems like a good man. He's apologized. His harmless deceit has been nothing but bountiful for you. I watched him at the pizza parlor last week, and an idiot could see he's very interested in you. I'm telling you, girl, if you want to salvage this thing with him, it's not going to take a lot of work, but you better try before it's too late."

Remy wanted to narrow the gap she had created, but he was the owner of the company, and she still feared that he liked her, but not much more than that. That thought alone was probably the source of most of her frustration about him. That, and the fear of rejection. Could they be together? Remy had no idea. She'd all but given up. He was everything she'd wished for—a hard-working, family-oriented man with a good sense of humor. And he was also handsome as hell. Lynn was probably right. She should at least give him a chance to explain. Her feelings couldn't be hurt more by an explanation, and it might help her find resolution one way or another.

She watched him through the kitchen window as he removed his mother's completely restored Schwinn bicycle from the truck. It was his surprise birthday present for her. Remy had introduced Bill to Teddy when they had brought the rusted mess to her neighbor's garage. A busy schedule had prevented her from checking on it during the restoration. A smile crossed her face as she watched him beam with pride at the bike as he leaned it against the side of the truck before closing the tailgate.

Bill stealthily approached the back door with his jewel. Remy held it open so he could muscle the bike inside. Along with her greeting, Remy gave him a big smile. "Mr. Keating. Why don't you hide it in the pantry for now and bring it out when people toast her big day?"

Lynn arrived slightly late. She had to close the shop after a busy Saturday. She looked stunning—her default look—and was met by Remy and shown through to the kitchen. The older crowd was milling about in the spacious living room, enjoying themselves. Anyone under forty seemed to gravitate to the kitchen. Remy knew her friend would want a glass of wine immediately after a long day.

Bill and Skip were leaning against the counter talking men talk—football or business or tools. Both pairs of eyes shot up when Lynn entered. By the look on Skip's face—Remy wished he would at least close his mouth—she could tell he was totally smitten at this point. He looked at Lynn like she was a sex grenade, and he was hoping he could pull the pin.

"Skip, do you think you could get Lynn a glass of wine and sit with her here at the island for a bit? She's been on her feet all day and probably wants to sit for a few minutes."

Not a sophisticated bon vivant, Skip stammered a bit, looked around for a place to put down his own glass when the counter was right in front of him, and managed, "Yeah. Sure. Of course. White wine? Gosh, Lynn, you look lovely tonight."

Lynn patted his cheek. "White would be fine."

Returning from the living room with Lynn's wine, Skip put a coaster down for her drink and fussed over her. "Can I get you something to eat?" asked Skip.

Enjoying the attention, Lynn said, "That would be nice. Thank you."

Skip was off.

Bill looked at Lynn and Remy. "I wish he'd move that fast at work. The harvest would already be in."

"*He's* such a gentleman," said Remy with a big hostess smile. She wanted to find something to busy herself with, but the caterers had everything covered.

Bill had sworn to himself earlier that he would try to mend the rift between them tonight. He'd get the lay of the land and wait for the right opportunity.

The four of them found themselves seated around the kitchen island. Lizzie periodically checked on them with various questions and just plain curiosity. They were mainly left on their own.

Bill found it amusing that all his daughter's questions were directed at Remy and not him. He also knew he was being scrutinized by Lynn, but thankfully, she seemed to be zeroing in mostly on Skip.

Lynn held Skip's hand. "That tan looks beautiful on you, Skippy, and you don't even have to pay for it."

"It's from lying between the vines at lunchtime, thinking about you."

"Be careful, young man," said Lynn as she stroked back his hair. "Keep talking like that, and I'm going to get a restraining order against you."

Winston came into the kitchen. "Remy, I can't thank you enough. Everything is perfect. You could be a party planner." Ever the gentleman, he spent time with the group, complimenting Lynn on having her own business, admiring the men for working through the recent heat wave in the fields, depreciating himself for being an old man addicted to air conditioning and a comfortable chair. His fit figure didn't support the lie. Remy and Bill knew he was an avid cyclist.

After he left, Lynn's impression of Winston matched Remy's when she first met him. "Oh my God, and I thought Cary Grant was suave, sophisticated, and handsome. Who does he belong to?"

After an enjoyable hour had flitted away, Lizzie came in to say it was time for cake and presents. All gathered in the living room. Toasts were made. Candles on the cake were blown out. Bill managed to sneak the bicycle into the room behind his mother.

"Happy birthday, Mom."

Martha turned and looked at the bike. Confusion covered her face until years of memories processed in her head and recognition loomed.

"Oh, my! It looks just like the bike I had when I was a girl."

"It *is* the same bike, Mom." Bill handed her a bunch of photos and documentation that Teddy had made during the restoration from the day it arrived until it was finished.

Martha was overwhelmed. She stroked the metal and the leather seat and started tearing up. Lizzie saved her when she came up and held her by the waist, staring in awe at the old bicycle.

"Wow, Grandma. You used to ride a bike? That looks so cool. Kinda like an old antique car. Can I ride it?"

"It wasn't just me who rode it, dear. It actually belonged to *my* mother, and she passed it down to me. Maybe I'll think about passing it down to you."

"You are so cool, Grandma!"

Martha turned to her son. "How did you ever think of this? I'm overwhelmed."

"Sorry, Mom. It was another of Remy's ideas. She found it in the barn the first day and pushed me to have it restored by her friend."

Martha leaned over and hugged Remy. "You are a wonder, young lady."

Helene came up and gave Martha a hug while she looked at the bicycle. "Okay. The spa day is one thing, but we won't be going on any bike rides together."

Curious, Remy asked, "What did you think of the spa, Helene?"

"Not bad, not bad at all. We've decided we'll be doing that again. Someone at the spa suggested trying a mud bath, but Martha and I balked. After all the mud we've slogged through in the fields, I'm not going to pay good money for the same experience. When Martha and I were young, a spa day was a Saturday afternoon lying on a blanket in the field with a bottle of bourbon. Today at the spa, they didn't have any booze. Next time, I'll bring a flask."

Toasts and presents were given. Things settled. The different groups went back to their conversations. Heading to the ladies' room, Remy passed Lynn in the hall.

Lynn winked at her friend and said, "I don't think I'll skip on Skippy. He may be a keeper. So far, he's been a quick learner. The hair is next. It doesn't look like he's used a comb since they baptized him." She feigned exhaustion for Remy. "I've got a lot of work ahead of me. I hope I'm up to it."

When Remy returned to the kitchen, she noticed Lynn and Skip deep in conversation. She didn't want to interrupt. Bill waved her over from where he was sitting in the breakfast nook on the other side of the kitchen.

It was time. Bill knew he had to be more aggressive, break down that wall, dispel her apprehension, help her see the light, talk to her in a language she understood. As she sat across from him, he took a large mouthful of wine, locked both hands around his glass, and leaned slightly toward her.

"Remy, you must know that I care about you. There was never any harm meant by my subterfuge, and it worked out tremendously for everyone. Why won't you forgive me?" Finally, he blurted out his reasoning before she could cut him off and dismiss him again. "I just wanted you to like me for who I was, without the family business being a part of it, to like me for being a regular guy. Can you understand that? I wanted to tell you several times, but I liked being just Chico with you. Is it possible for me to ask you out on a date, to start over?"

A long pause that seemed ages to Bill lingered as he watched Remy processing his confession and declaration.

"And how do I know your intentions are honorable *this time*, Mr. Keating?"

Bill understood this. He'd been studying *Pride and Prejudice* and other videos to pick up the language, all those weird expressions, that country-house jargon. Bill would play them all if it helped. He'd play that Darcy guy. He'd play that Colonel Brandon character. Hell, he'd even play that idiot Mr. Collins if it would help. He should have loaded up on more Hallmark movies, picked up some more modern pointers. Bill realized he had close to zero experience with women; he had dated little since his wife left years ago.

Frustration and desire won out. He could feel himself going off script but couldn't stop. "I think about you all the time. You're a wonderful person. I want to spend time with you." There, it was out. He slumped back in his seat, exhausted. Then he remembered one of his great rehearsed lines. "Of course, why would someone as beautiful as you notice a poor, besotted wretch like me?"

Her response was another long, wary look from intense, slightly squinting blue eyes. "Poor, besotted wretch?"

He wasn't immediately dismissed. Good. Like the strike of flint against stone, hope was rekindled. "Yes, yes. I read it in one of those historical bodice-ripper books you read. See? I'm trying." He lowered his eyes, a little embarrassed, but what the hell. "I thought it described how I feel."

"I do not read *bodice-ripper books*, Mr. Keating. I read classic romance novels."

Was there a difference?

"Of course, of course," stammered Bill. "See what an ignorant buffoon I am. I've been in the wilderness for so long. I need a strong woman like you to help guide me back. I'm mired in a swamp of romantic ignorance. I need someone to help me. I want you to help me." He took the cuff of his shirtsleeve and wiped the sweat from his brow. The other hand grabbed his knee to stop his foot from tapping. "You've got me all flustered now. Can't we go out on a trial date? I promise to be a perfect gentleman."

Another pause, and Remy's features softened. Still with the erect, guarded posture, still the hands folded in her lap, she spoke slowly and softly. "So, Mr. Keating, let me summarize so I can better understand. You want *me* to lead you away from your life of deceitfulness and help you with romance?"

"Yes, Remy." He pulled out his carefully rehearsed closing line, the clincher from that Darcy guy in *Pride and Prejudice*. "You're too generous to trifle with me. One word from you will silence me on this subject forever."

Bill took a big gulp from his glass of wine. He was spent. He'd given it his best. Mute now, he waited anxiously for a reply.

A slight smile, a hint of approval stopped his heart from sinking.

"Excellent, Mr. Keating. Was that from the book or the video?"

Careful. Was that a trick question? "Huh?"

"Well, Mr. Keating, in the book and the Colin Firth miniseries, Darcy says to Elizabeth, 'One word from you will silence me on this subject forever.' In the Keira Knightley movie, they leave out the 'on this subject.' So you must have read the book or watched the video."

"The video. Yes, it was the video." Bill wiped some sweat from his forehead and waited again, wondering if he was handling this right.

Trying to keep it together, Remy moved her hand briefly to her breast. This whole long declaration from him had her considering skipping the lady-gentleman stuff altogether. Raging hormones surged through her body. She felt her unbreachable Hadrian's Wall collapsing. The poor thing was trying so hard. She hadn't even thought about the fact he had money, but she knew it would sway a lot of women. Certainly, had he told her who he was, it would have changed how she acted with him—but because he was the boss, not because of the money. He seemed so vulnerable sitting there, baring his soul, offering that admission. Her heartstrings had been plucked. She hadn't misread her Chico. She was succumbing to his advances. Passion was overcoming her, and not the *Pride and Prejudice* and *Sense and Sensibility* kind. Oh, no, no. She felt like *those* women in *those* bodice-ripper books—a smoldering, passionate woman. Christ, where was Lynn? She was afraid she would jump on the guy. Right here in the kitchen!

Remy gathered herself; composure returned. She checked that her façade was still intact—erect posture, pleasant but indecipherable look on her face, hands folded in her lap. "Well, Mr. Keating, you seem to have been working on your honesty and sensitivity genes. Let me ponder on it for a bit. Please excuse me for a moment."

Starting to rise, Remy had to grip the table for support. The hardwood floor felt like quicksand beneath her feet. Catching herself, she made for the powder room, anywhere she could think in private for a few minutes.

Remy leaned against the pewter sink set in a mahogany cabinet. She could feel her pulse in her neck and wrists as she looked in the wood-framed mirror. Low, flattering light disguised the tension in her face.

You misread the situation. He cares for you. You cut him off before he could explain. And the explanation was so simple. Why had it never entered my mind? Hurt pride be damned, go back in there and give a little encouragement. Let's see where this goes.

With hope restored, possibilities scrambled her brain. Carnal lust pulsed through her veins.

He still sat alone in the corner. Nervous, peering into his empty wineglass, the poor thing looked like he'd been in a train wreck. At the island, Lynn and Skip were still consuming each other, the female wolf chatting up the unsuspecting sheep.

Remy settled herself across from Bill. Wariness was evaporating, but her guard hadn't fully collapsed. Erect posture, hands in her lap, she looked at the expectant face across the table. "You're forgiven, and, yes, I'll go out with you."

There, it was out. She wondered why he had the deer-in-the-headlights look. She thought her declaration quite simple.

Finally, he spoke. "That's great. Um, that's good. Yes, yes, I really want that."

Good. He's more nervous than I am.

Bill made a tentative offer. "Can we go back to my place and talk, have a drink together? I'm nervous talking to you with all these people around. Lizzie is staying here tonight with her grandma." From his expression, he was thinking that maybe he shouldn't have said that last part.

Remy was glad he'd said that last part. But she enjoyed watching him sweat and didn't want to make it too easy on him. "Are you asking me to go to your house *unchaperoned*, Mr. Keating?"

"I am."

He got the hard, silent look for what seemed an eternity.

"Very well, Mr. Keating. I'll follow you in my car."

Chapter 17

They arrived at Bill's house, about a half mile up the hill from his mother's. It was smaller than Martha's home, and Remy could tell it was custom built. It was an old country-style design with a large, covered front porch below a steep-pitched roof looking out over the broad landscape below. She could picture him sitting in one of the dark-red Adirondack chairs after a long day, taking in the peaceful view.

Bill opened the car door and house door for her. They entered from the back of the house and paused in the kitchen where Bill nervously rummaged through the fridge for some wine. Remy could feel the tension dripping off him.

As he started to open the wine bottle at the counter, Remy placed her hand over the bottle. He looked into her eyes as she put both hands on his shoulders and pulled him close. Hovering in the air above her, the Brontë sisters joined Jane Austen. They looked on from a discreet distance, eager to see how their Remy would handle this precarious situation. How would she write her story? Would decent, proper conduct be maintained?

It was over. Her surrender complete. Unable to control herself any longer, Remy held his gaze with hers. No words were spoken as she raised her lips to his. The feel of his arms around her increased her passion. Minutes passed. Deep, long kisses heightened the pleasure of their hands roaming over each other's bodies before they fumbled with their clothes like high school kids. Bill paused, gently pushed away, took her hand, and silently led her to his bedroom.

The Brontë sisters and Jane gagged and threw their hands up at the same time. Two words that none of them would ever have used shot through their collective minds—*carnal lust*.

The two lovers were most assuredly not followed to the boudoir.

His rough worker's hands were gentle on her body. His lips, coveted for ages, were magic on hers. Urgency did not win out. Neither spoke. Sensations were slowly explored. Time was suspended. She thought he would devour her breasts. Moans encouraged him. Remy enjoyed the firmness of his chest and thighs as her hands moved over them, sometimes softly, sometimes more intensely. The air conditioning was perfect, but the room felt like the heat in the barn. Sweating bodies moved together until exhausted. Finally spent with him beside her, Remy was in ecstasy over the whole unexpected experience. Quiet talk about their feelings took up some time before they intertwined again. Attempts were made to make up for months of suppressed desires.

Begrudgingly, Bill let her go home. Remy had insisted since Lizzie would be here early in the morning from her grandmother's. She would take no chances with the child.

The new Honda slid silently under the sycamore tree. Even the birds above did not rouse from their sleep. No longer would the tired, noisy old Toyota announce her arrival late at night. No one in the house was awake when she slipped into her bed at one o'clock in the morning.

Intoxicated by her newfound love, physically spent from expressing it, Remy found that sleep easily enveloped her. How could life change so dramatically in a few hours? Had she done the right thing? The dark dream stole its way in. Her literary companions from bygone years wanted to throw a damper on her joy.

Lady Catherine de Bourgh, with her twelve or fourteen chimneys, was hovering over her, laughing cruelly. "You're a scarlet woman. Your family is ruined."

Locked in her dream, unable to escape, Remy shifted her head to her left. The Bennet sisters were sneering at her. "You're condemned to the hinterlands with Wickham," barked Elizabeth. "You'll take Lydia's place." To her right, the Dashwood sisters, Elinor and Marianne, gave her reproachful looks. "You've cast your lot with Evil Willoughby. Your sisters will never find worthy suitors now."

Startled awake, Remy slowly found her bearings, casting off the disdain of her old-world critics. She flopped back on her pillow and smiled. The reality of what had transpired earlier that night jumped to the front of her thoughts and was logically evaluated.

Being a scarlet, wanton woman didn't feel so bad. Why did the scarlet, wanton women always get all the bad press? If the girls back in the eighteen hundreds missed out on the whole scarlet, wanton woman thing, it wasn't Remy's fault. Guilt? Not a bit. Happy? Yes. He smothered her with pleasure and love. Smothered was a good thing. If Hallmark and PBS cut her off, so be it. Lynn was right—life out of airplane mode wasn't so bad. How could anything on earth be that joyous? Soon she'd be with him again.

Smiling, she remembered how she'd melted into his arms as he explained more about his deception. How he'd liked the way she treated him when he was just Chico, and their relationship hadn't been tainted by the knowledge of him being the owner. How he'd been dazzled by the casual, direct way she spewed out one creative idea after another. How he didn't want to spoil it for himself, which was wrong. She'd laughed at one point when he tried to blame it on the Mad Duchess, but that didn't fly enough to get off the ground. A light punch on the arm brought him back to his profuse apologies.

Bill had never felt like this before, not even back in high school with his ex. Wanting Remy for the past months hadn't prepared him for finally having her in his arms, the touch of her soft skin, the smell of her, the way his hands moved over her curves. She'd poured the same energy she had for her work into their lovemaking. She consumed him. There were so many facets of her to enjoy—the way she made him smile, how she lost herself in her work, when she was calm in his arms, when she was animated out of them. He needed this woman in his life. He'd been given a chance and vowed not to let it slip by.

Sunday afternoon, Lynn and Remy enjoyed some precious downtime by Lynn's pool. Bill had gone shopping with Martha and Lizzie, stocking up on school items for the coming year. The women tucked themselves in the corner of the large communal patio away from the few other condo occupants, taking advantage of the perfect weather. The sun, combined with a light breeze, offered a rare treat. Between the two beige chaise lounges, on a small table, rested Lynn's assortment of fashion magazines and the owner's manual from Remy's new car. She was still figuring out all the buttons on the dashboard and screen.

Lynn said, "Skip passed all the tests. I've decided to keep him around." She shifted in her chaise and looked at Remy as she reached into her small cooler on the ground to retrieve a drink. "You're quiet today, and you have a certain glow about you. What happened last night? Do you want to spit it out, or keep me in suspense?"

Remy knew she'd be hounded and badgered until she offered something about the previous night. Keeping her eyes closed, face fixed forward, basking in the sun, she said, "Well, you'll be happy to know that we've resolved our differences. You were right, once again. I misinterpreted the whole thing. Have your laugh and get it over with."

Lynn was not about to be brushed off. "That's it? That's why you're so shiny and bright today? No, no. Spit the rest of it out."

Remy knew something else had to be offered, something definitive but tasteful. "Well, we...we shared a passionate encounter."

Lynn's long legs shot off the lounge and her feet rested on the patio as she leaned over her friend. "A *passionate encounter*? In English, does that mean you got laid?"

"Lynn, you're being vulgar again," said Remy. She kept her eyes closed so she wouldn't have to look at her friend.

"Oh my God, you little trollop. Stay right here. I'm calling the archbishop to get him over here for an exorcism." She pointed to the other residents, out of earshot on the far side of the pool. "Give me details, or I'm going over to those people to tell them there's some sexual deviant sunning herself by our pool."

Remy knew she wouldn't give up. She relented and told Lynn about the passionate speech Bill had given her, how all of her feelings had changed, how he really did care for her—a lot. She explained about the ride back to his house. What followed received a brief, respectable summary. Modest reserve must maintain limits.

"That's it? That's all you're giving up?" She playfully poked Remy on her arm. "What about the *swollen member* and *pulsating loins*? Sheets thrown on the floor. Neighbor's phone calls to keep the noise down. Did he slowly drip champagne along your long, squirming body? Was this passionate-encounter stuff done in the bedroom or on the kitchen floor?"

"Lynn!"

Lynn noticed Remy turning red and lightened up. She gave her a soft slap on her thigh. "Good for you. I told you that you had it wrong. This is great news. I'm so happy for you, honey. We must go out on a double date so I can ask the Chico guy about last night."

Remy knew she was being wound up. She went on the offensive. "How would you feel if I asked you about all the details of your sex life, about your *test-drive* with poor Skip last night?"

"Well, he *was* really nervous when I took all the bondage stuff out of the drawer." Lynn gave Remy a knowing smile and a wink. "But men usually are the first time, aren't they, dear?"

Remy scowled at Lynn, put her earbuds in, and reached for her Honda owner's manual, signaling this conversation was over.

The sun rose on another beautiful day. Men listened to the grapes threatening that they would soon be ready. The human beehive at the production facility stirred. Until the grapes made up their minds, the workers occupied their time with various assignments and preparations.

Intimate time together for Remy and Bill was awkward with Lizzie at home in the evenings. The two thieves occasionally stole precious time together at Bill's home when Lizzie was at school. Two teenagers playing hooky. One weekend night, they sought out a motel room after an intimate dinner, all so sinful and deliciously anti–Austen. Amends were made by spending extra time at night with Lizzie or going over Remy's plans for the new tasting-room design at Bill's dining room table while Lizzie did her homework. Remy loved it all. It was bliss. Caught up as they were in the newness and immediacy of the experience, I love yous were not exchanged, future plans not discussed. This was not the time for pressure or planning. This was time to embrace the feeling of being with her Chico, enjoying being a guide for Lizzie, and rising to the challenge of her dream job.

They both agreed to keep their relationship between them. Early days. Remy may be new at romance, but her whole life had been grounded in reality.

The plans for the new offices and function center were being bandied about between Martha and the architects. She had the last word for the office-design portion, and she and Remy together had worked out the basics of the building. Remy organized her ideas for the creative part of the museum and tasting room. She collaborated with Bill on the technicalities—refrigeration, stocking and storage, traffic flow, and particular areas for visiting professionals were still outside of her expertise. All of Sarah's needs were considered and worked in. After the basics were set, Martha would be consulted. Professionals could then handle lighting, color palettes, and other items to make the design work.

The next weeks found Juan, Bill, and Skip in the fields babysitting the grapes and in the winemaking facilities checking and rechecking equipment. When the harvest arrived, everything had to run fast and smooth.

Remy put all her ideas in order. Plans and drawings covered her tables in the barn. All the battered, broken antique winery equipment had been set to the side during the cleanout. Whenever she could corner him, Remy imposed on a patient Juan, asking him to explain the function of each piece, which parts were missing, and whether they could restore them.

"I'll be honest, Chica. I don't know what some of these things are," said Juan. "I'll bring my father over. He'll know. He used to work here back then. He'll enjoy this, and I've got to help up at the winemaking facilities. He probably worked half of this stuff when he was young."

True to his word, the next day, young Juan dropped off old Juan and introduced him to Remy. Pulling her aside for a moment, young Juan said, "If he gets tired, can you drive him home? We don't live far."

They communicated in Spanish until Remy realized that the equipment terms were beyond her. Old Juan's solution was they speak in English.

A purpose in life renewed, the spry old man took on the responsibility as consultant and educator. He would call up his cadre of older, retired wine workers. With an expectant smile, he promised they would scour the area as far as Napa for parts and other missing antique wine equipment. The old guys were back in the game.

Martha noticed Remy and Juan Sr. from her window. She immediately made her way to the barn. She wrapped the older man in a hug. "Juan, it's been ages. You look younger than your son. We're blessed by your visit. What brings you here?"

"It's good to see you, Martha. I'm here to help Chica sort through all this old equipment. My son doesn't remember half of this stuff. Chica and I will figure it out."

Excited to see her old friend, Martha said, "Both of you sit at the table in the shade. I'll be right back." She returned a short time later with three cups and a large communal coffee thermos from the office kitchen.

Old Juan said, "My son says Chica is a worker. You got lucky, Martha."

Years shed away as Martha laughed. "I remember you used to call *me* Chica my whole life until I returned from college." She looked at Remy. "When I finished school, he called me Señorita Keating. I guess I became a woman then. It took me weeks to get him to at least call me Martha."

Old Juan said to Remy, "I remember when Martha was about a year and a half or two years old, still in her diapers, learning to walk in the bumpy fields. I was a boy then. When the harvest started, we only had this vineyard behind us. Martha's mother had me bring over half of an old oak wine barrel. She filled it with a foot of fresh grapes. Her mom tucked her dress up and lifted baby Martha into the barrel with her. They would play in the barrel and crush the grapes with their bare feet." Old Juan looked at Martha. "You had the time of your life feeling the grapes give way under your small feet. The red grape juice was all over you. You and your mom laughed the whole time. It took her an hour to clean you up. The next day, you waddled after me, pulled on my pants, and pointed at the barrel, wanting me to fill it with grapes again. I remember you cried for an hour when your mother said no."

Martha almost teared up. "I never heard that story. It's lovely. My God, I've known you since I was born."

Remy, touched by the story, was trying to picture Mrs. K in a diaper and crushing grapes with her bare feet, but her synapses couldn't fire up the image.

"And I helped build this barn," said Juan. "It was good work for me over two winters." Lost momentarily in the distant past, Old Juan smiled to himself. "Your father always found something for a few of us to do so we didn't have to move around looking for work. He was a good man."

They reminisced for almost an hour before Martha excused herself and returned to the offices. Then they got to work. Remy and Juan Sr. selected and laid out all the relevant and restorable old equipment and tools in a display that would be understandable and entertaining to visitors.

Over the next few weeks, the old-timers threw in a bonus—a gold mine of old black-and-white and faded color pictures of early workers, many of them operating the antique pieces and tools. It was a photographic journey of planting, tending, cutting, moving, crushing, processing, storing, and bottling the precious liquid. Old movies and videos were out there somewhere, but that would be another quest.

Not being good with scaled drawings and plans, Remy used cardboard, old wooden boxes, and whatever she could find or borrow to make a mockup of the space. Muscle wasn't a problem. Juan Sr. was just outside most of the time with two or three of his cronies fixing and restoring, painting and varnishing the old equipment. Long, drawn-out lunches with the old-timers in the same area she'd had breaks with Juan and Chico were courses in wine history for Remy. Not wanting to be left out, Martha would occasionally grab a coffee and join the group. She was as bright-eyed as Remy, listening to all the old stories, funny tales, and serious anecdotes about her parents. Many of them were new to Martha.

A battered notebook and pen were always with Remy. At night, Bill would sometimes have to explain some of the terms and processes the old men threw at her. Weeks in heaven would never match this time.

After a while, with Bill's input, they decided where new additions would be integrated into the old structure. They were ready to take it to Martha for final approval.

Chapter 18

The grapes screamed they were ready. *Carry us off to fulfill our purpose.* Everybody jumped. Workers flooded the fields, answering the grapes' demands to be picked.

The pros organized the first day. On day two, the offices emptied except for one person manning the phones. The tasting room cut to the minimum staff. The entire company was in the field, experiencing the basics of what their livelihood rested on—the grape harvest.

Bins littered the fields. Tractors groaned all day. Cutting aromas permeated the air. Birds, bugs, and bees scurried to safety. Shirts stuck to sweating skin. The crushing machine waiting expectantly. The grapes laughed; they were finally getting out of the sun.

In the closest field, three long rows of inviting fruit braced themselves. It was time for the annual picking challenge.

"Are you ready, old man?" Blade in hand, Bill waited on Juan in the next row, cranked up like Seabiscuit at the starting gate, ready to gallop down the track.

Juan was finishing up showing Remy how to cut the stems properly. She and Martha would be together on the third row. Theirs would be a leisurely pace.

Martha paused and whispered to Remy, "This is always worth a laugh. Bill hasn't beaten Juan down a row since he started in the fields when he was seven. It's one of his big dreams in life."

Yawning as if he were about to lie down in a lounge chair at the beach, Juan said, "Chico, Chico, Chico. Why do you embarrass yourself like this? Especially now, in front of the ladies. I've spent half my life trying to teach you how to do this at an easy pace, and you still screw it up. I tell you to watch the elegant old gazelle ballet dance down a row with the finesse of a fencing master, and you still rampage around like a donkey on drugs with an ax. Please, Chico. Please try not to kill any of the plants this year.”

They began.

Bill took an early lead. Juan always let him get an early lead. They were halfway down the row. The women, far behind both men, paused and watched in amusement. Juan was drawing even, barely sweating.

“You were faster when you were ten, Chico. If this is too much for you, the ladies can find something for you to do in the office.”

“There’s a long way to go, old man. Don’t choke on the dust I’ll be kicking up in your face.”

Many of the workers paused to watch the end of the race. Martha and Remy abandoned their task for a few minutes. They walked down to watch the finale, both knowing not to verbalize any remarks as Juan teased his way in front of his student of years past.

Nothing new this year. Juan finished ahead of Chico and stood there with a bottle of water for the younger man. “You’re getting closer every year, Chico. Maybe when I’m eighty, you’ll win.”

They shook hands. The two men separated and got back to their respective supervising duties. Juan directed the other workers, making sure bins were close, filled, and dispatched to the processing plant, taking phone calls from other areas, and solving vineyard problems. Bill marched off to the plant to help Skip organize the incoming grapes and start the processing work. Helene Schneider was picking at the same time farther north. Space had to be ready for her incoming supply. Several weeks of hard, extended hours awaited both men.

Remy looked at the departing Juan in awe. “How does he do it? He’s so graceful the way he moves down a row. It looked as if he were doing half the work of Bill.”

“You just saw an example of the Tortoise and the Hare. Years and years of that graceful, smooth, relentless pace by Juan. Bill always wants to start fast and slows down at the end. Years ago, when the two of them would be out all day, not just for a ceremonial row or two, Juan would be way ahead of him by day's end." Martha stood in her old work boots and worn jeans and wiped her brow. "We'll do another hour and get the hell out of here. Now I know why God invented young people."

Remy smiled and moved to the next vine. "I'm surprised Winston didn't come out this morning."

"That's a joke, right, dear?" Martha snorted. "It would take him an hour to get out of his jacket, tie, and cuff links."

Routine drifted in. Several weeks passed, and the long workdays continued. Remy would finish her days at the barn and then take food up to Bill or cook something in the small employee kitchen off the tasting room next to the processing buildings.

As the sun went through its setting ceremony, a soft breeze would creep in from the west, visible from the high perch on the hill, sneaking through the valleys. The coolness would wrap around them at the outside table as they ate and enjoyed the magnificent view. With everyone gone, it was peaceful. Quiet. Some evenings, they would spy foxes moving around at the edges of the fields. Some evenings, spiraling hawks and vultures would entertain them. A flock of wild turkeys might cackle at them as they casually walked across the parking lot. Coyotes sang to them from distant oak grooves.

Remy pointed and asked, "Why has that field on the far hill and a few of the others farther down the valley turned all those beautiful fall colors while the adjoining fields are still green?"

"The field right below us is the one you picked a few weeks ago," Bill answered. "The other ones you see changing colors were picked a while ago. The plants know when they've been picked. They lose their leaves and go to sleep for the winter. The green fields have either just been picked or are waiting for their turn. We must keep watering them until they're dormant. When they're picked, the plant's juices run out the cuts, and they could die if the plant moisture isn't maintained until they heal."

Their alone time together up on the hill reeked of romance. Long conversations, quiet looks between them, and funny anecdotes about their day's work were all exchanged.

They were two adults without a private space for them at home. Sometimes Remy would gauge how tired her man was, and sometimes she would suggest a more intimate activity. Their favorite place together was under one of the majestic, massive oak trees that gave the winery its name. There, they were hidden from view, surrounded by wild shrubs on a gently sloping hill about fifty yards from the warehouse. Alone on a picnic blanket under the tree, they would explore their newfound love. Senses were aroused and pleasures indulged. They satisfied each other with new avenues discovered and enjoyed. Long groans and muted cries, yearning moans and soft sighs were heard nearby.

These unfamiliar sounds unsettled the native occupants of the woods and vineyards. Deer, wandering too near the couple, would tweak their ears and be on their way. A mother raccoon, tripping across the lovers, lowered the small black masks farther over her children's eyes, diverting them to another path. Upset squirrels scurried above, demanding to know why a blanket covered their acorn dinner. The heads of baby birds were shoved deeper into their nests by concerned parents. The chatter of various birds announced that this behavior was unacceptable. All the creatures were unanimous about one thing. It was dusk. Night is *their* time in the vineyards. Humans should know to go home if they wanted to do *that* sort of thing.

Remy's car had been emptied of all the old romance novels. Her favorite characters were locked between their covers, safe on the bookshelf at home. No longer would they be allowed up the hill to cast aspersions on her moral conduct.

The fog was coming in. A gentle breeze wrapped around them, holding a hint of the coming cold teeth that would be biting into them as autumn deepened. The sides of their blanket were flipped over them. Each was lost in thought as they lay tucked together, enjoying the landscape in the valley below. A fleeting question of where they would hide in winter drifted across Remy's mind before she found refuge in her dream world.

"Wouldn't it be wonderful to live up here? You could go out in the vineyards at dusk with your antique purdy shotgun from

London and shoot a pheasant for dinner. The hunting dog would bring it back to you clenched between its soft jaws."

"I have a golden retriever," said Bill with a hint of sarcasm.

She turned slightly, not wanting to move his arm from around her, and pinched his cheek. "A retriever? See, you're already halfway there." She lowered her head to his chest, indulging in her wistful fantasy. "We should talk about servants. I'm not sure how many we'll need. You should have a valet, me, a lady's maid. A cook, certainly, and perhaps a scullery maid?" Remy propped herself up and caressed his cheek. "On second thought, the only servant I need is you. Forget the pheasant. I can send you down to the market for some partridge or eel. I'll even buy you an umbrella to take with you on your horse in case it rains."

It was Lynn's idea. Four for dinner at her place on Saturday night. Over the last few years, she'd spent a lot of money on china and silverware, and damned if she wasn't finally going to use them. The metal-framed, glass-topped dining table was set. Placemats, folded napkins, water, and wineglasses complemented the china. Remy arrived early to help, and the boys would come later. It would be a salad and beef stroganoff. Lynn understood that men were easy. They wanted meat. Vegetables, potatoes, or noodles were just dressing.

Remy took in the beautiful table as she carried a bag into the kitchen. "And what provoked little Miss Homemaker to raise her fin above the water and prepare this feast?"

"Every time Skippy takes me to dinner, it's combat grabbing the check. He's like Mr. Macho Wage Earner from the last century." Lynn turned from the sink and put her hands on her hips, mimicking Skip's deep voice. "'I can afford to buy you dinner.' Sometimes he brings flowers when he picks me up. Christ, I'm surprised he doesn't bring me corsages to wear. I figure if I cook for him, he won't keep emptying his wallet on me."

Remy pretended to swoon. "Oh my, the great Man Manipulator is morphing into Caring Cathy. What's next? Are you going to buy him slippers?"

Lynn paused, momentarily lost in thought. She lifted the spoon she had in her hand and pointed it at Remy. "Not bad, girl. Not bad at all. Sometimes when he comes over, his feet *do* hurt, and he always has on those massive boots with soles made from car tires that you rustic people have to wear. Why do they cover the ankles? Is it so the snakes can't bite your legs?"

"Laugh all you want, but Bill's bringing some of that expensive pinot you like. Now, aren't you glad your Skippy is safe running around in those fields?"

"Good point. I like that pinot. You and I could only afford to buy that stuff at Thanksgiving or Christmas." A rare serious look crossed Lynn's face. "Maybe we're both getting lucky with men." She returned to the pot on the stove.

Remy pulled some things for the salad from the fridge. "The dining room table looks great. Where did you find the flowers? They're a pleasant touch."

"The florist around the corner from the salon saved my life. I grabbed a bunch of flowers that looked good and casually mentioned they were for the dinner table. She noticed they were all tall flowers and people wouldn't be able to see over them." She pointed her spoon at the flowers. "She made that arrangement up for me while I waited. I'm learning."

"Well, Skip and Bill will love them. I'd forgotten how long you labored picking out that china and silverware. The dining room is finally getting used."

"Good. I won't have to fight Skippy over the check, and it's closer to the bedroom." She gave Remy one of her teasing smiles. "Passion can be so immediate, don't you think? He and I may have to excuse ourselves early. You and Bill can wash up."

Last week, in an appalling lapse of discretion, her mind absorbed by her happiness, Remy had confided to Lynn how romantic it was in the evenings alone on a blanket under the stars up at the facilities. She had waited for some remark from her friend, some tactless comment about her sex life. None had come, only a loving, understanding smile.

"Lynn, don't start. I know you'll be a proper hostess and will remain with your guests until the night is over."

"Oh, sorry. This from the girl who ruts in the fields like some farm animal?"

"Lynn!"

Lynn laughed. "What? Did you think that little slip of yours last week wouldn't get shoved down your throat sooner or later? What do you do afterward? You know, with the sap and leaves all over you, the animal hairs on the blanket, and God knows what kind of bugs. Is there a shower up there, or do you just plop yourself into the closest water trough and get on with your day? I must ask Bill tonight."

Skip arrived first, disappointed to see flowers already on the table. Lynn gave him a peck on the cheek as she took his flowers from him. "We'll put them in the bedroom." Bill followed with two bottles of their best pinot, which earned him a hug from both women. Lynn took the bottles. "We'll put these on the table."

This was their first dinner together, and Remy was nervous about what Lynn would say. Her friend had a knack for keeping a conversation lively, not afraid to nudge against the border of appropriate conduct. Remy made sure her foot had easy access to Lynn's under the table, should limits need to be fortified.

But there was no need. Tonight, Lynn was the perfect hostess. Multiple topics were addressed, and funny stories exchanged. After a few glasses of wine, Lynn turned to Bill. "You've been spending long days working for the past few weeks. When are you two going to sneak off for a relaxing weekend? Skip says the pace is getting back to normal after the harvest rush." It was also a hint for Skip. If he didn't get it, she'd hint harder later.

A little flustered, Bill said, "Well, jeez, I hadn't thought about it, but it's a good idea. How about you and Skip? Any plans to get away?"

Lynn raised her fork and pointed in the direction of her bedroom. "Ouch!" she said after a bump from Remy's foot under the table. She glared at her friend. "I was pointing toward Lake Tahoe."

"Lake Tahoe is in the opposite direction, Lynn," said Remy. Her friend was loosening up from the wine. Best to change the subject. Taxes? Production yields? Toxic chemicals in the salon? Anything to keep her away from sex.

Chapter 19

"The forklift," said Remy. It was the next week, and they'd finished their evening meal at the picnic table on the hill.

Bill slowly shook his head. He wasn't a prude, but there were limits. "Jeez, honey, I don't think we can do it on the forklift."

The punch on the arm came, accompanied by, "Idiot! I want to learn how to *drive* it. Is everything in that sick mind of yours about sex? Isn't it enough that you've already made a wanton woman out of me?"

"Ha! That's the pot calling the kettle black. What about what you've done to me? Old demon lust hasn't lost your address." Bill's smile wrinkled into a suspicious frown. "Why do you want to learn to drive a forklift?"

"I want to learn everything around here, and they've always fascinated me. I used to watch them out behind the market unloading the trucks. Come on, nobody's here. I can't kill anyone." Remy did a poor imitation of sulking. "I thought you liked me for my mind, not just my body."

Knowing it was a losing battle, Bill relented. She was curious about everything at the production facilities and would badger him until he explained things. He'd already had to climb up on vats, through the maze of crushing and bottling equipment, to show her how it all worked.

"Okay. Let's go, but you'll have to be careful. We'll just drive today, no lifting and moving stuff. If you catch on, maybe I'll let you move an empty pallet around."

Bill looked around. "Where's Lizzie?" She'd been with them every night this week.

Winston had cajoled Martha into taking a week's cruise to Alaska. Mrs. K had instructed Remy to pick up her messages from Cathy, the receptionist. "Stick your foot in the water," was how she'd put it. "Call them back. See what they want. Call me on my cell. I'll tell you what to do." It sounded simple enough.

Remy said, "Don't worry. Lizzie's in the tasting room doing her homework. She only wanted a sandwich." With Martha gone, Lizzie had come to the barn after school every day. They drove up to the winery after Remy finished her day. "I gave her some more work this week with me at the barn. She's sharp, follows directions well. You'll be getting her time card."

"Yes, I know. She told me she was 'stashing some bucks for Christmas.' She was so excited about being able to pay her part of the spa-day gift for her grandma's birthday. You're creating another money junkie like yourself. She's even starting to sound like you."

Remy knitted her brow and pointed a finger. "Maybe you missed the meeting, Chico. I am Martha Keating's *personal assistant*. I think technically, I'm your boss. Forklift. Now." She rose from the table and was halfway to the warehouse when she looked back over her shoulder. "Let's go, old man. Time is money."

She was a four-year-old with a new red wagon. Bill shouldn't have taught her how to pick up the empty pallet. Up and down the aisles she went, up and down in the air the empty pallet went. They spent an hour before he called it a day. Bill removed the keys, afraid she might try to drive the forklift home.

Crisp October air announced that fall was upon them. Plans for the new offices were being worked on. The county had approved the small additions to the barn for the new tasting room, and work had begun. Restoration of the old winery equipment moved along with Juan Sr. and his friends, and restoration of the old flatbed truck to display in front of the buildings was near completion. The tasting room should be open within a few months.

Wrapped in her jacket, Remy escaped the construction noise and moved to her car. She needed to run some errands in Santa Rosa. It was overcast, and the wind had risen, adding to the chill. She checked that she had her list and tossed her backpack and some things to drop off in the passenger seat. The owner's manual told her how to turn on the heat for the first time.

She spotted the beige Mercedes in front of the diner when she drove past. It was hard to miss since it was parked beside Bill's truck. His ex-wife was getting into her car, while Bill held the door. Remy was past them before she could see anything else. Why was she here? Why was Bill with her? It unsettled Remy. The night before, Bill had told her he wouldn't be at work until late afternoon. He had things to take care of. Remy remembered that he'd sounded stressed, not his usual self. She convinced herself not to worry. Their weeks together had been a fairy tale for Remy. They trusted each other. Nonetheless, although I love yous had not been exchanged or futures discussed, Remy had been thinking about the next step they hadn't yet reached. It had only been a few weeks, but she wondered if he had thought about it also. The Mercedes and the beautiful ex unnerved her. Was he harboring doubts about sharing his and Lizzie's domestic life with her?

Remy continued on with her errands and returned to the office that afternoon. Around two o'clock, she drifted into Martha's office, There were some aspects about a marketing issue she was wrestling with, and she needed a second opinion. Mrs. Keating was not happy when Remy entered. She had just put down the phone—slammed down, a better description.

"Christ, that woman is thinking about moving back into the area," said Martha with undisguised venom.

The comment startled Remy. Recalling the beige Mercedes, she knew the answer but had to ask, "What woman?"

"Maggie, my son's ex-wife." She caught herself immediately. "Oh God, I shouldn't have said anything. My son was just asking my advice before he spoke to anyone."

Advice? Spoke to who? Spoke to me?

It was a comment that could impact her life, that could bring down a devastating typhoon of destruction on her happiness.

Remy collapsed in her usual chair across from Martha. Speech eluded her.

Martha said, "I always thought that girl was a schemer when she was in high school, and time has proven me right. Evidently, she just divorced the rich husband and wants to come back to her roots, to be closer to her family and spend more time with her daughter. Or so she says."

Remy regrouped, tried to sound conciliatory while the back of her brain raced through all the implications this could have on her and her growing relationship with Bill. "Perhaps her maternal instincts are kicking in late. Maybe she realizes how important her daughter is or could be to her."

Martha growled, "That woman never had a maternal instinct in her life. Her sole purpose in life is to fool men. God knows, I watched it with my son. I knew back then that anything I said would be ignored, so I just kept my mouth shut." Martha's pot was starting to boil. "She left her baby daughter. What kind of woman does that?" After a few seconds, the old warrior settled and managed a half smile. "I guess I shouldn't be too hard. At least we got Lizzie out of the whole mess."

Remy's biggest fear found a voice. "I saw her at the plant once. She's beautiful."

Martha leaned back in her chair, scowling as she spoke. "Not the half of it. She's smart, too. She has all the equipment to be a manipulator and seducer. Why do some women, with all of those gifts, end up morally questionable?" Martha shook her head. "Well, that's a conversation for another time."

Bill had never talked about his ex with Remy. She sent a probe out. "How does he feel about her?"

"Not a clue. He never, and I mean never, talks about her, hasn't in twelve years. All I ever get are mundane facts like Maggie called and wants to take Lizzie for a week in July, or Maggie called and wants to know what to get Lizzie for Christmas, stuff like that. No one knows his feelings toward her except him. I remember he was crushed when she left. It took him forever to get over it, if he ever did."

Unable to hide the tension in her voice, Remy said, "Do you think she wants to get back together with him?"

"God, Remy, don't say something like that. Not for your sake, or mine, or Lizzie's, or my son's." Martha threw it out on the table. "I know you two are getting close, and I couldn't be happier about it. You'd be my dream daughter-in-law. And now you've just raised the specter of that creature returning to haunt our lives." She looked up to the ceiling and absently rubbed her neck. "I have to think this through. Does that witch want my son's money now that her last well has run dry, or is she doing some long-range planning to get Lizzie's when she gets older? She must know that both Bill and I have trusts set up for the child. She's our only living heir. If Maggie's last husband had any sense, he'd have made her sign a prenuptial agreement, and that woman now needs money to finance that wasteful life of hers."

"Hell." That was all that Remy could muster. A heavy metal band called Bad Ramifications was playing in her head.

Stress was visible on Remy's face as Martha asked, "When do you see Bill again?"

"Tonight, after work, up at the warehouse."

Martha wanted this sorted. Quickly. "If he doesn't bring it up, I think it's best to come right out and ask him. Tell him I slipped, and don't forget to add it was because I was so upset. Don't let it eat you up inside."

Remy slumped out of the office. Depressed and distressed, she stumbled back to the privacy of the barn.

Martha stared at the empty space by the door. Great, she thought. That shrew Maggie wants money for designer shoes she'll wear once and clothes that will be in the thrift shop within a month, and that lovely girl who just left is learning how to drive a forklift. Remy had gone on and on about it after Bill had taught her. Martha had laughed when Remy suggested putting a big box on the forks and driving the kids around the parking lot on Halloween. That girl was always thinking.

Martha spun her chair around and gazed out the window into empty space, reflecting back to when Maggie had made the announcement she was leaving for the big city without her daughter. Martha had met with her privately. She'd offered a modest monthly allowance for a year until Maggie was settled and found work. The greedy woman had beamed as Martha slipped the papers giving Bill full custody across the table.

Maggie had quickly signed. At least that problem wouldn't mushroom should the woman return.

Martha felt helpless. Her son had always been impossible to read when it came to Maggie. Did he still harbor feelings for her? Had Martha been foolish in hoping that Remy could bring happiness and companionship into Bill's life?

Fear woke up after the first prick of adrenaline. That's how it worked. It expanded into a weighted ball in the pit of Remy's stomach, then it yawned and stretched, working its way around every muscle in her body. Its tentacles worked their way up to her brain and delivered what it delivered best— terror.

Remy sat frozen in her folding chair. The table in front of her was covered with forgotten plans and projects. Construction noise around her went unnoticed. Never in her twenty-six years had she experienced this kind of crushing despair and crippling helplessness. She had always been in control of her life and could do nothing about this looming calamity. *What's going on? What's to be done?*

In time, Remy stumbled to her car. She'd accomplish nothing work-related this afternoon. Sanctuary was found in her room at home. Colonel Brandon jumped up on the bed, licked her face, and snuggled at the side of her thigh. He could sense she was upset. He was there for her.

Scared? Who came up with that puny six-letter word? Remy rolled out other options. Terrified. Devastated. Crushed. Sad. Hopeless. She could trot through the alphabet for hours.

He's for me. It's him or no one. This far down the path in life, Remy had never known love could be like this. All those early romance writers had never come close to describing the destruction wrought by love lost. Well, it wasn't their job, was it? Their job was happy endings. Why couldn't she end her story up on the hill, lying on the blanket alone with Bill forever? She'd been good. What sin had been committed for her to deserve this? She'd only wanted a decent job that she loved. That's all. Not Darcy. Not the money. Not the mansion. A decent job. Now she was close to having it all, and it could all disappear in an instant, a millisecond, in the proverbial snap of fingers.

His ex-wife was beautiful and smart. That's what Martha had said. Could she worm her way back into Bill's life? How susceptible was he to that face, that body? This was a woman well educated in bending a man to her will. If Maggie had intentions, Remy felt she could offer pitiful competition. This was the mother of his child. This was his first love and high school sweetheart. The depth of the hopelessness was a vise on Remy's head, being tightened by fate.

Love was the culprit. She thought about how she felt when she was with him. Focus would drift when her eyes lighted on anything that reminded her of him. Paragraphs on the page would be read and not registered. Her body sang sultry songs whenever he approached her. Hair would be pushed back. Nails would press into her palms. Thoughts would not be completed. Sensuality would replace blood in her veins. Desires surfaced. Scenes were imagined. Thoughts of shameless mating held no shame. All this only added to her distress. She felt the ball of fear deep in her gut, felt its tendrils wrapping around every muscle in her body, felt it creeping toward her head. If he got back with his ex, she'd have to leave the company. For her, there'd be no choice. She couldn't comprehend not going to work at the winery, couldn't comprehend not seeing Chico, couldn't think of an alternative. This had to be addressed now, before it crushed her.

She didn't remember driving to the warehouse. The steering wheel almost cried under Remy's intense grip. Damp eyes focused straight ahead. Her surroundings were nonexistent.

Bill was coming down a ladder, carrying some small boxes from a shelf, when she entered. With her red eyes and tension radiating from her tight facial features, it was obvious something was wrong. She stopped six feet from him, white knuckles visible on hands clenched in front of her.

"What's the matter, Chica?" His name for her when they were alone.

No rehearsed lines, it burst out. "Your mother let it slip by accident. It wasn't her fault. She was upset when she hung up from you this afternoon. I had just walked into her office. Your ex-wife is moving back?"

Bill, looking confused, stayed in place and shrugged. "Nothing for you to be concerned about."

That was it? Remy's shoulders trembled. She was frozen in place, lips quivering as tears formed in the corners of her eyes. Her devastated expression pleaded for some explanation, some meaning to what was happening. Had she massively misinterpreted their growing relationship? Her knees felt shaky. Was this to be the defining disaster of her life? Had she been carrying the weight of love for both of them? She didn't know how love worked, didn't know about the subtleties, hadn't figured it out yet. She'd just broken through the door and thrown her heart at him.

She started shaking as tears ran down her cheeks.

"Whoa, Remy. What is it?" Bill walked toward her, drawn in by the distress, the fear, and the tears.

In a broken voice, she said, "She's Lizzie's mother, and she's coming back into your lives. She's beautiful. You never talk about her. I saw you hug her and kiss her in the parking lot of the tasting room." Remy's sobs grew as she continued. She fought to get it out, knew it was coming in spurts. "I saw you with her at the diner this morning. Do you still love her? Are you going to try and make it work again?"

Bill stood there, perplexed, trying to figure out what this was all about. Then comprehension flooded his head. Clarity surfaced. He slowly put the boxes down and closed the small gap between them. His voice was calm, soft, and slow as he took both her hands in his. This had to be fixed. Right now, and very clearly, any doubts completely erased. "Oh, Chica, I'm sorry. Instead of saying it was no concern of yours, I should have said it was no concern of mine." Bill raised his hands and lifted her face. "*You* are it for me, Remy. *You* are everything to me. You are everything she is not—loving, loyal, a worker bee, concerned about others. You're smarter and more beautiful than her." He ran a hand softly across her cheek, brushing away a tear. "I have zero interest in Maggie. Any hugs or pecks on the cheek you saw were only to keep peace between us for the sake of my daughter. All of my passion, all of my interest is only for you. You're what's important to me." Bill pulled her into a hug and stroked her hair. "I love you, Remy Reilly." He'd never uttered those words before. He pulled back enough to look into her beautiful eyes. A smile lit his face. "There, it's out. I've finally said it, and now I can tell the whole world."

Years of caution in Bill's life were dismissed in seconds. For weeks, he had always wondered if this joy with Remy could really last. Long-term thoughts and dreams had not been expressed between them. They'd been too caught up in the present, bathing together in the wonder of the here and now. Now, he asked for her feelings.

"Are you comfortable with that, Remy? Do you feel the same about me?"

She tightened her arms around him. "I love you so much! I never knew what love was before you. I don't think I can exist without you. Please tell me you love me again."

Bill gently pushed her back so he could gaze at those lovely eyes again. "I love you, Remy Reilly."

Arms locked around each other, they made their way to the employees' kitchen. Two glasses and a bottle of wine were carried out to quiet table overlooking the valleys to the west. Serious and light admissions of love bounced back and forth across the table. Hands were temporarily unlocked so sips of wine could be taken. In time, their blanket was retrieved, and they lay under their oak tree, bringing new distress to the furry and feathered local residents of the fields and the trees.

The fall air chilled as the sun retreated. Bill turned to Remy. Another problem had to be addressed. "Can you come home with me while I tell Lizzie about her mother? I have to get this over with, and I have no idea how she'll react. Sometimes she hides her feelings better than I do."

Remy was in the kitchen preparing dinner, allowing Bill some privacy while he broke the news to his daughter. From the family room next to the kitchen, she heard Lizzie's lament. Crying confused most of what Lizzie said, but Remy understood she didn't want to live with her mother. It was a cry for help. Remy could picture the tears flowing, the anxiety rising. Bill's voice was calm and soothing, but he wasn't selling it well.

Remy calmly wiped her hands, walked to the family room, and sat beside the distraught child. Bill was trying to regroup himself in front of the girl's anguish.

Remy put an arm around Lizzie and pulled the child into her embrace. "You don't have to move, Lizzie. Not at all." Calmly, slowly, having had lots of practice with her younger sisters, Remy took over. "You're in complete charge. I guarantee it. Would you like me to explain?"

After delivering the initial shocking news, Remy knew anything Bill said would be held in question. He was the villain of the moment. Logic was relinquished to Remy.

"Yes, please." Lizzie folded into Remy and gave her father a disapproving look.

"Okay. Pay attention." Remy shifted around to make eye contact. The girl had to focus. "If you have any questions, just ask. This is adult talk, but you'll get it."

A tentative, teary nod of assent.

"Your father and grandmother, knowing that they never ever wanted to lose you, made sure of it years ago when you were young. They guaranteed it very simply. Do you know what parental custody is?"

"Yes. Some of the girls at school have divorced parents, and problems come up with that sometimes." She gave a pleading look toward Remy. "I'm not going to have a problem, am I?"

Remy stroked the child's head. She put her face close, locked on to Lizzie's eyes, and gave her a big smile. "Not even close. Unfortunately, you're *condemned* to stay here with your dad, close to your grandma, and no one can budge you. Years ago, your grandma and your father had your mother sign over full custody to your dad. Do you know what that means?"

"I think so."

"Let me make it simple for you. It's rock solid. Just like now, your mom does have visitation rights. You really should see her, maybe a lot at first. Remember, she is your mother. She only wants what's best for you, and she loves you very much."

A slight change in the Lizzie's expression signaled to Remy that she may not have slipped that last part by the girl. Kids weren't stupid.

"I don't have to move?"

"Never. Now, I think you should give your dad a big hug for making sure, years ago, that you wouldn't ever have to go anywhere."

She hugged Remy before bolting across the sofa into her father's arms.

Things settled at the dinner table. Lizzie stabilized. They reinforced her situation calmly several times so it was crystal clear. Bill agreed that Lizzie should see her mother more when she moved back to the area. It was the right thing to do.

After their meal, Remy said, "Now go to the dining room and start your homework. You don't need to help with the dishes tonight. I'll be there in a few minutes, if you need any help."

When they were alone doing the dishes, Bill asked, "How did you know about the custody agreement? I'd have never thought of telling her about it."

"Your mom told me this afternoon. You should call her. She was very upset." Bill pulled her into a hug. Remy kissed him on the cheek and pushed him away. "Go ahead, call your mom now. I'll finish up here."

As he turned to go, Remy placed a hand on his arm. "She's a wonderful child. Did you notice what she said about how much she loves you and her grandma? How you complete her world? You've done such a good job of raising her. She's learned all the lessons a parent is supposed to teach—good manners, thoughtfulness toward others, a work ethic, accountability." Remy wanted to take the weight off the evening. She patted his cheek. "You may screw up a lot at work, Chico, but you're passing parenting."

"My mother has a lot to do with it." Crisis over, Bill's humor returned. "She's always so patient with Lizzie. Raising me was a lot easier on her. If I brought home a bad grade from school, she'd stick bamboo slivers under my nails. The teachers couldn't see the marks." To emphasize his sick humor, he lifted one hand and rubbed the fingers with his other hand. "They really used to hurt."

He got a silent, tolerant look. Remy knew she would have to put up with these appalling excursions into his warped humor.

Bill took her in his arms. "Now that Lizzie's okay, how are you? Are we clear about my feelings for you? Any more doubts?"

"Tomorrow is Friday. Can you take me to dinner and tell me all over again?"

Chapter 20

Martha was waiting for Remy as she drove up to the barn. Before she could get out of the car, Martha opened the passenger door and jumped in. "To the diner. Breakfast."

"That's a nice offer, Martha, but I've already had something."

"So have I. Drive."

Comfortable in their far corner booth, the two ladies ordered coffee. Martha got to it. "That ne'er-do-well son of mine called last night to tell me about how you calmed Lizzie down after he told her about Maggie moving back." She raised both palms in the air. "Why is my son still a buffoon? When I asked about you, I got a lot of gibberish, stumbling and mumbling from a three-year-old." Martha reached for her coffee. "Tell me what happened—not with Lizzie—with you two. I barely slept."

Before Remy could say anything, Martha pointed and said, "Wait. Grab me one of those croissants. I'll need it to absorb the acid from all the coffee I'm drinking today."

Serene, fulfilled, happy Remy Reilly was back. Mentally, Remy was in heaven. Physically, she was drained from the previous day and night.

"Short version, your son and I are in love. It was all sorted out last night when I went to the warehouse. It was very emotional, but I'll spare you the details. Maggie's moving back turned out to be a good thing. I can tell you he has no feelings for her. His interactions with her over the years have simply been to keep things nice for Lizzie's sake." Remy paused, collecting her thoughts, wanting this to be okay with Mrs. K. "Do you mind that we're seeing each other? I really love your son, Martha."

Palms up again, expressing hopelessness at the world, Martha said, "Please, not another buffoon. What's a female buffoon called, a buffooness? Didn't you hear me yesterday? You're my dream daughter-in-law. As far as work goes, I was afraid of losing you. I'm starting to feel very comfortable delegating things to you. When Winston and I were away, I was actually relaxed. And that idiot son of mine almost screwed it all up. A grin grew on Martha's face. A new idea loomed. "I know what. Now I'm delegating him to *you*. If he screws up from now on, I'm holding *both* Juan and you responsible." Executive decisions over with, Martha slumped back in the booth. "Gosh, honey, you've just made me a happy woman." She turned and waved for more coffee and bit into her croissant.

Time to lighten things up, thought Remy, a little payback for Martha's son. She put on a serious face. "Bill told me he was always concerned that you might stick bamboo slivers under Lizzie's fingernails for bringing home a bad grade like you did to him as a boy."

"Yes, yes. When I wasn't beating him with a shovel or forcing his head into the toilet. Poor Bill. If I did any of that for poor grades, he wouldn't be alive now. His father was the one who kept him on the straight and narrow. Lizzie has been a dream compared to him. That girl is smart. She does well in school. Intelligence and common sense must have skipped a generation."

Remy reached out and held Martha's hand. "You know you're being too hard on yourself. Your son is about as close to perfect as one can get."

"Boy, are you deluded. You must be in love." Martha was pensive for a moment. "You should know, even before last night, Lizzie adores you. She talks about you all the time. You'll have no problem there if the two of you... Well, how should I say this... If you want to take the next step."

Next step? Jesus, there was a next step? Remy hoped there would be a handrail somewhere.

It was upon them. The week after Halloween was the employees' harvest party. Martha, Remy, and Lizzie had completed the preparations over the last few weeks. Bill, Skip, and Juan had put the decorations in place. The warehouse was ready. Flaming tiki torches lined the long drive up to the warehouse. The vines were asleep, oblivious to it all. Dark clouds filled the sky with the promise of rain after months of dry weather. It was a welcome sight to anyone involved in Sonoma County agriculture. The week before, an asphalt crew had filled in the potholes on the road so they wouldn't worsen over the coming winter months.

Orange and black crepe ribbons sagged from the rafters, along with big cardboard leaves from the craft store in town. Stacked pumpkins welcoming guests were held in place by scarecrows that flanked the doors outside. Food and drink tables took up one side, a DJ was set up on the other. In the center, a large open space had been left for socializing and dancing. Happy people milled about the room. Thanks and relief that a good harvest had been completed and set down to rest shone on the smiling faces of those present.

Remy glanced around the room. She was in love and had her dream job. How good could it be? She was with her Lord Billy the Absent at a grand soiree. The warehouse was her country house ballroom. The hanging decorations were her massive chandeliers with flickering candles. The DJ in his vintage Rolling Stones T-shirt and baseball cap on backward was her string quartet in tuxedos. She was standing beside the grand dame, Martha, who had her consort, Winston, at her side. It was heaven—plain and simple. She imagined Jane and the Brontë sisters smiling down on her from the top of one of the tall wine vats.

All eyes turned as Skip and Lynn came up to them. As usual, Lynn looked like a goddess. Lynn didn't do country casual. She was done up in a form-fitting blue dress. Her high heels brought her eye level with a rebranded Skip in an open-necked white shirt, sports coat, and slacks. The group chatted, and Remy tactfully shunted Lynn aside.

"What did you do to him? The hair, the clothes? God, he's handsome."

"Small rewards." A mischievous glint came off Lynn's eye. "He's been performing up to expectations. Besides, I enjoy playing with his hair." She giggled. "He gets so nervous, and I have to take him into the bedroom to calm him down. This is all a little strange. I *really* like the guy."

"Lynn! That's wonderful!"

"Yeah, I'm shifting stuff around next weekend at the salon. We're going to Lake Tahoe. All these lovey-dovey feelings are a bit strange. Did you feel the same way?"

"I think we'll need a long dinner to go over *that* subject. Don't you feel guilty leaving the shop on a Saturday? I still feel guilty not going to the market."

Lynn said, "Remember Harriet, the lady I worked with for that one year in San Francisco after I finished school? Do you remember last year when she was getting tired of working in the city, and I lured her up here to work for me? Well, she loves it around here." Lynn glanced around and lowered her voice. "I'm offering her a partnership. She's terrific at what she does and brings a lot of new customers in. I don't want to lose her. We can both make great money, keep the quality up, and take a few weekdays and alternate weekends off. It'll be win-win for both of us."

Remy was thrilled for her friend. They could spend more time together when they weren't both exhausted. The news about Lynn's building relationship with Skip was a bonus. "That's terrific news." Knowing her friend's disdain for outdoor activities, Remy gave her a rare jab back. "Just think, next year you can come with Skip and help with the harvest. You know, pick grapes with me on the first day. It'll be great, both of us together out in the fresh air."

Lynn looked at her friend as if she had just returned from Mars. She looked down at her long, manicured nails, lovely dress, and shiny, pricey shoes. She stroked the dress as if it were already contaminated with dust. "Have you taken leave of your senses?"

Martha, Bill, and Juan mixed with the crowd, thanking employees and customers for their support. As the food and music took over, Remy and Bill stood together watching Lynn and Skip maul each other during a slow dance. The music changed to a fast song.

Bill, his arm around Remy's waist, said, "During all those years of working weekends and going to school, did you ever learn how to dance?"

Remy looked at him as if he were a simpleton. "Dance? Me, dance? Michael Jackson wrote a song about me. That's right. 'Dancing Machine.'"

Remy jumped about three feet in front of him and turned back. She bent slightly at the waist and twirled her hands around in front of her to the sound of the music. She then did the mesmerizing thing with those her graceful arms, hands, and fingers, pulling him toward her. "Come on, old man. Why are you standing there like a lamppost? Let's see what those feet can do besides walk you into trouble."

She danced him to the point of exhaustion. Bill finally convinced Remy to take a break. They retrieved refreshments from the bar, and the two made their way outside to one of the quiet tables away from the people and the music. The promised rain had not yet arrived. Bill, warm from dancing, placed his sports coat over Remy's shoulders to ward off the fall breeze creeping in through the valleys from the ocean to the west.

"I have a friend in Ontario, Canada, close to Detroit," Bill said. "You'll get a kick out of this. The town he lives in is called London—London, Ontario. He's asked me to come up and look at a property where he wants to start a vineyard. I was thinking of going at the end of the month or the first week in December. Things are settled around here, so it's a good time for vacations. Juan and Skip will have no problem without me." Bill had been thinking about Remy's lack of vacation time, her limited travel experience. "Would you like to go with me and actually get out of California for the first time?"

Remy almost jumped in his lap. "You want to take me on vacation to *Canada*? Would we take an airplane or drive? I've never been on an airplane!"

"Wow. We'd fly into Detroit and then drive for an hour or two. It's beautiful country. It's not like we're going somewhere fancy like New York."

Exhilaration was replaced by reality. Remy's mood came down a notch. "Would Mrs. K let me go? I haven't been here that long. We're working on a lot of stuff right now."

"I think I have a little influence around here. If she balks, there are secrets that could be revealed." His voice lowered. "Did you know that Hannibal Lecter took her cooking class on preparing sauces to use with vital human organs?"

Remy's mood meter shot up. "Yes! A real vacation. Would it be like a long weekend?"

"No. It would be at least a week."

"Yes!" The practicality machine kicked in. "Do you have a suitcase I can borrow?"

Bill endured the Question Machine for about twenty minutes before they made their way back inside. Remy rushed ahead to Martha. Bill was stalled by some of the employees wanting to thank him for the party. He watched over their shoulders as Remy talked to his mom for a bit and then gave her a hug. Remy then bolted over to Lynn and Skip. Seeing her rush around, Bill thought she looked like a four-year-old who had consumed too much sugar on Halloween.

When he came up to Martha and Winston, his mother said, "Whom do we know in London, Ontario, Canada?"

"Never mind, Mom. It's a surprise."

Knowing not to press it, Martha said, "Well, make sure she has a good coat. It's cold up there this time of year."

The following Saturday, Martha and Winston took Lizzie for the night to give the two other youngsters some alone time, some privacy at Bill's house. Remy prepared a dinner for two—steak, mashed potatoes, and French-cut green beans, his favorite. She was glad she hadn't fallen for a chef. Her man was easy. The table was set perfectly. Candles glowed in the dim light.

After dinner, over a glass of wine, Bill excused himself for a minute. When he returned, he placed a bag on the table. "A present for the trip." He leaned over and kissed her on the head.

Remy looked at the shopping bag from a store she couldn't place. It was the second gift a man had ever given her, and it was being given to her by the same man. On either side of the bag's carry straps, Bill had put a small piece of duct tape to keep it closed—gift wrapped. Macy's wouldn't be hiring him for Christmas, but Remy didn't care. She retrieved a knife from the kitchen to cut the strong tape. A new backpack materialized from the white paper inside. She ran her fingers over the soft blue-gray leather and sparkling-gold clasps and zippers. It was beautiful. Where did he find something like this? She jumped up and wrapped herself around him. "It's lovely. Thank you so much."

She put it on and walked around the room, feeling like a fashion maven. "Lizzie will be so jealous."

"I know you're attached to that ratty, duct-taped, nylon thing you've had for years, but you can still use that for work. Please use this for the trip and when we go out. People look at me like I'm Scrooge when I'm with you."

He sat and watched her open and close all the pockets, adjust and readjust the straps, fascinated by her new treasure. When he could get her attention again, he said, "Speaking of Lizzie, I spoke with her last week about us."

Remy's focused immediately.

"She was over the moon that I finally said something to her. I was told it's about time. She asked me if you would be moving in before I had a chance to bring it up delicately." Bill looked up toward the ceiling. "Kids today catch a lot more than I would have when I was young. Anyway, she'd love to have you move in as much as I would. What do you think?"

Remy got up and moved into his lap, shaking slightly, almost tearing up. "I love you so much. You just made me the happiest woman in the world—again. Is it okay if we do it after the trip? I'd love being here with both of you for Christmas." Always a step ahead, she leaned back, smiled, and patted his cheek. "And my sisters will love it. They'll each finally have their own rooms."

Chapter 21

She'd been instructed to get a passport. Instructed that Canada was another country and required it. He had to spend the entire trip to the San Francisco airport making up stories about his friend in London, Ontario. Bill had been vague and dismissive for the previous few weeks about all the questions. He'd never been to London, Ontario.

At the airport, after check-in and passport control was completed, Remy ambled down the hall, marveling at all the people. There were colorful outfits from different corners of the world mixed with the more subdued clothes of American businesspeople. The international terminal at San Francisco hosted them all. Shoulder bags of straw, nylon, leather, and cloth held necessities for long flights. Her eyes drifted to the airplanes waiting outside. She'd never been this close to a big airplane. They were sleek, shiny *Game of Thrones* dragons waiting to lift her into the sky. What would Jane Austen have thought? Remy could travel in warm luxury halfway around the world in the same time it took a cold, sparse carriage to get to London.

They stopped at a shop to buy water and snacks. Remy didn't know you couldn't take water past security.

Seated in the boarding area, Remy rifled through her new backpack and pulled out one of her books. "Would you like to hear about Ontario? Toronto is the capital. It's on Lake Ontario."

Bill looked down at the book. *Was that a tour guide for Ontario? Where did she even find a tour guide for Ontario?*

"Why don't you tell me on the plane, honey. We're early, so right now I'm going to get us some coffee. You stay right there."

When he returned, Remy looked distraught, a disappointed little girl with her hands clinging to her new backpack. "Chico, I think we're at the wrong gate. That sign over the counter says London, *England*."

Bill's shoulders slumped. Irritation clouded his face. "Not again. Please, not again. This is the second time that damned travel agent has done this to me." He turned to Remy and took her hand. "I'm so sorry. We'll never get to the other gate on time. It looks like we'll just have to go to London, *England*. I hope you're not upset."

Bewildered, Remy tried to sort this all out. "But I've bought a tour guide for Ontario."

"I know, honey. You're right. It's a bad idea. You probably wouldn't like England anyhow." Bill did a good act of looking crushed. "I wanted this to be a wonderful trip for you. Maybe we should just go home." He started to get up.

Remy pulled him down. She'd been sorting while Bill was talking. "Home? Are you *crazy*? This plane is going to *England*. And we have tickets!"

Her head was spinning. Would she walk on the same streets Jane had when she'd gathered ideas for her books? City scenes from the videos and movies danced across her mind. He'd said before that many of the old buildings were still there. Big Ben and Parliament, the river Thames, and massive stores all flashed behind her eyes. "What will we see? What will we do?"

"Well, many of the things you read about and watch. We'll do a day trip to Bath, so you can see the Assembly Rooms and the costume museum. You'll be amazed at what women had to wear back then. We'll take a boat trip down the Thames from Greenwich to Big Ben. We'll ride the Underground all over London."

Remy's mouth rounded in awe. "The Assembly Rooms in Bath, where they socialized and danced all those years ago?"

"The original ones," he teased her. "You can lean against the same doorjamb as Jane Austen." He did a poor imitation of mesmerizing with his hands. "Picture Jane throwing down her cigarette and grinding it out on the floor so she could grab her pencil and jot down a new idea."

Bill wished there were seat belts in the waiting area to keep her in her seat.

Remy settled. He'd gotten her good this time. Mere yards away, a gleaming, silver carriage was waiting to whisk her away on her dream trip. She wagged a finger in front of his face. "You've deceived me again."

"I have."

"You're worse than Mr. Wickham, worse than Evil Willoughby, worse than all of them."

"I am."

"And you don't even regret it."

"I don't."

"But you promise never to deceive me again like this?"

"I don't."

A seat belt wouldn't have held anyway. In an instant, she was in his lap, right there in the boarding area in front of all the people. Embarrassing kisses landed on his face.

The ring was in his carry-on bag. He'd wanted to give it to her in London but decided to put off asking her until Christmas. A proposal couldn't compete with her excitement over this trip.

Remy held his face in both hands. "I don't care what Mrs. K says about you, *I* love you."

About the Author

Jackie Campbell is a writer, an artist, and author of *Rebranding Remy Reilly*.

Jackie draws on her years of travel, her love of humor, and addiction to romance novels in order to help people have a laugh. She thinks a good romantic comedy novel is the perfect vehicle. When not traveling around looking for ideas, Jackie lives in Marin County, California.

For questions or comments, contact Jackie at:
jackie@jackiecampbellauthor.com

Call to Action

Thank you for reading. Reviews are a major help to authors. If you enjoyed this book, please consider leaving a review. It will take only a few minutes and would be greatly appreciated.

Also by Jackie Campbell

Alicia Darwin Sorts It Out

Alicia Darwin seems to have it all: wealth, fame, an acting career she cherishes, and a boyfriend the tabloids approve. But a sudden breakup and a healthy dose of straight-talk convince Alicia that she needs to make some changes in her highly controlled world.

Alicia flees London for a break in the mountains of Northern California, where she finds herself sharing her alone time first with a bear and then with an only slightly more civilized creature – her rescuer, Jay Connors. A widower raising a teenage niece, Jay has created a life that is serene, if not blissful, in his small town. After meeting Alicia, he wonders if he'll ever experience serenity again.

Alicia Darwin Sorts It Out is a humorous romantic romp in the forgotten world of normal people, far from Miss Darwin's entitled lifestyle.

Reviews for *Alicia Darwin Sorts It Out*

Comments from the New England Readers Choice Contest:

"This book is exceptional on so many levels"
"Absolutely loved this book. You had me from page 1!"
"I enjoyed it and will look for more from this author"

Kentucky Book Club review-

"General opinion from each of us was how well written and detailed this book is. Characters are cleverly portrayed with an added flair that you do not see in most romance novels. People from two different worlds coming together always has its challenges, but you managed to "Sort It Out". Our group gives this book full marks."

www.ingramcontent.com/pod-product-compliance
Lightning Source LLC
Chambersburg PA
CBHW021154110726
47900CB00002B/564